D0673140

DREAMING

"What do you want her to be, Matt?" asked Betty, calmly.

"Who?"

"The sleeping one."

"Want her to be? I don't *want* her to be *anybody."* He choked and stopped speaking.

"Not even in a dream?"

"A dream?" He was shocked and astonished. "You mean I've got designs?"

"No, I don't mean sexy designs. I mean another kind of dream. A dream of fair woman." Betty was wide-eyed.

"Tell me more," he said, relaxing suddenly and sitting down on the sofa. He had a feeling that something was going to break open and he was feeling desperate enough to be glad of it.

"She's so beautiful. She's so helpless. She's so empty."

"Empty?"

"Her spirit isn't there," said Betty solemnly.

He looked at her as if she had gone mad.

But Betty went on recklessly. "So you can dream it's anything you want."

"So that's what I'm doing? Dreaming?"

"Aren't you? Don't you want to? Doesn't everybody?"

CHARLOTTE ARMSTRONG

DREAM OF FAIR WOMAN

ZEBRA BOOKS
KENSINGTON PUBLISHING CORP.

ZEBRA BOOKS

are published by

Kensington Publishing Corp.
475 Park Avenue South
New York, NY 10016

First Zebra Books printing: November, 1992

Printed in the United States of America

Chapter One

He went through the hospital lobby and out the front door, aiming himself like an arrow for home. He crossed pavement, and began to thud briskly along the path, worn into the ground by short-cutting feet across the shabby little park where, on either side, the lumps and tufts of neglected grass retained, in June, only a little green from winter rain. But Matt, broken out of routine into the late sunshine, moving fast, could not help feeling an inappropriate pleasure. There was nothing exhilarating about a prompt and resolute response to intimations of catastrophe.

Poor Ma. Poor Peg. Tumbling out choppy sentences on the phone, without preliminary. Not exactly asking him to drop everything and hurry home, but needing his presence. "I'm all alone here," she had said. He hadn't stopped for questions. He would be there in ninety seconds — to put in train whatever had to be done in these unhappy and undesirable circumstances. Poor Peg.

Yet, to be reasonable, if his mother rented rooms to strangers she inevitably risked witnessing some stranger's fate, sooner or later. He guessed his mother had used that weaseling phrase in her shock, softening shocking truth. At least she hadn't said "passed away" — a euphemism which Matt particularly despised.

He wouldn't have expected Peg Cuneen to have called for someone to hold her hand, even in such circumstances. She had always lived with a gusto of her own. But one's mother, Matt thought, must inevitably age and depend. In which case he would be, without question, dependable.

So he raced the park, crossed pavement again, loped up the walk to the old stucco house on the corner. The familiar doorknob leaped to his hand. She called his name. He bounded up the stairs. There she was, sitting in Betty's small arm-chair in the back bedroom, with her small feet flat on the floor. There was something odd and ominous about her sitting down.

Peggy Marks Cuneen looked up at her tall son and said with bright shame, "I'm sorry, Matt. I'm all right, now."

They were a pair not much given to caresses, so he put his own brand of comfort into his voice. "O.K., Ma. Don't you worry about a thing. I'll stick around until the doctor calls back. What happened?"

"Well, I don't know." Her face pinched. "She rang the bell early, not five minutes after you left. She looked worn out — I thought she'd probably spent the night on some miserable bus ride. And she dragged her suitcase right up with her. So I don't think she cared so much what the room was like, just that there *was* a room where she could rest." Peg darted a nervous glance at him. "She had the money. I didn't take it. We didn't settle much. There wasn't time. The phone . . ." His mother tilted her head and called out, "Betty?"

Betty Prentiss thumped fast up the stair carpet and whirled into her room, where they were. "Oh, Matt, I saw you tearing across the park. Peg, what's the matter?"

6

"I'm all right," said his mother. "I'm all right, dear. It's that girl."

"Oh?"

Matt said, over his mother's head to his contemporary, "Well, see, I guess this character just up and died."

Betty was a small girl with short dark hair, a freckled nose, and brown eyes, set deep. She had a mannerism, a way of lowering her head and looking up from the caverns with an effect of intense attention. She didn't pull this trick, in the moment. Her face was peeled of expression, bare in shock.

Then Matt felt his mother's small strong hand winding itself into the flesh above his wrist. "Oh, *did* she die?" wailed Peg. *"When* did she die?"

He looked down, all signals off. "I'm sorry, Peg. I thought that's what you meant."

"Oh, no, no," cried Peg, letting him go and pushing at her own abundant dark hair. "The whole point is that I'm not going to *have* her dying. Not in my house. Not of neglect, anyhow. I told you. I said, 'She won't wake up.' I don't know why she won't wake up. It's weird. It scares me."

Matt had the immediate impulse to go and see, but his mother grabbed for him. "Don't you go in there. Who knows whether it's catching?"

Betty, who had rallied in a twinkling, said, "If it is, then I've caught it. I talked to her this morning. So I'll go."

She went with a flash of legs and whirl of skirt. But Matt, who couldn't believe that whatever-it-was was "something catching," stayed and studied his mother.

Peg said to his puzzled scrutiny, "I guess I'm being pretty silly."

Matt grinned at her. "Well, I'll tell you. If this character is pouring off any such powerful germs as you're imagining, then the whole town is already in

7

epidemic. Where had she come from? Where had she been?"

"I don't know, dear."

"She came on a bus, you say?"

"Well, I don't *know* that."

"We're not exactly on any transcontinental bus lines. How come she came *here?*"

"She saw our sign. She might have been all night on a train."

"We're miles from any railroad station. Not likely."

"Well, she did come here," said Peg tartly, "so that much has to be likely."

"She came on foot?" Matt didn't correct her logic but dug for facts. "With a suitcase? Not in a car?"

"I didn't see or hear a car."

Then Betty said nervously from the doorway, "She just seems to be sleeping. Did you call Uncle Jon?"

"Yes. He's going to call back."

"Well, then, you've done all we can do," said Betty soothingly.

Matt was inclined to agree. He struggled to begin at the beginning. "You didn't think she was ill, when she came? No visible symptoms?"

"I thought she was just terribly, terribly tired." Peg said and added with nervous irritability, "I told you."

"I thought so, too," said Betty gravely. She crossed this spacious room, that had been Matt's own when he was a little boy and sat down on her bed, winding her good legs around each other. "See, when Peg had to go down to answer the phone, I took over. Well, I mean, I told her about sharing the bathroom, and which towel bars she could use and where Peg keeps stuff, and all that. I thought she was exhausted. Or else—preoccupied."

"What do you mean, Betts?"

"Oh, kind of not quite all here. I had the feeling that she wasn't quite getting my messages. Or else she didn't quite care, you know?"

Matt was listening intently for some facts, not impressions. "What did she *do?*"

"Well, she closed the bathroom door," said Betty with a drawl, "and used the facilities, I presume. When I heard her come out, I was ready for school. So I put my head in at her door to say I'd see her later." Betty's eyes flickered. She put her head down. "That's about it."

Matt said, "What I can't figure out, Peg, is how come you decided that this girl absolutely had to wake up. You thought she was pretty beat and needed to rest. So why didn't you just let her alone to sleep it off?"

"You don't understand," his mother said.

"That," said Matt promptly, "is what I just intended to convey." And he grinned at her, fondly.

They were nothing alike, mother and son. Peg was not tall, and on the plump side. Her features were, however, strong and sharp. She had a long and pointed chin, a fair-sized straight nose, and bright brown eyes under well-defined brows. Matt was tall, and in the body, on the slender side. But he had a round head, well covered with sandy hair that insisted, unless he had it cut to a mere bristle, upon curling riotously. His nose gave a first impression of being stubby but in profile it was seen to be straight and well cut, but set at a slightly flattened angle to his face. He had blue eyes, set merrily, and a good mouth that grinned often. Peg wore a keen and driving air. Matt appeared to be easygoing. But they knew themselves to be essentially the other way around.

Peggy Marks Cuneen had, long ago, abandoned a warm clan in New York to marry Dr. Peter Cuneen of Southern California, with whom she had fallen permanently in love one summer, when she had been very young and visiting her college roommate. She had not regretted one moment of her choice, had made a cheerful and resilient doctor's wife, borne a fine son, had always been able to settle cosily into her surroundings, informing them with her own spirit. Now that she was a widow, Peg did no moping but kept busy with good works, liking nothing better than the bustle and confusion of group activities.

Matt, who considered his mother just a touch scatter-brained, and soft to a fault, to let herself in for so many committees and chairwomanships, was not convinced that she could understand him by methods of her own. She had lived, before he was born, with a man who kept himself also in the aloof position of one who was fascinated by sequences and consequences in nature and delighted in sorting them into coolly observed patterns.

So now Peg gathered her wits to present her memories of this day in a way that would sound "reasonable" to him.

"Well, it was Mrs. Ransom on the phone about the Red Cross and in a terrible twit . . ." Peg groped for order. "Let me see. Betty went off to school. I was buzzing around downstairs until time for my luncheon. I came up, of course, just before I left, but she didn't answer my tap on the door. I didn't like to disturb her. So I left a note and her house key on the hall table. Well, when I came back, about three o'clock, the key was just exactly where I had put it. So I came up to see if we could, you know, get straightened around. She hadn't said how long she'd want the room and all." She gave Matt a guilty, defiant lick of her eye.

"When she didn't answer, I cracked the door, and she was sound asleep. So I let her be. I changed my clothes and put the roast in . . . Oh lord, the roast . . . !" She looked at her wrist. "It's all right," she said, seeming to comfort them. "The oven's on low. Where was I? Yes, then, about four o'clock, I got to thinking that she hadn't had a drop to eat all day long. So I fixed a little snack. . . ."

"She wasn't going to board here, was she?" her son said. (Betty boarded here, but Betty was different.)

"I don't fancy anybody starving," said Peg indignantly.

"O.K. O.K." Matt winked at Betty, but Betty didn't twinkle back. She was wound up in a leggy knot, seeming rather tense and solemn.

"Well, she was *still* sleeping." Peg's hand began to be dramatic. "And that was the first time I really tried to wake her up. Well, she wouldn't! So I left the tray. But it was beginning to make me nervous. A little later, I came up and tried again and"—her right hand made a violent slashing motion—"I tried *hard.*" Peg fixed a stern gaze upon her son. "And the point is, Matt, *of course,* I wouldn't have tried to wake her up if I thought I could."

Matt jingled some change in his pocket. This was the kind of remark that always surprised him by making sense. "O.K.," he said indulgently. "Go on."

"So I called Jon Prentiss. He wasn't there. Betty hadn't come in. I guess I panicked. I'm sorry. I shouldn't have called and taken you away."

"Why not?" Matt was very calm. "Tell me, did this dame speak up, at all? Did she, by any wild chance, tell you her name?"

Peg said, "Her name is Dolan. Wasn't that it, Betty?"

"Oh, Peg, I don't know. Seems to me that's close, but not quite right. Olin?"

"It could have been," said Peg, with an air of gracious tolerance for the opinion of another.

"Did she have a first name?" inquired Matt, a little too patiently.

Betty folded in her lower lip and shook her head at him, ruefully.

"She didn't say," Peg told him.

Matt put his hands in his pockets and lounged against the wall. "To recapitulate. She told you her

11

last name but you aren't sure what it is. You don't know where she came from or how she came or why. You didn't ask her how long—"

"She needed a *place*," his mother interrupted. Then she added from no train of thought that Matt could follow, "I don't say I took to her, especially."

Betty said, "Maybe we should have been able to guess that she was coming down with something. But we didn't. So don't pull any hindsight on us, huh, Matt?"

Betty was sticking up for Peg. She was almost family. Her mother was Peg's roommate of old, the very one that Peg had visited so fatefully, long ago. Betty, whose parents had moved away north, was just finishing her first year of teaching in an elementary school not too far from Peg's house, where she was a paying guest and a courtesy niece. She stood to Matt as almost a sister, since in some long-gone days they had played together as children.

There had been a hiatus while Matt was off to one college, and Betty, in her time, to another. But the ancient friendly entanglement of two families had even found Matt his marvellously convenient part-time job, as a lab technician, in the little private hospital across the park from his mother's house. It was Betty's uncle, Dr. Jon Prentiss, who had found the job for him, the doctor being on the staff and a close personal friend of the Administrator, a certain Fred C. Atwood. So that Betty was, in a sense, also something like the boss's niece.

Now, both mothers were delighted to have Betty living under Peg's loving wing. Both mothers took care not to utter, by word or pen, one word on the subject of the desirability of a romance between their children. Neither mother had fooled anybody.

But there was no romance. Or even dates. Matt, who was earning himself a Ph.D. in bacteriology the hard way, had no funds for squiring girls, especially not almost-sisters.

He grinned at Betty now and said, "Just lining up the facts. And here's one we had better be sure of. Is it *true* that this person in the front room won't wake up? I guess we'd better let the doctor determine that."

"Oh, I wish she would! I wish she would!" said Peg emotionally. "Go and try. *You* try. Both of you."

Matt met Betty's eyes. There was nothing to do but obey. Betty unwound her legs and jumped up. Matt followed her.

Matt understood his mother better, now. Having been a doctor's wife, no doubt Peg could guess at some of the possibilities here. If, indeed, this stranger had fallen into some kind of coma, then one had to consider the brain, and disease of the brain was no common cold. The fact that a stranger in the house was very possibly *going* to die was an idea more upsetting than a stranger already dead. It was just like Peg to feel that she could not allow it.

At the half-opened door of the front room, Betty hesitated and looked up at him from under her brows. He brushed it off as just one of her looks, not stopping to catch and consider his brief impression of some kind of warning, some kind of foreboding, some quality of presentiment that had nothing to do with the possible mortal illness of a stranger. He winked at Betty, pushed at the door and went in.

This was a big square room with one side to the park and one to the cross street. It was dim, the shades being drawn, but by no means dark. Matt realized that he had become rather unfamiliar, these days, with the upstairs regions. He never came here anymore, unless it was to carry out some necessary repair. When his father had been alive, this room had been his parents', and, he realized now, rather a holy place to him. Now he went tiptoe, feeling helplessly intrusive, toward the double bed.

There was a girl lying on her back in the very middle of the bed, the covers drawn discreetly up to a point just below bare shoulders. She seemed to be soundly and sweetly asleep. Her breathing was slow and easy, her face serene. He could not see her hands. Nothing but the face and the hair, which was spread upon the pillow, a medley of blonde streaks, some butter-color, some gold, some almost white. Her eyes were closed. He could not see the color of the eyes. She was young, but no teenager. She was full woman, but young and fair. The skin was without blemish, smoothly tanned to a soft gold. The mouth was a perfect mouth, healthily pink, unpainted. The nose was small and straight, the line of the cheek smooth and perfect, with the cheekbones stunningly placed to give the whole face a dainty elegance.

Matt caught himself not breathing. He forced a swallow. He could feel, behind him, a kind of pressure from Betty, from her silence. He, then, was to act? But it was impossible to call out "Miss? Miss?" The English language needed a word like Mademoiselle or Fräulein. Matt went close to the bed.

He wished, now, that he had kept on his white lab coat. He more than half expected, or at least hoped, that the girl would waken after all, at which time strange-man would be one thing but strange-man-in-a-white-coat quite another. Matt was no doctor, having changed his mind about that, but he had the dangerous little knowledge. He did not know quite how to go about this. Mustn't be violent, surely.

He bent and took hold of one of those bare shoulders. It felt like satin to his suddenly coarse fingers. He shook her by her shoulder, gently. The girl slept on. She seemed limp, but not a lump. She was living.

He put his mouth down close to her ear. "Hey, you? Wake up! Come on, please? Wake up, will you?"

It was absurdly embarrassing. His voice hung out there. Nothing happened. Matt straightened, feeling unnaturally flustered. He didn't like any part of this, didn't like this sense of having intruded upon a shrine. He didn't like something in the quality of Betty's attention. He didn't like not knowing whether the girl was naked. And he wasn't going to ask his mother!

He went to the foot of the bed, ripped the coverings from their moorings and threw them back a little. He took hold of a small bare foot and shook it, almost roughly.

Nothing happened. She slept on, seeming in perfect peace. Matt knew he held in his hand a strange thing, a perfectly unblemished woman's foot, with straight little toes, well-kept but unpainted toenails, the smooth flesh tanned to the same faint gold of the face—a foot as beautiful as marble, but by no means as cold.

He let it go, covered the foot quickly and turned away, achieving an air of decision. "No use getting tough, I guess. That seems to be that." He made for the door. He wanted to be out of here.

Betty gasped behind him, as if she could not breathe properly, "It's a little bit uncanny, you have to admit."

But he didn't have to admit it, because the phone rang downstairs, and Matt leaped gladly to descend and answer.

Betty Prentiss drifted along to her own room, shook her head to Peg's look of inquiry, and sat down on the edge of her bed again.

"You know, Peg, it was so funny, this morning . . ."

"What was, dear?"

"What I said to her. She was standing in there, with only her slip on, looking . . . Well, you know how she looked. So kind of fey? And I said to her, 'Gosh, you look as if you could sleep for a week'."

"Did you really?" said Peg softly. "That *is* funny!"

In their female minds moved a recognition of the

15

strangeness of all things, the pure chanciness of the whole world, the prevalence of omens, and a sense that the threads in the texture of life did not all run square. In the same eyeblink, they agreed that neither would mention this "funny" remark to the men.

Dr. Jon Prentiss, having once upon a time introduced his brother's fiancée's house guest to a certain young Dr. Cuneen of his acquaintance, was old-friend-of-the-family indeed. He was also wisdom and authority. His incisive voice soon told Matt exactly how they would proceed. The place for the girl was in the hospital. She should be examined there, and all possibilities explored. He would send for her. Meanwhile, would Matt take care of notifying her people?

"I hate just shipping her off," Peg said.

"Oh, come on, Ma," Matt argued. "You can't take care of her here. You didn't guarantee a nursing service. A contract to rent doesn't say 'in sickness or in health' like a marriage service." He must comfort his mother's stricken air with cool reason.

"Just the same, I don't like it," she said, uncomforted.

"It's nothing to like or dislike," Matt lectured. "It's something to *do*. And we'd better go rummage around in her things and find out who the devil she is and where she came from, so we can let her own people know."

"I suppose," said Peg, without moving. She didn't like the idea of rummaging, either.

"Don't worry," said her son. "We'll do the dirty work. Come on, Betts."

Betty said, "We'll take care of it, Peg. It's the only thing *to* do."

"I know," said Peg. And yet . . . she knew more than she could say. She seemed, to herself, to be feeling something in the situation that the young folks

16

didn't feel at all.

In the big dim room again, Matt glanced once at the girl, who slept as before. Then he forced a deep breath and began to look around. Betty went to pick up a black handbag from the dresser top and he left her to it. There was a grey suitcase, an old one, much battered, lying on a straight chair and, thrown over it, a short white wool coat. Over the back of the chair was spread a black dress of some sleazy material, and a white slip, which even to his eyes seemed very plain. On the floor, a pair of low-heeled black pumps lay drunkenly under stockings that coiled where they had been dropped.

"This kid," he concluded to himself, "is neither rich nor tidy." He opened the closet door. Nothing hung in the closet.

Betty said in astonishment, "Hey, Matt, there's absolutely nothing in her purse but money!"

"What?"

"Look. Not a handkerchief. Not a lipstick. Just a roll of green money."

"How much?"

"Two hundred and fifty bucks. No silver. No change."

"That's peculiar. No I.D.? No license? No credit cards?"

"Not another thing!"

"It's un-American," he said. "Try the suitcase."

So Betty went over to the chair, lifted the white coat gingerly aside, and opened the case. She began to itemize in a low voice. "One nightgown. One cotton robe. Corduroy scuffs, pretty beat up. One, two, three panties. One pink toothbrush." She lifted both hands high. "That's *it!*"

"This is ridiculous," Matt said, rubbing his head. "You know that?"

"It's pretty wild." Betty began to feel in the coat pockets. "One grubby handkerchief," she announced, "and positively no monogram." She whirled to the dresser and began to open drawers.

Matt pursued the idea of a monogram. "Does she have a watch on?"

"I don't know."

Betty made no move, so Matt went resolutely to the bed, groped in a warm place under the covers for the girl's left arm and lifted it into view, exposing as he did so, flashes of gentle other flesh. The arm in his grasp was relaxed, but throbbed alive. He looked down at the watchless wrist, the ringless fingers, the blunt unpainted fingernails. He let the arm and hand down gently, outside the coverlet.

His mother spoke quietly from the open doorway. "Who is she?"

Matt said, with too much breath, "Not a thing to say."

"Nothing?" said Peg, as if she had half expected this. "Poor child."

Matt, who felt as if he'd put on blinders, who was canceling his peripheral vision, who would not look again at the girl on the bed, saw his mother's face begin to pinch. He said warningly, "Now, Peg!" He thought she was going to cry.

But Peg said, flatly, "Then I guess she's mine."

"What are you talking about? Now don't be like that, Ma. You're *not* responsible."

"I am. Until we find her own people."

"Peg, there is no law —"

She put up her chin and said, "I can't help *that*."

Betty Prentiss, who was running her fingers around the edges of the white paper lining of a dresser drawer, felt as if fingers were running up and down her spine.

Matt said crossly, because he was feeling a touch of panic and knew not why, "O.K., Ma, but try not to take it *too* hard. Will you, please?"

They heard the ambulance in the street and Matt

went tearing down the stairs to let the men in. Motion was relief. He didn't like this, didn't like it at all.

When he had gone, Betty turned her head to look at Peg. Peg was looking back at her, dark eyes a little defiant. "If you don't understand, then you don't understand," they seemed to say. "But my life is my life, my self is my self, and I have to do what I see to do."

"I wish she hadn't seen *your* sign," said Betty. She told herself it was too bad for Peg to have been so put upon by chance.

Chapter Two

There was an old-fashioned, round, pedestal table in the corner of Peg's big kitchen. That evening, Betty Prentiss sat sideways behind it, sipping coffee and contemplating the possibility that she was in love.

Matt was at the table, too, just finishing his late supper. Tony Severson was there, bouncing with curiosity and pumping them as urgently as he could.

But Betty wasn't saying much. *Do* I want to marry Matt Cuneen? she was asking herself. If not, what am I doing here, anyway? Why don't I take my own apartment or take one with another girl, or a whole flock of them, and live the life with the double dates and all the intrigues of my peers? Why do I hang around with a proxy mother like Peg? I don't need a mother. And why haven't I gone all out for summer travel, which is the thing for us school teachers to do? Why didn't I arrange to go to Europe, like everybody else, with Kleenex and camera? Looks as if I wanted to stay right here. And why is that?

Something in the back of herself had evidently decided that Matt was the man for her. It wasn't a new idea. Naturally not, with their mothers feeling as they did, and even Betty's uncle simply assuming that one day a wedding would come to pass. To that generation, the match seemed so suitable, sensible, desirable, and safe that it made itself. As a match, Betty thought highly of it too. She and Matt were equal in status, as compatible in interests and in values as might be, and long acquainted. It ought to work.

But now, she thought ruefully, to be just about the opposite of star-crossed lovers was not the most attractive thing in the world. Not for Matt. And not for Betty, either.

It wasn't suitability. She didn't know what it was, but it wasn't that. How come she suddenly knew that it *was*, at all? She didn't know how she knew. But now that she knew, what was to be done?

There was another thing. Betty was well aware of a tradition that had grown up here in the last five years, since Dr. Cuneen had died and Peg had resolved to stay where she was in the big house, to move herself and Matt down into the wing that ran off at the back, to rent her two upstairs rooms, and by this means, pay her house taxes. She had not been left destitute; neither was she affluent. But Peg managed, in her own way, very well. She enjoyed having young women in the house and invariably, if they showed any signs of wanting to be mothered, Peg mothered them.

But her friends and neighbors had made a running joke of the fact that almost every one of Peg's girls had, in her day, rolled a speculative eye at the son of the house, the so personable and eligible son who lived there too. So Betty knew that she had fallen heiress to a pattern that might take some breaking. How many counts were there against her? One of his mother's roomers, playmate from the cradle, recommended by their elders, no surprises.

How could Mr. Matthew Marks Cuneen, boy scientist, not in the hunting mood, evasive by long practice, and feeling like her big brother, besides, be enticed to realize that Betty was the one for him?

Some old-fashioned methods were just too corny to consider. For instance, she was not going to try to "make him jealous" because of Tony Severson, who

21

came around from time to time. Tony worked for a newspaper, not a big-city paper but a semi-local sheet that had its yellow tinge. Young Mr. Severson was not spending any of his traditional pittance to take Betty to shows or nightclubs. He liked to come by casually and pick her up of an evening, ramble around the town with a good companion, drop by a pizza parlor or a hamburger stand, or often just to drop in and sit here in Peg's kitchen and talk. He didn't want to marry Betty and nobody was going to think so.

Hmm. Well, now. The solution of this problem was going to take a little serious planning and effort, now that she seemed to know what the problem was. She stole a glance at Matt's face. Yes, she liked his face. She liked his hands. She liked . . .

Sex? she presumed. Well, sex was all right with her, but she didn't quite know how to begin to flirt with him, if that was the word. He could be, she guessed, rather impervious to signals of that sort. From good old Betty Prentiss.

She wasn't sending any such signals at the moment, not being decked out at all. She had on a pair of blue capris, an old white shirt, and no shoes. Her dark hair lay wild on her head. She was just good old Betty, at home in his mother's kitchen, with her bare feet on the rounds of the chair.

She wasn't beautiful and strange. Betty blinked and began to listen to the conversation.

Tony Severson was the kind of young man who turned a wooden chair around, sat astride of the seat, and rested his arms upon the back rail. His reddish hair stood up and his little hazel eyes roved foxily from face to face. Peg had told him about the mysterious stranger and Tony was bound that there was more to know than he had been told.

"You guys aren't expert room-searchers," he was

22

arguing. "Why won't you let me go up there with ye olde fine-tooth comb? You've missed something. There has got to be a clue to this dame's identity."

"There hasn't got to be," Matt said, "and there isn't. So you won't go up and snoop around, because who needs you?"

One had to be rude to Tony. He invited it. He was always cheerful in the face of rudeness.

"Take a matchbook cover," he went on arguing. "That could be a clue, for instance, to where she'd just been. Does she smoke, by the way? And say, has anybody scraped under her fingernails?"

"For her name and address?" inquired Betty

"Ah, come on. A clue to her occupation, maybe. You guys got no Sherlock blood? Does she look like an office worker? Or maybe, you should pardon the expression, like a school teacher? What does she look like, anyhow?"

Matt was poking at the sweet roll that was his dessert and he neither spoke nor looked up until Betty's silence seemed to surprise him.

So Betty looked away and answered in a deliberate drawl, "Well, I'll tell you, Tony—she is absolutely gorgeous."

"Hey! Hey!" said Tony, between delight and suspicion. "You're not putting me on? How? How do you mean?"

"A beeyootiful blonde," said Betty and thought, Listen to me sound pure cat. She glanced slyly at Matt. He was munching his roll.

"A real doll, eh?" said Tony, making gestures that outlined huge breasts in the kitchen air. "I mean with all the standard equipment, yes?"

"I presume so," said Matt with the regulation leer.

So Betty let her breath in slowly and deeply. She now perceived, with a little hoot of silent laughter, that fate had played the old-fashioned "jealous" trick on her. It had worked very well. *This was*, suddenly, how she knew that, in love or no, she certainly did not want *anybody else* to have Mr. Matthew Cuneen. Well, well, she said to herself, mysteriously smiling.

Matt was trying to conceal his irritation. He had leered as he was expected to leer. But he was thinking morosely that if they had been able to say that the stranger was an ugly old woman with a moustache, Tony would have lost interest in the business. Matt didn't think the girl in the hospital was any of Tony Severson's business, especially since Tony's business was always public business. Matt wouldn't permit Tony upstairs, to poke at those few pitiful possessions. He didn't fancy the helpless girl being made the center of a circus, newspaper style. Let Tony go peddle his papers somehow else.

The hospital, in the person of Dr. Jon, had been somewhat dismayed when the girl's identity had proven elusive. Nothing, of course, deterred the whole staff from the task of diagnosing and, if may be, curing her. So she was as safe as she could be, in good hands, and Matt wanted things to be let alone. He didn't want Tony stirring up trouble. Not his kind of trouble. Matt rather wished his mother had kept her mouth shut.

The dining-room door was swinging and in came his mother with Dr. Jon Prentiss behind her. The doctor was a stubby man with broad shoulders aggressively squared, and a very straight broad back. His face was rugged and habitually stern. He was a no-nonsense man. But he greeted Betty with affection and endured an introduction to Tony with courtesy.

"We don't know yet," he said to their questions. "Tests tomorrow." He sat down and Peg poured him coffee and fetched him the saccharin. He and Peg were very fond, but there was no nonsense between them.

"How old would you say she was, Doctor?" asked Tony briskly.

"About Betty's age."

"Young and beautiful?"

"Well designed," the doctor admitted.

"And no idea who she is?"

"Not unless somebody's been around here, inquiring for her." The doctor took the negative answer from their silence and began to sip.

"I think," said Tony, speaking from the position of a young man of the world, "you would be well advised to call the police, Doctor."

"Police!" Peg exclaimed.

"Well, sure, Mrs. Cuneen. See, maybe somebody reported her missing. Missing Persons, see, is like a lost-and-found department and what you've got here, you've got a 'found' girl." Tony looked pleased with himself.

Dr. Jon was looking at him over his cup, fixing him with his stare that could scatter nurses like petals in the wind. But Tony said blithely, "I'd be glad to make the call *for* you, Doctor."

Dr. Jon said, "The police knew nothing about her, as of three hours ago."

"Oh, I see. Well, sir," Tony was less patronizing this time, "could I suggest something else? If you would like me to get hold of one of our photographers to take a few pictures, my paper would be glad to print them. Might be the way to find out who . . . uh . . . lost her."

Matt said lazily, "Why don't you keep your nosy nose out, Tony? Nobody needs you."

"Ah ha," said Tony, shaking a finger. "Maybe you do, old boy. What about the power of the Press?"

Dr. Jon was looking at him thoughtfully. Betty said nothing. But now Peg slid into a chair beside the doctor and said, "It might be a way."

"Ma," said Matt. "Now, you don't want that kind

25

of thing. Believe me, you don't realize what Tony and his paper can do to you."

"I wouldn't do a thing in the world to her," said Tony indignantly. "I love her! Don't I, Mrs. Cuneen?"

Peg clasped her hands and said, "I keep thinking of her people. How could they come *here,* to inquire? She just happened to see my little sign out on the lawn. How could anybody know she would see it?"

"A point well taken," said the doctor. "I can tell you this. It is advisable to find her people quickly. We need her medical history."

"As a public service," crowed Tony, "I'll get the photographer there first thing in the morning. I'll come myself."

Matt said, "Don't do it."

"Why not, dear?" his mother asked. "I don't want anybody thinking about trouble for me."

"I don't think it's a *good* idea for anybody," he said, unwilling to be more specific because he was not going to add any fuel to Tony's highly inflammable imagination. So he offered an alternative to the doctor. "Why not let the police trace her?"

"Because they said it is not their province," the doctor answered promptly. "No law's been broken. No crime is involved."

Betty had her feet on the floor now, and she felt Matt's shoe nudging her ankle. "I don't like it, either," she said at once, and sought his approving eye.

But Peg said to them gently, "It's nothing to like or dislike. It's something to *do.*"

And the doctor said with a Jovian nod, "Right. I think so. I'll make the arrangements."

"Then I'll lay it on," cried Tony joyfully. "Be very glad to, Doctor. I'll get it a good position. I'll write the story myself." He sounded as if this should reassure them as to literary quality and humane discretion. It did not reassure Matt in the least. But he kept

26

quiet until Tony, babbling promises, had taken his leave.

Then Matt said, "I think we forgot something, sir."

"What was it *we* forgot?"

"That it isn't quite normal," Matt said, bearing up nobly under the doctor's eye-beams, "for a person to carry *no* identification whatsoever. Not even an old letter. A scrap of paper. Or so much as an initial."

Betty was with him in a flash. "Sure, because everybody carries some dumb thing. You mean it's not an accident?"

"My point," said Matt, grinning congratulations at her. "So I ask you this. Is it possibly, deliberate? Suppose she doesn't want to be identified?"

The doctor was frowning. "Why wouldn't she want to be identified?"

"We can't know *why*. But that doesn't mean it might not be so."

"The fact remains," said the doctor judiciously, "that if we are going to save her life, we need all the information about her that we can get. I wouldn't worry about offending her, myself."

"I wasn't quite worrying about *offending* her," Matt said. "We might do worse. We might put her in some position she was trying to avoid."

"In danger, even," Betty said.

Peg's hands fluttered alarm.

But the doctor turned to Betty and said, mock-solemn, "From the Mafia, I suppose?"

"*Or* a reasonable facsimile." Matt remained cheerfully obstinate. "There are some contributing indications. She came unusually early in the morning—looking as if she had not slept at all—to a strange house, where she took what seems suspiciously like refuge. She carried nothing with her to tell who she really is. She wasn't forthcoming."

The doctor countered at once. "She was on the brink of an illness, which fact manifested itself as fa-

27

tigue. She took refuge, as Peg says, because she needed a place to rest. She took a strange room because she was travelling. Witness the suitcase. I doubt the very remote possibility, that she intended to hide from physical danger, should prevent us from trying to save her from a very real and undeniable physical danger by any means we can. She is safe where she is, as far as the Mafia is concerned, *or* its reasonable facsimile. From some emotional problem, she can be rescued later. But we do not yet know what ails her, in the body, and we had better find out pretty soon."

"Oh, Jon," said Peg woefully.

"So we'll let this newspaper appointment stand, I think," said the doctor. "Agreed, Peg?"

"Yes," Peg said. "Yes. She mustn't die because we neglected *anything*."

"Matt? Betty?"

The doctor was taking votes, but the conclusion was already clear.

"I guess we lose, Uncle Jon," said Betty for them both.

So the doctor said he had to get along home. He told Peg, sternly, not to worry. She had done and was doing the best that she could do. As would he. So he went off, carrying as much as he could of the trouble on his big shoulders. Peg went quietly off to her bed.

Matt and Betty sat on, in the kitchen.

Matt had almost forgotten that she was there. He was a little ashamed of his argument. Not that it hadn't been of some import. It was, however, more of a rationalization of a reluctance. An instinct?

He was remembering now, seeing with great clarity in his mind's eye, the little private room where they had put her. She was not in isolation, not yet. Just before he had come home, he had looked in and seen her lying on the high bed, seeming enshrined. It was

28

funny how that feeling had been transferred from the room upstairs. It had stopped his breath for a moment.

They had given her a nurse for the night, instructed to observe to the motion of an eyelash. She was a pleasant woman of middle years, named Selma Marsh, whom Matt knew casually. She had been in attendance with a devoted awe, he mused now, as if she were handmaiden to a fair young queen, where the lady lay in whiteness mellowed by one yellow light, lay like Elaine on her barge. Now where, he wondered, wrenching away from the vision, had that Elaine-image come from? An old *child's* book?

Then Betty spoke up reasonably in his mother's kitchen. "If she was running away from something, she might have given us a phony name."

Matt stirred, feeling as if he had been too rudely awakened. "She might have," he agreed. "It could follow."

"I'm pretty sure, you know," Betty went on, "that she never did say 'Dolan.' And she didn't even answer when Peg asked for the rest of it. Maybe she hadn't made up a first name yet."

This grated. Matt got up, taking dishes to the sink. "Oh well, Tony gets to have his fun, and all will be revealed by the power of the Press."

"I suppose so," said Betty. "But I sure wish . . ."

"What?" he said, waiting to turn the hot water on.

"Oh, just that Peg wasn't taking it so darned hard. There's nothing more for her to do."

Matt turned the water on and held his cup under it. He seemed to know that Betty was wishing *he* wasn't taking it so hard. He felt a little curl of resentment. *He* wasn't taking it that hard. But if his mother felt responsible, what was he supposed to do? He had to be responsible, too. He hadn't asked for it. He shut off the water and said, "At least it doesn't have to bother *you*." He knew he had stung her. He shouldn't

29

have. Surely he needn't wave a big fat KEEP OFF sign for Betty Prentiss!

"Hey, hey, old Betts," he said to her frozen face, "I didn't mean that." And then he did it again by saying much too formally, "Would you excuse me?" before he headed for his bed.

Chapter Three

The next morning, Thursday, Matt walked across to the hospital and found Tony in the corridor outside the girl's room, involved in an argument about lighting with a photographer, two doctors, and a nurse. Matt stood by, silent, non-interfering, and barely breathing, while the job was done, and when they had closed her door, where she still lay sleeping he suffered the gleam in Tony's eye, and Tony's mindless bubbling thanks, and watched Tony go scurrying off to stir things up.

He wasn't due in the lab until noon. He had to go out to the University to register for the summer session. He might as well go. He needn't ask any questions of the doctors, since he could tell by the very atmosphere that they had not yet decided upon a name for the girl's condition. They were not conclusion-jumpers.

So he tore himself out of there, raced through the park in the pleasant morning, took the car he shared with his mother and drove his twenty miles, since — although he was lucky enough to be able to walk to work — he went a rather more normal Los Angeles-area distance to school.

Matt did his dreaming in a practical and organized fashion. He had every intention of becoming, one day, an important scientist, for which reason he meant to be, first, well trained and then industrious. He would go steadily, step by step, upon his way to achieve something, and it would not be wealth. He had ambition, a goal, and a plan. Upon which he proceeded, without romancing. He had long ago decided just which courses he would take this summer and why. He knew what hours would be best and which instructors, and what textbooks he must buy.

This morning, it all seemed very cut and dried.

Betty Prentiss went to her school and her third-graders as usual, but this was the last day, and when she had gone through the short session and had turned in all her reports, she drove back to Peg's house, feeling at a loss.

What would she do now? Would she look for a summer job, as she had half-planned to do? No, not today. It was an afternoon for brooding quietly, clearing the head, perhaps making full plans.

But she kept seeing that girl, hearing that girl's voice, going compulsively over and over that brief encounter.

The funny thing was, that girl had not, awake and moving, struck Betty as being so darned beautiful. Oh, a reasonably fine collection of physical attributes. Yes, of course. But she had moved as if she were weighted, spoken in a voice without volume or emphasis, seemed dull, dusted over, without radiance. That could have been her illness coming on.

What had she said? Very little. She had said, at sight of the front room, "This is nice. This is nice." But without enthusiasm. How could anybody say such a thing without enthusiasm? Nevertheless, that girl had. Then she had said "Thank you" a time or two.

Then she had said, reeling with weariness, mumbling, "My name is . . ." Dolan? No. Olin? Tollin? Bollen? Rollin? Polling? Pol*ing?* The sound would not come back to Betty's ear with any satisfactory clarity.

When Betty had heard the phone and taken over, volunteering to let Peg go down, she could remember no strong response to her friendly chatter. When she had uttered that prophetic sentence, about sleeping, had the girl smiled? Yes, surely she had smiled. A slow sleepy smile? An absent-minded grimace?

Well, it was a mystery that would soon be solved. "This, too, shall pass," she told herself, mockingly.

Peg had a guild meeting in the afternoon. She said nothing to the ladies about the incident of the sleeping stranger. Matt had warned her, gloomily, at breakfast that she'd be answering questions soon enough. But Peg had a running argument with herself that went around and around like a broken record. I mustn't worry. They are taking care of her. But if she dies and then her people come, will I say to her mother, "I didn't notice. I had a room for rent. She had the money. Who would expect me to notice?" But I mustn't worry. They are taking care of her.

The whole day had a paralyzed feeling to it.

The girl slept.

Matt slipped along to Room 124, just before he left for home, and by this time Mrs. Marsh was on duty again and glad to see him.

"I sit here," she told him, "just kinda plugging with my nerves for her to wake up. Every time she stirs I think she might open her eyes. And just, you know, suddenly — be all right? I don't usually do that. But I can't seem to help it. Wears me out, too."

Matt said he knew, but himself felt no such thing. *He* was not plugging with all his nerves for her to wake up. And this was odd. He stood a while, forcing himself to breathe the quiet air, the air of peace in this place. All his nerves seemed to sag away from tension when he was watching her, where she was sleeping so peacefully. They had been feeding her through a vein. She looked perfectly healthy. Perfectly serene. He didn't want to know the color of her eyes.

When Mrs. Marsh sighed in his ear, "She's such a lovely, lovely thing," Matt woke with a start.

"Well, take it easy." He clapped her on her sturdy shoulder and went away.

But his feet dragged on the park path. It was strange. It was very strange. *Too* strange. Suddenly he felt he ought to shake the strangeness off. Or go back and shake that girl to sensible consciousness.

In the evening, he grimly hit the new books he had purchazed. Betty watched television with Peg. Tony didn't come around. The evening had a paralysed feeling to it.

In the morning, Friday, Matt dashed out to buy Tony's paper, since it was not the regular fare of the house. There she was, at the top of page three. The photographer had done a good job. The reproduction was superb. Folds of white fabric lay beautifully shadowed. The whole picture was composed on a diagonal and was absolutely compelling. No one could resist looking at it, and surely if anyone had ever seen that exquisite face before, he would recognize it.

It made Matt's scalp creep.

Peg's name was in the story which began, "A mysterious beauty lies in sleep . . ." (And turned Matt's stomach.)

Peg's phone began to ring, as he had predicted. But it was only one violently curious acquaintance after another.

Matt, for whom there were no classes until a week from Monday, mowed the lawn and tinkered with the car. The morning crept.

Just before noon, he raced the park and strode down

34

her corridor, bracing for anything. But there was nothing. Mrs. Marsh was not on duty at this hour. The nurses on the floor were attentive enough. Her door was ajar. Matt thought she seemed too vulnerable, too exposed.

He tipped in and went closer. They were taking very good care of her. She was immaculate. He studied her face. Not a grain of powder (as Matt innocently thought make-up to be) on that skin. Not a smidgeon of lipstick on that mouth. A face, a body, intact and unadorned, and warm asleep. Like a child, he thought. He had seen children asleep. But she was not a child. A woman? What was she? Does she dream? he thought.

He snatched at his obligation to be where he ought to be, and not in here. And went away, trying again to shake off whatever it was she made him feel. A funny thing, it wasn't goatishness. No, but a planlessness, a drifting feeling. He seemed to have no plot, no plan, about this girl. He didn't seem to hope or fear. He just wanted things to stay as they were. He didn't *want* to know who she was. But that was ridiculous! He *had* to want to know. He'd better forget the whole thing and do some work.

At about one o'clock, Peg was tidying away the traces of a meal when the doorbell rang.

A few ripples had reached her by this time, thrown into the pond by the picture and story in the paper. Another paper had telephoned. A man calling himself an occultist had telephoned. Peg had told the former that all she knew was in the published story and had refused to be sold an electronic crystal ball by the latter.

Now she trotted to answer the bell and found an obviously prosperous middle-aged gentleman on her doorstep. She caught the idea of prosperity quickly, partly from the lines of the car standing at the curb and partly from his clothing. Peg was nobody to know one make of car from another, nor was she a connoisseur of men's tailoring, but she knew, just the same, when money had been spent.

"Mrs. Cuneen? My name is Leon Daw. I wonder if you would let me come in and ask you a few questions? It is in regard to the young woman whose picture was in the paper. You see, I may know who she is."

"Well, then, come in," said Peg eagerly. "We are very anxious to find out who she is because, I'm afraid, she is quite ill. Poor child."

"Then I suppose I hope," he said piously, "that she is not my niece." He gave her a pained smile as he stepped inside. "There are reasons," he said, "why I have come here instead of going directly to the hospital. Would you be good enough to tell me what you know about her? She came here on Wednesday, did she?"

Peg took him into her living-room, where he waited politely until she was seated and then drew up his trouser knees by expert habit. He was rather a bland-looking chap, in his forties, she surmised, with a face and a body that seemed an intricate arrangement of curves. He had a well-fed look, pinkish skin on cheeks plump enough to be unwrinkled, a tonsure of pale brownish hair around a pink bald spot. His light blue eyes were quick and sly enough to send her some admiring glances, as if a busy little brain were saying "What a nice woman!" His mouth was narrow but high, what could have been called a rosebud mouth had it not been so heavy of lip and masculine in size. He looked smooth. Smooth was the very word for him. Even his voice was smooth, with a purring quality.

Peg told him rapidly all she knew, which was so very little. "She gave us a name," she continued, "but we didn't quite understand it. We haven't let the . . . well, the newspapers have that. But I'll tell *you,* of course." She told him. "Does it mean anything?"

36

"No," he said, with a sigh. "No, but if she is my niece, I can conceive of reasons why she wouldn't have given her real name." He stared at her a moment, with his strange mouth part-way open. "Would you be good enough, Mrs. Cuneen, to look at *this* picture?"

He handed her a newspaper clipping, a poor photograph taken at an airport obviously. There was a girl, standing out against a distant background of a disembarking crowd. "Could that be the girl, do you think?" he purred. Then he sat very still.

Peg studied the picture. This girl, for all one could tell under her boxy jacket, had an excellent figure. Her legs and ankles were good. She was slim. She stood with an easy air of dominance. She looked as if she had poise and force. Her head was bare, her blonde hair piled high. The shot was full face, not profile, and showed only the oval shape, the well-spaced features which were in no way distinguished by any striking emphasis of chin or nose or eyes.

"I don't know," said Peg. "I suppose it could be."

"Then you see nothing that contradicts?" he pressed her.

"No. No. She's a very good-looking young woman."

"Yes," he said. "Yes, she is. Poor Dorothy. I don't understand this, you know, Mrs. Cuneen. But I saw such a resemblance in this morning's newspaper, I felt I must check."

"Of course."

"Tell me, did anyone besides yourself see her or speak to her?"

"Oh, yes," said Peg. "Wait. I'll call her."

So Betty came down.

Betty had the immediate conviction that Mr. Daw was a bachelor. This screamed to her from everything about him. A high-living bachelor who liked women. He had that assessing and exploratory air. She looked at his clipping and agreed with Peg. It might be. Nothing said it couldn't be. So Mr. Daw turned on what he,

37

no doubt, thought of as his charm and asked her to recount her impressions of the girl who had come here on Wednesday morning.

Betty hadn't much to tell him, either.

"Well," he sighed, "I am sorry I have no other picture of my niece, none recent enough, that can be of any help. Except this one, which was taken when she flew in, on Sunday morning."

"Why don't you go over to the hospital where she is," said Betty with real curiosity, "and see?"

"Yes," he sighed, "I must do that. I did hope that you ladies could tell me something that would — well — knock out the possibility of her being . . ." he hesitated . . . "Dorothy Daw."

Peg, who knew the name, gasped.

"What?" said Betty, looking at her in bewilderment. But she too seemed to have heard that name somewhere.

"Because of the publicity," purred the man. "My niece, poor child, was born prey for the newspapers. She happens, Miss Prentiss, to be the tenth richest young woman in the world."

"Oh," said Betty and then burst, "But her things! This girl, our girl, had the cheapest kind of clothing. All worn and old, and cheap in the beginning."

"Is that so?" He sat back and pursed his already naturally narrow mouth. "That is certainly very, very strange. Is there anything among her *things* that would make it impossible for her to be Dorothy?"

"I don't know what that could be," said Betty.

"I don't either," he confessed. "But she had, for instance, no checkbook? No jewelery?" They shook their heads. "Well, I'm stumped," he said to them both. "I want to do whatever is the right thing." He spread out his hands. Peg nodded in sympathy. "But I do *not* want to bring in Dorothy's name at all if that is not necessary. She has had enough pawing from the Press in her day. Now, she only just came back, on

38

Sunday, from a year's stay in Uganda."

"Uganda!" said Betty, the syndrome, "Africa,-tse-tse fly — sleeping sickness" leaping into her mind, and then being quickly cast out as popular science in the worst sense. "Is your niece missing?" she inquired.

"She may be," he said gravely. "She may be. I put her into a cab for the airport on Tuesday, right after lunch. But she was wearing a very good suit, a little feather hat," he was making gestures, "hand-made shoes and bag to match and carrying a white train case. If this *is* she, then where are those things?"

"Where was she going?" asked Betty. "Are you sure she didn't get there?"

"She did not get there,"said the man, sadly. "I tele-phoned this morning. Her friends in San Francisco had not even expected her. She had not phoned them or wired. So *that,* you see, is a little mystery in itself. A coincidence?" he purred.

Betty began to believe that the girl was Dorothy Daw. "Was there anything," she leaned forward to ask, "that she might have wanted to run away from?"

"My dear, I don't know." He looked startled and spread his hands again. "I do not know. She didn't say. She came in, on Sunday. I met her and took her to my house, of course. I am her . . . well, not her legal guardian anymore, since she is too old for that . . . but I manage the . . . er . . . estate for her. Dorothy doesn't want to be bothered by the financial chores and so she hires me to do them." He smiled and the corners of his mouth turned up rather saucily. "I hadn't seen her for . . . oh, more than two . . . I should say almost three years. She travels, you know. She goes where she pleases. We simply had a reunion. Nothing at all was said about her wanting to . . . how did you put it? . . . run away. I see, of course, what you mean. I suppose it is possible. I suppose she could have tried to . . . disappear, shall we say? To have be-come anonymous? She might even have gone to the trouble of a disguise. I don't know. I can't say. It is true that she . . . rather dreads the United States. She hates walking in the limelight. She had much too much of that, years ago. That's why she travels. She says that in the United States she is *least* free."

He sighed. "So you ladies assure me that you cannot think of anything . . . ?"

Betty took a moment to divine his meaning. She felt he was putting it backwards, in some curious way. Then she answered, with Peg, that they could think of nothing to deny that the girl might be Miss Dorothy Daw, the tenth richest young woman in the world.

"She wore no make-up, though," said Betty. "No nail polish. Nothing at all, of that sort."

"That could be Dorothy," he said. "It is a strange thing—or maybe it isn't—how a person who has always had a great deal of money will be the one to care very little about some of the things money will buy. Things that . . . how shall I say this . . . that would be budgeted for, by less prosperous people. As a matter of fact, I can imagine that she was on . . . well . . . a poor-but-honest kick."

"She sounds," said Betty, "like a very unconventional person."

"You could say so," he said, with a trace of bitterness. He became suddenly a little impatient. "She is not conscious? She doesn't speak? What *is* this mysterious illness? Is it really serious?"

"I don't think they know what it is yet," said Peg, in a fluster. "They would have let *me* know, you see. I have considered myself responsible because, after all, she was taken ill in my house."

"Oh, my dear lady," he said, his pale lids fluttering, "how good of you to be concerned about a poor stranger—as she must have seemed to you. But if she is my niece, of course you must feel relieved of *any* burden. With our deepest appreciation."

40

Peg couldn't answer. Betty went with him to the door.

Then Peg called after. "I'll phone my son, Mr. Daw. He works at the hospital and he can guide you. Show you just how to get to see her. I do hope—I do hope that she will soon recover."

"So do I," he said, "which goes without saying."

With many thanks he bowed himself away.

When Betty returned from the door Peg was already on the phone, pouring the whole story into Matt's ear.

When she had hung up, Betty said, "I don't know, Peg. It looked as if she never had worn any jewelery. No watch or ring marks."

"Well, but if she was being poor-but-honest in Uganda for a year . . ." sputtered Peg.

"She sounds whacky," said Betty.

Matt was on the hospital steps when the big black car came slipping around the park. Mr. Leon Daw took no account of regulations. He left his vehicle in a doctor's slot beside the entrance and came to where Matt was standing with somewhat of a bounce.

"You are, of course, that very kind Mrs. Cuneen's son," said Mr. Daw, shaking hands. (Matt didn't care for being told who he, of course, was.) "And I must say to you," the man continued, "that if this girl *is* Dorothy Daw, I'll want your advice as to how, in some substantial way, we can show your mother our profound gratitude."

Matt felt himself freezing.

"I'll want Dorothy under my own doctor's care," Mr. Daw went purring on. "The very best of everything. Poor dear. Do you know what this illness is?"

"They'll find out," Matt said. "She's in good hands."

"Of course. Of course," purred Mr. Daw, scenting offence taken. They pushed into the lobby, where he stopped. "By the way, did *you* see or speak to her that Wednesday morning?"

41

"No, sir," said Matt. "By the time I saw her she was . . . sleeping." His throat swelled.

"I see." Mr. Daw began to walk. "Now, how do I find her?"

"I'll take you there," Matt said stolidly. The man had the right.

"Dr. Cuneen . . ."

"Mister . . ." Matt corrected quickly.

"I see. Then, *Mr.* Cuneen, you can't tell me whether her condition is serious and if so how serious? Or whether she . . . will recover?"

The man had stopped again. His light blue eyes peered at Matt under arched brows that gave his face an expression of skittishness. "I want the truth," he added, as if with great daring.

"Nobody knows the truth yet," Matt told him. "For that reason alone, it is what you would call serious."

"But do they think she will come out of it?" Daw asked impatiently.

"Possibly. Possibly she will never regain consciousness," Matt felt weary of the layman's demand for a "yes" or "no" answer, as he told the truth.

Then suddenly, as the blue eyes went wincing and blinking away, Matt fell-in-hate with this fellow. It was like a conversion. He was absolutely sure that he did not trust this Leon Daw, did not like him, in fact, loathed everything about him, his looks, his mannerisms, his very flesh. Matt did not want the girl to turn out to be Miss Dorothy Daw, the tenth richest young woman in the world. He did not want her to belong, in any way, to Leon Daw. He did not want this man to take the sleeping girl away.

But Matt led him along the main corridor. There was a truth about her and it must stand.

They turned into the side corridor and saw a knot of nurses at the far end of it. Matt lengthened his stride, taking them swiftly to that open door, halfway along.

In Room 124 the sun slanted through the blinds, but she lay sleeping in soft shadow.

Leon Daw went tiptoe, soft as a big cat, towards the bed. Matt went with him, watchfully. "Not too close," he warned. He didn't know why. Daw's face seemed pinker and it was gathered to solemnity.

"Ah . . ." he breathed. Then he whispered, "How long has she been this way?"

"Since some time on Wednesday," said Matt, in normal tones.

The man glanced at him nervously and then back at the girl. Matt looked at her, too. They had skinned back her hair and tied it somehow; it lay smooth and neat to her head. Her face was totally revealed, pure, serene, quiet in beauty.

Matt heard Leon Daw suck in his breath. "But she *will* wake? She *will* wake, won't she?"

Matt could only shake his head.

"What are the chances?" the man whispered urgently.

"Do you know her?" Matt countered. "They don't know anything about her. They have no clue. Who is she?"

Leon Daw wiped his mouth with his fingers. "Ah, yes. Ah, poor dear Dorothy. Yes, this is she."

"Are you sure?" said Matt crisply. ("So be it," his mind said, "alas.")

"Of course I'm sure." Now the man used voice, but softly. "I've known her since she was"—he took out a handkerchief—"a baby. She's not my blood niece, you know. Her grandfather married twice. I was a stepbrother to her father. But I took the name. We are family. All that's left. How young she looks, to be . . . so . . . so stricken." He turned away and Matt followed him out of the room.

"Now, then," said Mr. Daw, putting his handkerchief back into his pocket. (Quite dry, thought Matt with a flash of anger.) "I asked you what the chances

43

are that she will wake. I do not want her waking up in a strange place—"

"I'm not a doctor," Matt said shortly.

"What are they *doing?*"

"Nothing, until they have a very sound idea what the trouble is. They'd better not."

"You mean to say they are doing *nothing?*"

"They are watching, testing. How can they do what they don't know yet they ought to do?" Matt was disgusted with a layman's idea of science.

"I see, I see." Leon worked his mouth. Then he said sharply, "Now then, to whom ought I to speak about taking her out of here immediately?"

Matt blinked.

"You *must* see that I'll want her somewhere where something *will* be done. I'll arrange it as soon as possible."

The man turned to walk and Matt turned with him, feeling an unreasonable anger.

One of the nurses came running. She was a young one with a rosy face and she said breathlessly, "Oh, Mr. Cuneen, have you heard?"

"What?"

"They know who she is, now!"

Leon Daw became as still as a cat.

"Her name is Alison Hopkins," the nurse went on excitedly. "She's a starlet in the movies. Her mother is with Mr. Atwood now."

Chapter Four

"Her *mother!*" burst Leon Daw on a gust of breath. "Her mother is dead! Her name is Dorothy Daw."

Matt looked at the angry face, the blue eyes popping from pink flesh, and felt an unreasonable inner leap of glee.

"Where is this so-called mother?" The man's poorly shaped mouth could be vicious. "What's going on here? Who is in authority?"

"I'll show you," said Matt mildly.

Mr. Atwood had a small office tucked away in the north wing. Matt tapped on the door, and feeling justified by this fantastic emergency, he opened it before he was bidden to do so. The Administrator was behind his desk, his head up, his look alert. Dr. Jon was standing beside him, stiff and frosty towards a breach of etiquette. In the chair at the other side of the desk there was sitting a woman, with her head swivelled around on a taut neck.

"What is it, please?" said Atwood hostilely.

"Mr. Atwood, Dr. Prentiss, this is Mr. Leon Daw," said Matt with crisp urgency. "He has just identified the girl in 124 as his niece Dorothy."

The men's faces understood and changed. The woman did not move. Perhaps her eyes became a little glassy.

Dr. Jon said, just as crisply, "This is Mrs. Bobbie

Hopkins. She identifies the girl in 124 as her daughter Alison."

Mrs. Bobbie Hopkins said, foolishly, "How do you do?" Then, belatedly, she gasped.

She was not a large woman, but one a bit too stout for her height, and sternly corseted in. Her hair was a reddish color that nature not only had not produced but probably never would. She had drawn all around her blue eyes with various colored pencils and pastes. Her mouth was painted a rich red some of which color was also on her front teeth. She had a burning cigarette in her right hand and now, as Leon Daw moved with his cat tread to look down at her, she squashed it in the ashtray with an emphatic gesture, as if to declare war.

"Madame," he said in his purring way, "if you are speaking of the girl whose picture was in this morning's paper, then I fear you've made some mistake."

"I don't know what you mean," said Mrs. Hopkins shrilly. "You out of your mind or something? That's my kid. I ought to know."

Matt backed up against the wall near the door to listen and observe. Dr. Jon seemed to have stepped back with the same intention. Fred C. Atwood, a man with a face like a bloodhound's, remained silent, although alert.

But now Leon Daw turned on the Administrator. "I don't know what you people think you are doing," he barked. "I want my niece removed, at once, for intelligent treatment, and away from any more wicked invasions by irresponsible people. I'll make the arrangements *now*. May I use your telephone?"

"You may not," said Atwood quietly, "until we know a little more about this. You say you recognize that girl?"

"I do. She happens to be my niece."

"Well, I certainly should know my own baby," cried the woman. "Say, who is this creep? What right has *he* got to come barging in here and calling me a liar? *Is* he

46

calling me a liar?" She was heaving at the bosom and she clutched it. "I told you all about it. When I saw her picture I was . . . Oh, I can't tell you how it hit me. Poor kiddie! That's my little baby girl lying there, so sick, and she might even die, and now this man . . ."

Mrs. Hopkins was preparing to weep. Matt, who had been searching her face for any resemblance, felt a flash of disgust with her feminine tactics. To weep would not alter the truth. But what was it? The woman's face was so made-up, so beaten into what might, with very low lighting and a good deal of charity, seem still young and fair, that although Matt conceded that she might once have been a pretty little thing, it was difficult to judge just now. There was the straight small nose, the well-rounded chin. But the resemblance, if such it was, did not constitute proof. Or even conviction.

"Listen," the woman sobbed, "I told you. She took off. I was looking for her myself because somebody wants her for a big part. I mean, *I* didn't know she was sick in the hospital, for crying out loud. I woulda been here, long ago."

It was Dr. Jon who told her to be quiet and by some personal magnetism held her so, as he began to pry into Leon Daw's knowledge about his niece's health. Had Dorothy Daw a physician in Los Angeles? Not that Mr. Daw knew. Where then, in what part of the world, had she been treated by a physician? Mr. Daw did not know. She travelled, he said haughtily. Had she had an illness, say within the year? Mr. Daw had heard of nothing important. He was a perfect blank. But he kept his control, although sweat appeared on his forehead.

"What about . . . Does Mrs. Hopkins know anything?" put in Matt.

The Administrator was shaking his head.

So Matt said boldly, "As you know, I admitted the patient on behalf of my mother, who holds herself responsible. I don't see how we can surrender this girl to either of these people until we are sure which one has the right."

Atwood was nodding gravely.

Leon Daw turned on Matt and said nastily, "If it comes to a question of proof, I am prepared to bring a few other people to support my identification. That is, if you are really refusing to take my word." His word, he implied, was backed by status and record, and they must be insane to doubt it.

Matt was unawed. "I understood my mother to say that your niece had been out of the country for years. So how . . . ?"

"I mean to bring people who saw her here, since Sunday." The man was furious and sweating.

"Well," cried Mrs. Hopkins, who had been held back long enough, "don't kid yourselves that I can't bring around quite a few people who know Alison."

"Didn't I understand *you* to say," put in Dr. Jon, "that your daughter had only recently returned from Spain?"

"That's right," said Mrs. Hopkins. "She came home two weeks ago. But her agent knows her, for God's sake. She's not exactly an unknown." The woman glared triumphantly. "She's in motion pictures."

"Ah, in motion pictures," purred Leon Daw, with enlightened contempt. "I see. I see."

"You don't see a thing," shrilled the lady. "You think you're so smart. Let me tell you, Alison is a dedicated artist. She's studied for years. She's had some very good credits. She's going places. And you don't go places without . . ."

"Without publicity?"

The woman goggled at him. The paint on her face seemed to detach from the skin, as if underneath there was another face.

"Publicity," said Leon Daw, "is just exactly what *I* do *not* want. So I think I shall find another telephone and

48

make some arrangements that will not be disclosed to the Press."

"Now you see here!" Mrs. Hopkins heaved herself out of the chair. "Mr. Atwood! Dr. Prentiss! I won't sit still for this! Nobody is going to take my own daughter away from me and you'd better not . . ." She threatened a fit of screaming, "You'd better not!"

Dr. Prentiss said coldly, "Sit down. Both of you." He was accustomed to being obeyed. They obeyed.

Atwood said, "Now, Mr. Daw, suppose you tell us how you think your niece came to rent a room from Mrs. Cuneen?"

"I can't tell you that," said Leon Daw promptly. "I am telling you that the girl is Dorothy Daw, who, by the way, never did arrive at the place where I had been told she intended to go." He was sitting down, holding himself calm. Sweat shone on his face, but his voice was steady. He went on to tell the rest of it, succinctly, and rather well, Matt had to admit.

Meantime, Mrs. Hopkins heaved herself to and fro in her chair making mindless gasps of outrage.

"So now," said Leon Daw finally, "I think we all have the . . . er . . . tolerance and human understanding to . . . er . . . perceive that this lady—because of a resemblance which, obviously, there must be—is finding herself in an embarrassing position. Unless," he added with sudden cruelty, "she is deliberately exploiting that resemblance for the sake of the newspapers."

"I," howled Mrs. Hopkins, "am a mother!" She was up on her feet. "So don't you call me a phony, you phony! I don't know what you want with my girl, but you won't get her. I may not have much money, but I can make a lot of noise. If you let him take her off and hide her from me," she howled at the men, "I'll raise the biggest stink you ever saw."

"On the other hand," said Leon Daw more coolly, "if you let this woman claim her, for even one moment, this hospital will be in quite some trouble."

Atwood spread his hands. The folds of flesh on his face lifted as he put his brows high. "This hospital," he said finally, "has accepted her as a patient. It is not our duty to find out who she is, except insofar as that would aid us to find out how to make her well. Neither of you are helpful in this respect. I suggest that you settle the question of her identity between you, if you can. And subsequently, one of you must prove it to the hospital's lawyer, so I should think."

"And to me," said Matt.

"And to me," snapped Dr. Prentiss. "In the meantime, I want no visitors for our patient this evening, and I would advise you both, very strongly, not to interfere with our efforts on her behalf. Now, I have work to do." A few strides, a wag of the door, a waft of air, and he was gone.

Leon Daw purred to the Administrator, "Who *is* paying her bills, may I ask?"

Atwood did not answer.

"I grant you mean to be cautious," said Daw getting up, "but you are both obstructive and insulting. How can you take seriously this freak of a stage-mother—"

"Can't you see he's a big fat liar?" shrieked Mrs. Hopkins. "And he'd better not call me names!"

Atwood had become strategically deaf.

Matt said loudly, "It's plain enough, isn't it, that my mother and I are going to stay responsible until this is cleared up?"

And Atwood said quickly, "Why don't you both *quietly* bring these other people or whatever proof you have? In the morning."

"Very well," said Leon Daw. "Meanwhile, I agree and insist that *nobody* is to see her. No more newspaper photographers. The Press is not to get anywhere near her."

Atwood seemed to be listening, but he did not speak.

"You can't keep this out of the papers!" cried Mrs.

Hopkins.

Leon raked her up and down with a look. "If you talk to the newspapers," he said scathingly, "my lawyer will be in touch with you, too." His face was pale now. His forehead wet. He seemed to have come to the end of some rope. He flung the door open and in a somewhat feeble imitation of Dr. Jon's departure, he departed.

Atwood rose and stood a moment, listening to the woman's noises. Then he said, aside to Matt, "See her out. Get her a cab if she needs one." He left them.

So Matt waited out a fit of weeping and wailing. At last the woman peered at him from one ruined eye and said, "Who is that man? Who is his damned niece, anyhow?"

"His niece is supposed to be the tenth richest young woman in the world," Matt told her.

Bobbie Hopkins opened her bag to reach for the tools of repair. Her face was ruined and old, the eyes were bleak. "Well," she said flatly, "too bad for him. That's my daughter in there, and can *I* help it if this is going to get in the newspapers?"

The eyes met Matt's. Hers were both shrewd and frightened. They veiled and fell, coquettishly. *"You* seem like a very nice boy."

"May I call a cab for you?"

"No, no, I got my car. But thanks a lot, honey." The underlying face, with its knowledge of defeat, was hidden now. "Listen, you stick to what you said, hear? Don't you let that rich bastard get my Alison. And you tell your mother, listen — I'd really like to stop by and all." She moved her mouth. Matt felt her thirst in his own mouth, suddenly. "She'll understand," said Bobbie. "She's a mother, too."

Matt said nothing. Bobbie Hopkins, having done a quick job, taken a swipe or two at eyes and lips, gathered up her handbag. "It certainly, certainly is," she said with strange detachment, "a crazy crazy situa-

51

tion."

And Matt felt wild. He said deliberately, "It *is* strange that her own mother can't tell the doctor anything that will help him save her life."

The blue eyes fled to the corners of the room. "I don't know. I just can't think. Listen, she don't live with me, you know, except since she got back from that lousy deal in Spain." Bobbie Hopkins pulled her image together. "But she'll be all right," she said in a high sweet voice of pious hope. "The good Lord isn't going to take my little girl away so soon. You'll pray for her, too, won't you, dear?"

Matt stepped aside to let her through the door. He was trying his best to feel sorry for her. He thought, savagely, that her brain must be the size of a peanut.

Chapter Five

Tony Severson, that evening, was preening himself. His story, with its intriguing developments, was being picked up far and wide. It would be on the late news on TV this very night. He was filled with naïve proprietary pride. He marched to and fro in Peg's kitchen, spreading his tail feathers, too exhilarated to sit down.

Matt, with a dampening air of austerity, kept reminding him that the power of the Press had promised the truth.

"Don't you worry," said Tony. "There's a pack of hounds on this thing now, and you couldn't conceal your own navel. It's my story." He looked at Matt defensively. "The cops aren't going to move on it. You said so yourself. And you say the hospital isn't going to hire any private investigator. So who is it up to whom? Yah. Yah. It's up to little old me. Because our readers are going to have their tongues hanging out for the real truth."

Matt wished he wouldn't keep saying "the real truth."

Peg was there, quietly dismayed but disputing nothing. Betty was there. Matt had a feeling that good old Betty was seeing his points.

He said, "Since when do your readers pant after the 'real' or any other kind of truth? Don't they prefer a story?"

"Oh wow!" cried Tony. "So it's a story! I love it. I love it. Is the Sleeping Beauty a missing heiress? Or a poor young struggling actress of humble origin?"

"Or neither one," snapped Matt. "The hospital's had half a dozen more phone calls from people who think they know who she 'really' is."

"I've had them, too," said Peg unhappily.

"Oh well," said Tony cheerfully. "You're always going to get the nuts. You knew that."

I knew it, Matt thought. But Dr. Prentiss, in his innocent integrity, hadn't known it. The doctor, much annoyed, had sternly banned any visitors and had slapped a sign on the hospital room and told Atwood that he would have peace or know the reason why. Atwood had met with the lawyer and the PR man and members of the staff, to no conclusion Matt knew about. He shuddered to think what might happen tomorrow when the papers ran the story of two possible identities. And such gaudy ones, at that.

So he was viewing Tony Severson with uncontrollable distaste.

Tony had turned up a good deal of past news about Dorothy Daw. She had been brought up on her mothers' Long Island estate. The father had died years ago. Inevitably dubbed the "madcap heiress," Dorothy had been a celebrity very young. When the mother died, Dorothy, then eighteen, had gone abroad to school, had turned up in smart resorts — with assorted escorts and rumors flying — here and there around the civilized world. But for the last two or three years, she had moved out of the news. She was getting a little old to be the newspapers' pet. She hadn't done anything very startling. She had been living, more or less quietly, among people who were exiles of one sort or another, but exiles with incomes, Tony would bet. Tony said the paper hadn't got on to anyone in Africa who was willing to gossip. Or at least they hadn't yet. So her recent doings lay in obscurity.

As for her character, she had been publicized as the perennial stereotypes spoiled little rich girl. But Tony had to admit that she had never been in any serious scandals.

He had a couple of old clippings, photographs. The resemblance was there. But the styles were strange. The impression was different.

As for Alison Hopkins, she was, indeed, a minor kind of actress. She had, indeed, been "making a picture" in Spain. That was about all Tony had on her. He couldn't do everything in one day, could he?

"Of course," said Tony now, "I've got a good hunch which one our little darling really is."

"Which you won't publish," said Matt waspishly, "until you sell tomorrow's papers?"

"Listen," said Tony, looking hurt. "I can't print it when I can't prove it."

Matt threw up his hands.

Betty said, "Look, Tony, you're among us chickens. Don't bother with your image, huh? You're going to beef up this story if you possibly can, and everybody here knows it."

Matt kicked her in the ankle approvingly. "Was it your shenanigans upstairs that gave you this hunch? That you can't prove? Excuse me. I should say 'scientifically prove,' of course." (And sarcasm would get him nowhere.)

He had been obliged to take Tony up to the front bedroom when first Tony had appeared. He had been obliged to watch Tony open the grey suitcase and take out every garment, hunting for cleaning tags and laundry marks, search the shoes for the manufacturer's name, list the numbers on the money. Tony had gone about all this with an air of great efficiency which had leaked away as he proceeded. There were no tags or laundry marks unless they were visible only in a special light. The shoes had come from a cheap chain, the bills of money were in no special sequence. Tony had finally pronounced all this to be police business, needing the organization.

"All I say," Tony announced now, "is that I get the message myself. It's intuition. You develop it with experience. Oh, this kid is Dorothy Daw, all right. And I'll tell you why. Because this Bobbie Hopkins, well . . . she's a type."

"A publicity-hungry stage-mother, eh?" said Matt. *"That* type?"

"Why, sure. So she jumps to a nice exciting conclusion when she sees the picture. O.K. When she gets there and looks at the girl, she *wants* to believe it's her darling daughter because what sport? Right? So she utters. And after that, she's stuck with it." Tony was confident. "She'll back down. Want to bet? But meanwhile . . ."

"Back in the headlines."

"Well, hell, Matt . . ."

Peg said, "Wouldn't she want that very sick girl *not* to be her daughter?" And Tony looked at her as if he could not understand a word she was saying.

Betty said vehemently, "The point is what *are* you going to do to find out the truth about this very sick girl?"

And Matt keeping quiet, letting anger boil about in his blood, felt grateful for her sharp good sense.

"Yeah, better tell us what you're going to do," he said quite amiably. "We are the ones who have got to be shown, you realize."

"Or get stuck with the bills, eh?" said Tony innocently. "O.K., listen." He bounced on his toes. "I got a line into the DMV. Say they had put their thumbprint on a driver's license. That would do it. Right? Also, I'm going after dentists. Say I dig up a chart of their teeth, either one. That would do it. Now, that's the kind of thing has got to be done. Match up the old fangs. Right?"

Matt's own teeth began to ache where they were

56

clenched.

"You see," Tony went on, beginning to make a disagreeable kind of sense, "we don't have any personality clues. This kid in the hospital is out like a light. So how can we tell what kind of kid she is? Now, if she'd have just lost her memory or something like that, we'd still have mannerisms and speech habits and stuff like that there."

"That should be so," said Betty calmly and thoughtfully. "But I heard her speak, you know. I saw her up and moving."

"Yah?" Tony pounced on her. "Yah?"

"But I guess," Betty went on slowly, "she couldn't have been feeling like much. I thought she moved, well—sluggishly. She spoke very low and didn't say much. She was . . . well . . . dull."

"She was ill," said Matt quickly.

"Yah," said Tony surprisingly. "Sicklied o'er. How about education? How about vocabulary? Grammar? Accent?"

"She didn't utter any sentence that needed any fancy syntax," said Betty. "No particular accent. Would you say, Peg?"

Peg shook her head.

"Well, now," Tony said, "I'll tell you. This Dorothy Daw, she went to finishing schools all over the map and she's been around the world a few times. Probably she'd have what you could call an International English. But this Alison Hopkins, she never went any farther than a high school in Arizona. Too bad, it wasn't the deep South."

Betty said, "I wouldn't know. I couldn't tell."

Matt said sharply, "Wouldn't an actress have studied speech?"

"Yah," Tony was frowning. "True for you. Could be. But see, we can't ask her to speak up now—and that's the problem. It has got to be something physical. Like say, if you'll pardon the expression . . . her marital sta-

57

tus?" He looked at them bright-eyed and feeling clever.

It was Peg Cuneen who replied to the word he had not used. She said calmly, "I don't believe you can prove anything of that sort, in these days." She looked him straight in the eye. *"Can* you?"

Matt managed to say in an amused tone; "You may be putting a little too much faith in 'scientific proof,' old boy. A bit of a risk, wouldn't you say? Suppose she wakes up and sues? Invasion of privacy?"

Tony had put on a hangdog look. "So I can't beef up the story with a bit of virginity." He was giving them hurt looks. "So how about some operation? Did one of them have her tonsils out or her appendix? Any objections? Did one of them ever break a bone? Should one of them have a nice big scar on her fair young hide? Hey, Matt, *you* can find out for me whether this kid in the hospital—"

Matt said icily and evenly, "You do a little research on scars and let us know. Then I'll be glad to see that it is checked out for you in some half-way decent way."

There was no scar. He knew that, already. Selma Marsh had told him. "Not a mark on her skin, anywhere. Honest, you know, Mr. Cuneen, it looks like she never *been* awake. Like she's been preserved someplace, in Cellophane."

Selma Marsh seemed to have established a bit of a cult. She acted as if only she and Matt belonged to it, as if they, in secret, worshipped what no one else quite saw.

Matt didn't discourage her. He didn't know how. He had listened and made no comment.

But he was not going to mention, in his mother's kitchen, what he had been told. He felt that he had just sounded pretty stuffy, but he was too angry to care much.

Betty said hastily, "But aren't they going to bring people around? People to swear?"

"Oh, sure," said Tony, whose foxy eyes lingered on Matt's face. "Eye-witnesses. And that's the worst kind. They can swear on their mothers' graves that they saw something with their own eyes, and it won't mean a thing. Oh, they'll bring! Leon Daw, *he* says he'll settle the whole business, his way, tomorrow. And more he will not say. Bobbie Hopkins, *she* isn't letting anybody in either, which would be peculiar—if she wasn't eight sheets to the wind and incoherent—or so I suspect. Or maybe she thinks it's good to play hard-to-get. Which . . ." Tony admitted ruefully, "it might *be*. Especially if she's a phony. But she's got a pack of nuts for neighbors, up there in them Hollywood hills, and they'd swear to anything, including saucers full of little green men. I talked to one whacky old biddy. She says this Alison has got an astral body or two of the faces of Eve. I can't print everything I hear, you know." Tony was plaintive.

"*Was* either of them married?" Betty asked. "That should be possible to find out."

"You think so, eh? Well, not Dorothy Daw. You can just about bet your boots. Unless it was in far-off Africa under some thornbush and kept very, very quiet. I'll have to try and find out about little old Alison. I did get to her so-called agent . . . and before he knew what was up, too. At first he had a little trouble remembering her existence. Seems much of an actress, she ain't. When he finds out what's going on he shuts up like a clam and starts thinking which studio he can peddle her to . . . I mean, presuming she comes to. He *wants* her to be Alison, see. There's money in it for him, maybe. So much for the real truth. Hey? Well, I've got work to do, chums."

It was Peg who had the grace to say, if ambiguously, "I know you have, Tony, and I know you'll do it the best you know how."

So Tony kissed her, gave the others a farewell glare, and went away.

Afterwards, Peg seemed to have taken heart. She said that Tony couldn't be the cynic he pretended. She said that they must not think of the girl in the hospital as being torn limb from limb in a contest to claim her. There had been a mistake and it would appear soon, who was mistaken. Truth must out, said Peg, and went off to her own room, enjoining them not to worry.

So Matt and Betty sat on in the kitchen. Betty was wearing a dress; a bracelet slid on her arm. It occurred to Matt that good old Betts was a female and one he dared question.

"Maybe I get a little steamed. Maybe I was wrong. But you tell me, would *you* care to have your teeth, for instance, discussed in the newspapers?"

"She wouldn't like it," said Betty softly. "I agree. The whole thing should be done more . . . well . . . more reticently."

Matt felt as if he had been blessedly understood. He sighed and stretched, relaxing. "Poor Tony, he means well, I suppose. It's just the way he goes at it . . . The way he . . . I'm glad you see what I mean."

Betty began to play with her bracelet. "You know, Matt," she said in a moment, with an air of quiet reason, "since Peg feels the way she does and since you have to go along with that . . ."

"I sure do. I'm glad you see that."

"And I do, too. You know how I feel about Peg."

"Why, sure." Now Matt included her, generously.

"Don't you think," she continued, "that it might be up to us? Why should we let Tony and his ilk take over and do it? Why shouldn't *we* try to dig up the truth about her?"

He stared at her. What she had said clicked down into his whole sense of things as they should be.

"Because," she added, "Peg is the one who will have to be satisfied. She'll want to be as sure as she can be that you turn the girl over to her own people and the right people. That's the way Peg is."

"Right." Matt stared at the refrigerator.

"And if there are just going to be more witnesses, swearing they know her, but on both sides, then Tony's right. There'll have to be some other kind of proof, somewhere, somehow."

"Somebody has got to find it and check it out with a little objectivity," he declared.

"I'd help. I'm kind of free. I've got a car."

"Maybe I can get free." He turned and beamed on her. "You're a good kid, old Betts. I hope you know that."

"Sure I am," she said, "and smart, too." But she thought to herself, Well, if you can't fight it, join it. That's what they say. Doesn't he *know* why he can't stand to think of any invasion of her rights to the privacy of her own body? Or am I wrong? No, I'm not wrong.

"Of course," she said, "if she wakes up she can just plain tell us who she is. Will she?" He didn't answer. "Will she die?"

"She doesn't change," he said. "There's no deterioration. Why should she die?"

"These things can just last, you mean?"

"They've been known to last." He stirred restlessly. "Tony thinks she's Dorothy Daw. I have a feeling that Dr. Jon leans that way too. For one thing there's plenty of money there to take care of her. I don't mean to say *he's* going to go by a hunch or a wish. That won't do." Matt frowned at the kitchen sink. "Just for the hell of it, what would you bet?"

Betty's intuition knew what answer he wanted. But she tried to think it over honestly. "Nothing tips *me* off that she has to be Dorothy Daw," she said at last. "In fact, I don't care what Mr. Daw says about this poor-but-honest kick. She wasn't living in a hut, obviously. Also, we are a long way from Africa and it seems darned odd to me that a girl with all those millions of dollars wouldn't have stopped off between planes

61

somewhere and had her hair done, or a professional manicure."

Matt said, "The female angle. Humph. *I* wouldn't have thought of that. You could be right. You know what bothers me? Say she isn't his precious Dorothy Daw. Then why is Mr. Leon Daw so busy saying she is? Is he just making a mistake?"

"I can think of another question. Whichever girl your1. . . ." Betty coughed . . . *"our* girl is, where is the other one?"

They looked at each other, Betty with her head down sending her look up to him, Matt with a gleam of admiration.

"That is a very good question," he said judiciously. "If we could just find the *other* one, that would settle it. Hey, it's a deal." He put out his right hand and she gave him hers. "One for all and all for one," he pronounced, as they solemnly shook their clasped hands up and down.

"I'll see what I can do, tomorrow," he said, "about getting time off. After all, *I* signed her in. I'm legally responsible. For that matter, the hospital ought to be glad if somebody goes about this whole mess with a little intelligence."

But afterwards, getting ready for bed, Matt wondered briefly about that echo from an old book. *The Three Musketeers,* he remembered now. How come he kept bringing up stuff he had read in some old book, long ago? Never mind. Consider the pleasure it was going to be to bend his brain towards an orderly investigation, a hunt for firm evidence, to a logical conclusion. He would have to be, he knew, especially careful and fair-minded, because he had a prejudice. He was not disposed to be crazy about Mrs. Bobbie Hopkins, but he fiercely, and unreasonably, disliked Mr. Leon Daw.

Betty, brushing her hair in the room upstairs, was thinking a little bitterly of her role as henchwoman. Matt was going to be the hero. Betty was going to be girl-aide and confidante. Maybe she ought to practice her dialogue, use a lively tongue, make quips, provide the comedy relief.

That was one way to look at it.

The other way was to believe that this alliance rested upon duty and reason in which they were joined dutifully in a reasonable fashion.

"Oh, boy," she said aloud, and crawled into her bed and lay in the dark and thought about the weird illogic of being in love and its devious compulsions.

Chapter Six

About nine-thirty o'clock on Saturday morning, Matt took himself to the hospital and, passing through what seemed to be an unusually crowded lobby, came upon Dr. Prentiss in the hall, pounced on him and explained his project. The doctor approved, with immediate grim enthusiasm, and went with him to talk to Dr. Parkes of Pathology, Matt's boss. Dr. Parkes took the semi-humorous attitude that Matt wasn't going to have his mind on his work anyway, so he had better take off — providing he spoke with Atwood first.

Matt was anxious to speak to Atwood and found that gentleman just about to face up to his desk. When Matt proposed that he investigate, as best he could, on behalf of the hospital, as well as for himself, the Administrator's folds of skin hung down sadly while he thought it over.

Then he pulled them into a smile. "You *should* qualify to sort this business out, Cuneen, being personally involved. So I am going to put another chore on you. You'll be just the fellow to deal with the rest of the claimants."

"Who, sir?"

"I am told that we have four, in the lobby right now and surrounded by newsmen. The Police Department has just sent us a man to keep them in the lobby and in order. We cannot have our routines disrupted. There has to be some system set up whereby these people — and there'll be more of them, judging from the ruckus in the papers this morning — can be tested out or got rid of, whichever is right. Right, in the interests of our patient first. And, of course, right in the interests of the hospital. We can't turn anyone away carelessly yet, since we do not *know* who the girl really is. But neither can we have the place overrun.

"I suggest to you, now, that only people who seem to be reasonably possible, as connections, be allowed to see her and those only during regular visiting hours. And be made to keep their distance when they do. I suggest the mask-and-gown routine for everybody. And no newsmen at all. Now, will you take this on?"

"Yes, sir," said Matt promptly. "I'll go talk to them. I'll take care to be here during visiting hours. Sir, has anyone come who was sent by Leon Daw or Mrs. Hopkins?"

"Oh, yes," said Atwood wearily. "Oh, yes. Two men from some restaurant. They say that, to the best of their knowledge, she is the Dorothy Daw who lunched with Leon Daw and another lady on Tuesday. A man and a woman who live next door to the Hopkins ménage say she looks like Alison Hopkins to them. They, *and* the Press, were all here by eight o'clock and I cannot allow another such scene."

Matt said he wished he hadn't missed it.

Atwood said he wished *he* had, and shook his head until his wattles waved. He said bluntly that he didn't know what to believe and therefore suspended belief. He had other matters to attend to. "We harbor a great many people who do not feel well," he said quaintly and then he shook hands with Matt, wished him luck in a mournful way, and turned to his paper work.

Matt went out into the lobby, which was a small one made to appear larger by the use of wall mirrors. Ten people seemed to be a mighty throng. There was a man in a police uniform standing quietly between the lobby

65

and the main corridor. He wore a gun and, for a moment, Matt thought the whole thing was simply mad.

Dr. Prentiss came up behind him and growled in his throat, "Leave this to me." He marched into the crowd and bellowed for all newspaper people to come to him. Then he led the pack out the front door. Matt almost laughed aloud at such Pied Piper simplicity. He quickly placed the guard on the entrance to the building and turned back into the lobby.

There were now only four people waiting there.

One was a tall woman of majestic proportions who was draped in a long white robe tied at her ample waist with a purple cord. She sat like Patience, meditating. One was a woman in mannish garb who looked hostile. A young man, very nervous, thin, and wiry, jumped up and demanded to be allowed to see his beloved, but errant, wife. The fourth was a mumbling old man in a dirty rumpled suit who seemed totally confused.

A pack of nuts! Matt quailed within, but he shut up the agitated husband and made them all a little speech. Surely they would not wish to endanger the patient in any way, or interfere with the work of the hospital or its rules. Therefore, they could not possibly be permitted to see the sleeping girl until two o'clock this afternoon. Meantime, he would speak to each in turn, right now. His name was Cuneen, and he was in charge.

The young man protested in shrill tones that his name was Martin Reed, that he had a wife named Eloise, and she was here and he must *see* her, right now.

So Matt took him, first, into a small office the other side of the entrance where they could not be overheard. "Has your wife a scar of any kind?" he asked.

"It wasn't *my* fault," the young man squealed. "She was only bluffing, anyway. The blade was dull. She hardly bled at all."

Matt ducked whatever tragedy was here by saying quietly, and repeatedly, that since the girl could not possibly be his wife Eloise, he could not see her at all.

66

At last the tormented man burst into tears and went away.

The old man, accustomed to defeat perhaps, was already leaving, mumbling that he had hoped his daughter would forgive him, after all this time. He'd be back. Oh yes, he certainly would, because she would surely want to be good to her poor old daddy who hadn't meant a bit of harm and it was twenty years ago, now, and he was tired.

Matt didn't expect him back.

The mannish woman showed her long teeth in a wolfish smile and said archly that she thought the picture in the paper resembled someone she knew very well indeed. A scar? Yes, poor Sybil had that burst appendix, a year and a half ago. So Matt told her she must seek elsewhere. The woman seemed to think she had been tricked and went, muttering maledictions from convictions of persecution.

The woman in the white robe stood almost as tall as Matt himself. "I telephoned yesterday," she boomed, "and told someone here that the girl's name is Kraus. She is my protégée. I had to be in court on an important matter, so I have come the soonest that I could. I cannot come back this afternoon. I have an important conference. May I see her now?"

Matt asked her about a scar.

"A scar where?"

"You tell me," he challenged, and to his surprise, she nodded sagely.

"I see that you are being careful," she boomed.

"You haven't answered my question, ma'am."

"I've noticed no scar," she said rather impatiently, "which is not to say there may not be one." She fixed her large soft eyes upon his. "Her name is Lilianne Kraus," she said with perfect assurance. "I phoned and said so, yesterday. Now, since I cannot return today and since I have nowhere to take her at the moment, will you tell her, please, that Alfreda *will* come by, very soon?"

"Since she is unconscious," Matt said, struggling against her combination of steam-roller personality and what sounded like woolly-mindedness, "I can't *tell* her anything. I don't think it is a question of taking her anywhere. She is very ill."

"I'm sure you think so," the woman said with great pity. "I shall come and heal her—not on the Sabbath, but in a day or so."

She bowed her head gravely and marched away.

A nut! They were all nuts of one variety or another. Matt sighed. He briefed the guard, who had been assigned to remain on guard for this day at least. He briefed the switchboard girl and the receptionist. As a further precaution, he went to the wing where the patient lay sleeping, gathered the nurses, and enjoined them seriously to speak to nobody—nobody at all—about any possible scars. He said it was very important. He was in charge of an investigation into the patient's identity and they must not answer *any* questions, because in so doing they might make his job more difficult.

He went away, butting through the clamoring pack of reporters who milled before the entrance, and hurried home.

But when he took off with Betty in her saucy little Chevy, he was feeling sheepish. Peg had sent them on their way with such innocent good cheer, with so touching a faith in their inevitable success, that she had made him feel like a Boy Scout.

He was driving. Betty held a book of street maps. They were armed with addresses from the morning paper. Betty began to be crisp. They must begin with the last time each girl was (so far) known to have been seen and try to trace her path from then on. This ought to lead them either to Peg Cuneen's front door, or to a girl who would be the other one.

So were they going to the restaurant?

Matt relaxed against this clarity and told her about this device of asking for news of a scar. He wanted to see Leon Daw first. "We can ask *him*. We can run the question in," he explained, "among others. Might settle it, then and there. Suppose he says Dorothy Daw *should* have such a scar. And that would do it."

"That would prove she *isn't* Dorothy Daw. Um hum. Did you see her this morning?"

"There's no point in my seeing her," he said, a little harshly.

Leon Daw lived no more than three miles distant, in a large Spanish house partway up a fashionable hill. The trim was freshly painted; the grounds were neat. They parked in his curving driveway. This was a prosperous-looking establishment, but not in terms of millions. "Doesn't he have Daw money?" Matt wondered.

"He manages it. He's hired to do it. That's what he said. He works for a living."

"Uh huh."

They rang, and, after a while, a drapery moved at a window. Leon Daw himself opened the door. He was wearing a red silk robe over shirt and trousers and made almost a caricature of wealthy-bachelor-at-home. There seemed to be no servants in the place. He greeted them grudgingly, having recognized them both, and led them into a spacious living-room, well appointed but airless, as if it were never used.

"I am in a state of siege," he told them. Then he smiled his fishy smile. "And how is Dorothy this morning?"

Matt told him patiently that there had been no change in the girl's condition and went on to say that he proposed to ask questions, on his mother's behalf and also on the hospital's authority. To this Leon nodded

69

gloomy approval. So Matt began.

"How old is your niece, sir?"

"Twenty-four, about to be twenty-five in July."

"Has she ever married?"

"No." Daw had adopted brevity.

"When was she last in this country?"

"Three years ago, in April. Not here. I flew east to see her at that time."

"Where had she been living in Uganda?"

Leon gave them a mailing address. "A small place, I believe. Just the place name, Mengo. But she gave up her house," he added.

"What was she doing there?" asked Betty, breaking in because she couldn't help wondering.

Leon Daw gave her a bleak eye. "She was living there."

"But did she live alone, Mr. Daw? Does she travel all alone? No maid or companion?"

"Sometimes. Sometimes not."

"This time?" Betty insisted.

"Alone, as far as I know. She certainly arrived alone last Sunday."

Now Matt took breath, but feeling that he was about to fumble the important question he shifted to another.

"When and where did you see her the very last time?"

"In front of a restaurant named Nickey's, on Wilshire Boulevard, last Tuesday, at one-thirty in the afternoon, when I put her into a taxi-cab." This sounded well practiced.

"She went off alone?"

"She did. I told the driver to take her to International Airport. She had a reservation for San Francisco." Leon looked at them sourly and then volunteered something. "By the way, I phoned the airline and she had cancelled that reservation."

"When was that?"

"On Tuesday morning," said Leon Daw, rather angrily.

"But you lunched with her that day," said Betty quickly "and she didn't *tell* you she had cancelled?"

"She did not. She didn't tell me she intended to disappear, either."

"And you don't know *why* she would want to do that?" Betty had taken over for the moment. Matt thought she was doing fine.

"I don't know. I don't know," said Leon Daw. "I know she dreads publicity. She'll love this." The man was irritable. He shifted in his seat. "There's another thing. Dorothy had called for an appointment with our . . . that is, the estate's . . . lawyer, St. John Cotter, on Monday, at about noon. It was set up for Tuesday morning. She cancelled *that,* by phone, late on Monday, telling Cotter she was going to San Francisco for ten days and would see him when she returned. I did not know she had wanted to see him. I don't know what about. Nor does he."

"It would be about money, do you think?" said Betty sweetly.

"I would suppose so."

A silence fell.

Then Leon opened his strange mouth and said, "The money belongs to Dorothy. It is not in trust, not waiting, say, on her twenty-fifth birthday. I manage it for her. I manage it well and am paid well to do it. The books are open. It is all there and it waits for nothing but Dorothy's pleasure. If she should die, then I suppose I'll get a good deal of it, but by no means all. Now, if anything but *these facts* are reported or insinuated — I'll go to law."

He looked at Matt and said nastily, "I hope you realize that you are preventing me from calling in physicians of my choice. Your doctors had better be competent."

So Matt jumped in. "I realize all that, sir. So you can tell me, for her sake, whether she had had any surgery or an injury? Anything of the sort that might

71

have left a mark or a scar?"

The man frowned. He played with the sash of his robe. "I have been trying to remember," he said almost in a whine. "I don't know. As a child, she —"

The doorbell played a sequence of gong notes.

"Excuse me." Leon Daw went to the window to move the drapery.

Matt rolled his eyes at Betty and she put her teeth over her lower lip and shook a rueful head.

Their host said, "Pardon me," and made for the foyer.

"Nuts!" said Matt softly.

"Try, try again," Betty whispered.

They heard a woman's voice in the foyer begin to speak and then stop abruptly. Was there whispering? They couldn't tell.

Now Leon Daw appeared in the archway with his hand under the smart elbow of a woman. She was tall, and slim to the point of emaciation. Dressed in high fashion, she might have been a model, except that her definitely hawklike face was time-worn. She must be in her forties. She moved with precision, in the perilously unbalanced gait of the model, and her voice affected a high drawl. "I'm so sorry, darling. I had no idea you were busy. Shall I go wait in the back room?"

Betty knew instinctively that the man of his house must do his living in that back room, and not here.

"No need," said Leon Daw. "They are leaving. Megan, dear, may I present Miss . . . uh . . ."

"Betty Prentiss."

"And Mr. Cuneen. This is Mrs. Megan Royce."

"How do you do?" the woman said. "Oh please, sit down." She seated herself with trained grace and did not cross her legs but sat erect, stripping off her gloves, holding her head tilted.

Leon Daw said coldly, catching Matt still on his feet for his manners, "Is there anything else?"

Betty said, "Yes. Will you tell us, please, why your

niece did come here this time? If you know, Mr. Daw?"

Betty's voice had taken on just a touch of an intention to charm. Matt sat down.

"To renew her citizenship," said Daw glumly. "To more or less check in with me, on her affairs, which she does from time to time."

"Oh," said Megan Royce, "you are talking about poor Dorothy."

"I am trying to understand," said Betty, "how a very rich young woman could be travelling around in shabby clothes, carrying two hundred and fifty dollars, no more no less, in an old black handbag."

"Isn't it simply *in*comprehensible!" said Megan Royce cordially. Her eyes assessed Betty's pink cotton shirt and skirt. "Of course, it may be that Dorothy was smart enough *not* to be smart." Megan relished her own mot. "Poor Leon. The publicity is *miserable*."

Leon said, "And if Dorothy is *not* lying unconscious in your hospital, will you tell me how she can possibly have *missed* the publicity? Or why she hasn't been in touch with me?"

"She hasn't been?" said Matt, rather stupidly.

"Of course not." Leon Daw was turning sulky. "I fail to see the point of your questions. Especially when you don't believe what I have already told you."

"Ah, don't be cross, darling," cooed Megan Royce. "Aren't we going right on down there now, where *I* can certainly settle the whole question?"

Matt looked at her.

"Oh, but don't you see?" she said, leaning forward with a straight back. "Leon took both of us to lunch last Tuesday. Not to let kitties out of bags . . ." She looked, insofar as she was able, coy. "Dorothy was to be *my* niece, too. It was the occasion for me to get to know her. And don't you think"—her glance went to Betty; she seemed gay and amused and very sure of herself—"that a woman observes another woman, rather intently?"

73

"Perhaps," said Betty, who was observing this woman very intently indeed. Everything about her, including the shrieking violet of her narrow dress, the purple hat that clung to the side of her head, the great roll of black hair that balanced it on the other side and was stabbed by an odd silver pin, everything shouted "Look at me!"

"So now," said Megan to Leon, "let's just go, darling. I am ready."

Matt said, "Will you wait until two o'clock, please? The hospital has had to set up rules."

"What rules?" snapped Leon.

"No one may see her outside of visiting hours."

"You are excluding *me!*"

"No more than all the others."

"All? *What* others?"

"Several," Matt said, not without relish.

Leon was popping his eyes. "This is ridiculous!" he cried. "Impossible! Criminal! I won't *have* it!"

"But there are so many poor *poor* souls," said Megan, "living in dream worlds. I suppose they have no drama in their own poor little lives. This dreadful mother? Or whoever she is?"

"The Hopkins woman is not being admitted?" Leon roared.

"No, sir, she is not. Except during hours, I am responsible."

"Then *you* had better expect my lawyer."

Matt got up. He put out his hand to Betty and she rose.

Leon Daw turned as if to lead them to the foyer, but Matt wrinkled his brow and spoke. "I can't remember. Did you say that your niece had an old injury or a scar?"

Both he and Betty knew, at once, that he hadn't pulled it off very well. Silence fell thick.

Then Leon said petulantly, "I told you that I couldn't be sure."

The woman said brightly, "I saw no scar."

Leon Daw said, "I haven't seen Dorothy in nearly three years."

"But I wonder," said Megan Royce. "*Would* she have confessed it, if she had crashed a car? And broken a bone, or something? You know, darling, you say you've scolded. Dorothy was a *reckless* driver."

Matt pounced. "She had a California driver's license?"

"I doubt it," Leon said. He was withdrawn and suspicious now. "She has never really lived out here on the coast."

"She did seem to adore this out-of-the-way place in Uganda," burbled Megan. "Oddly enough, I had the impression she intended to go back there. Didn't you, darling? Poor Dorothy. Well, perhaps she can—once she gets over this strange illness. As she will, won't she?" Her bold eyes were inquiring of Matt and at the same time fawning on him. She was announcing that she found him an attractive male.

"I can't say," he answered. "Thank you and we'll go, now."

Megan said, "Shall I see you again, at the hospital? At two, wasn't it?"

"I'll be there, Mrs. Royce."

"How nice!" she drawled. "Leon, darling, I can very well go alone, then. You know that if *you* step out of here, the goblins will get you. Whereas nobody will pay the slightest attention to *me*."

She didn't believe a word of this. She was a woman who behaved as if she were beautiful and dressed to attract all eyes. "Mr. Cuneen will take *me* to see her. Won't you?"

"Yes, ma'am. Anytime between two and four."

Matt and Betty left the house.

A familiar car was parked out at the curb. In the front seat of Betty's car sat Tony Severson with his feet up on the dash. "Hey! Hey!" he cried. "How did you make out? Did he tell you anything?"

"Not much," said Matt gloomily.

"Hey, who was the dame in the purple hat?"

"Name of Megan Royce," said Betty. "They are engaged, or so *she* said."

"I don't believe it." Tony whistled. "Old Leon is supposed to have been playing the field for a hundred years. I wonder what she's got on him."

"Tony, would you get out of there?" said Matt impatiently. "We've got places to go."

"Goody, goody," said Tony, getting out. "Where? Where? I'll be right behind you."

"Why?" said Matt belligerently.

"Because, old friend and buddy, the hospital says *you* are official. *You* can get in. So whither thou goest, I goest . . ."

Matt said, "Oh, shut up."

He settled into Betty's car and said between his teeth, "I can't stand that kind of woman."

"What kind?"

"That clotheshorse," he said, surprising her with the term. "What makes old Megan so sure *her* testimony is going to settle everything? She'd as soon lie as look at you, for my money."

"There's not going to be a fingerprint on a driver's license," said Betty. "We didn't get too far with the scar bit."

"We'll have to try it on Bobbie-girl. Um boy — and *there's* a female for you."

"Misogynist?" Betty said lightly.

"They've got a curious conviction of power," gloomed Matt. "A very curious idea about how to win friends and influence men."

"Where are we going?" she asked in a moment.

"To that restaurant. That's our trail." He was feeling very grim.

Betty said, "Hey, Matt, even if I happen to be female —"

76

"Oh, come on." He thought she was going to resent his crack about the opposite sex.

"It struck me," she said, "there was one little point, Watson—"

"The dog in the night-time?"

"More or less," said Betty. "Didn't Megan refer to poor Dorothy, at least twice, in the past tense?"

"Oh, come on," said Matt again. "That *proves* something?"

Betty didn't answer. She was examining, with curiosity, her own sensation of a cauld grue.

Chapter Seven

The *maître d'* at Nickey's was called Arnoldi. He held a sheaf of menus before him as if he would feel naked without them, and spoke in a soft rapid voice. His eyes kept wavering from Matt to Betty and, now and then, to Tony Severson who stood behind them, keeping quiet, listening hard.

He remembered the young lady who had lunched here with Mr. Daw, on Tuesday, very well. Mr. Daw had arrived first, worried lest Miss Daw had come before him. But she had arrived in a cab, a few minutes later. Mr. Arnoldi had pricked up his ears when she had called Mr. Daw "Uncle Leon." It was his business to know who people were. The cabby had carried in her suitcase and it had been placed in the checkroom. There had been a little discussion, Mr. Daw wanting to have it put in his car, proposing to drive her on to the airport, the young lady insisting that this wasn't necessary. Mrs. Megan Royce had then arrived. Arnoldi knew her very well. She ran a smart shop about a block away. She had, in fact, managed a few fashion shows in the private dining-room, for some ladies' groups. A clever woman. She often lunched here with Mr. Daw. There had been a discussion of plane time. Arnoldi himself had volunteered to be helpful and have a cab ready for Miss Dorothy Daw, at the right moment.

The three of them had then taken lunch at that corner table. Oh yes, the girl in the hospital was definitely the same girl. Arnoldi had studied Miss Dorothy Daw's face, since she was a celebrity and he must call her by name the next time she appeared. He had taken Russ Hanson, their waiter, with him to the hospital this morning, since he, too, had been able to study her face. No, Hanson wasn't in yet. Too early. Nor was the hat-check girl in yet. Mr. Anoldi was sorry—always glad to do what he could, of course, but it was nearing the restaurant's busiest hours and he did hope his subordinates need not be diverted from their tasks.

Miss Daw had been wearing, he told Betty when she asked, a brown suit and had carried a brown coat which had been checked. A blouse of some bright color, not quite orange, not quite red. He had told this to newsmen only this morning. Here he gave Tony a special nod. Always glad to cooperate with the Press. When the cab had come—

Matt interrupted with a question.

Yes, Arnoldi had called the Yellow Cab Co., as usual. Yes, he did happen to know the name of the driver. It was Willson. Chuck Willson, he believed. The man was more or less regularly on call for Nickey's. Now he had told all this, in a spirit of helpfulness, not only to the Press but to the police, and now, as he understood it, to a representative of the hospital itself, and he begged—

But Tony had come to startled life. "Hey! Why did you tell it to the *police?*"

"Because they asked me," said Arnoldi with a pained smile.

"They came *around?*"

"Certainly."

"When? *Who* came?"

Arnoldi put on elaborate patience. "An hour ago." He fished up a card and read from it. "A Lieutenant

79

Clarence Tate."

Whereupon Tony hit himself on the head with his palm, cried, "Oh, wow!" and darted off.

Arnoldi said, more rapidly than ever, that there really wasn't any more to tell. The cab had come. She had taken her coat on her arm. Mr. Daw had carried her suitcase out. As to its color, Arnoldi was not prepared to say. Mr. Daw had come back and rejoined Mrs. Royce at the table for five more minutes. And that was all, really.

By the time Matt and Betty had thanked the man and gone out into the parking lot, Tony's car had vanished.

"A fine old friend and buddy he turned out to be!" said Betty. "What did he mean 'Oh, wow'?" She was feeling a little frightened. Why the police? Something must have happened. Something must have changed.

Matt said he didn't know. He stood on the pavement, gazing up to the line of far hills. Then he said abruptly, "I'm going back in and make a couple of phone calls. Wait for me."

He called the hospital and spoke to Atwood, who knew nothing about the police, had no news, knew of no developments. The girl slept.

Matt hung up and stood still, watching the mark of moist fingers fade from the place where he had been holding hard. Then he called the Yellow Cab Co. and asked for a cab, to be driven by a certain driver, to be sent to Nickey's. He was willing to wait until the right driver could appear.

When he came out and told Betty that Chuck Willson would be along, although it might take a while, he scarcely heard her say that this was clever of him.

He was turning in his mind the piling up of probabilities. He was afraid the girl was Dorothy Daw, after all. Why afraid? Who was *she?* A poor little rich girl? A young woman running away? From what, he wondered? A refugee from the limelight? That didn't seem frightening enough. What about Alison Hopkins, a poor little poor girl, running away from another "lousy deal" that her looks *and* her mother were pressing her towards, to her dismay? No, there would have to be something much more . . . well . . . urgent, from which to run away. Something dangerous?

And if so (whoever she was) had they, in their very concern, made her vulnerable to her enemies?

Betty Prentiss, waiting silently beside him, thought to herself that Betty Prentiss was a rather remarkable woman, not to be chattering. She thought to herself, No, just smart enough to realize that he wouldn't hear me, he doesn't see me. Old Betts is a kind of nothing-shadow, a kindly blob, whose virtue, at the moment, may be that she owns a car.

When the cab came, Matt gestured Betty into it, got in himself, and said to the driver, "I represent Cooper Memorial Hospital. I want to talk to you about the girl you picked up here last Tuesday. Go down the block and park."

"Oh, nuts," the driver said. "Listen, I just been talking to the cops about this chick. I can't waste all day."

"We'll pay your meter," said Betty sharply.

Matt blinked at her and then grinned. (Watch it, buddy, thought Betty grimly, I might be real.)

When the cab swooped down upon a curb, two blocks farther along, the cabby turned around, took off his cap, and wiped his forehead. He was a middle-aged man with a grainy skin and hard intelligent eyes. "Yah, yah," he said, "I knew I'd get it sooner or later, when I seen the morning papers. O.K., I pick up this girl. One-thirty, Tuesday. You want to know what she was wearing. So I'll tell you what I told the cop. A little bitty flame-colored hat. *That* I remember. So the fella who comes out with her, he tells me to take her

81

to International. Western Airlines Terminal, he says. They kiss bye-bye. But we get about six blocks from here and *she* says to me, 'Driver, I want to go to the Union Railroad Station.' Where she gets out, she pays, *and* she tips me good. *And* she goes inside and that's that. Now, you wanna run up my meter any more or what?"

Matt was frowning.

"She had a suitcase?" asked Betty, finding nothing better to ask in her bewilderment.

"That's right. One of those classy white jobs. I run around and haul it out. There's a pack of redcaps. But this Miss Dorothy Daw—the tenth richest girl in the world, eh?" He rolled his eyes. "She don't hire no redcap. Last I seen of her, she was picking up that suitcase with her own lily-white glove. Now, what anybody wants to make out of it, let them make. Where to, friends?"

"Wait a minute," Matt said. "Why did the police want to know about her?"

"Who knows?" said Chuck Willson. "Not me, brother."

"You told *them* all this?"

"Sure did. What have I got to hide? So? Back to Nickey's?"

"Wait. Did you *talk* to her at all," said Betty earnestly, "on the way?"

"Well, I let drop a couple of remarks, but she don't want any. Some do. Some don't."

"Did she look as if she didn't feel well?"

"Nope," said the cabby cheerfully. "She looked good to me."

"You recognized her picture in the paper?"

"Nope."

"No? Why didn't you, I wonder?"

"Because what *I* see is a pretty blonde in a hat. And so what? I get all kinds. In the picture, it's black and white. She's *got* no hat."

"But you said—"

"Look, I know *I* had that pick-up at one-thirty, didn't I? When I read *that* in the paper, *this* morning."

"Why didn't you call the hospital?" broke in Matt sharply.

The cab-driver said, "You know, I was thinking about doing just that." He grinned as if to say "and nobody can prove different." He waited for another question. When none came, he started his vehicle, cut a sharp U turn.

At Nickey's, they paid in silence and the cab took off.

They retrieved Betty's car. Matt looked at his watch. "Union Station? We've got time."

"That's our trail," she answered.

Neither of them said what both were thinking. The police would already have been to the railroad station.

Whatever there was to be found there, the police would already know. They were following a beaten trail.

But there was nothing to be found out at the railroad station. The very small cluster of redcaps professed not to be able to remember what had become of the girl in a brown suit and a small bright hat who had arrived in a cab, near two o'clock, on Tuesday, and carried her own luggage. Yes, there had been some police detective asking around. Just about an hour ago. Yes, sir. Yes, ma'am. *They* knew not why. They knew nothing.

So Matt and Betty went in and walked down the whole line of ticket windows without finding anyone who remembered having seen any such person. End of trail.

They must hurry back to snatch a bite with Peg, and then Matt must be at the hospital for visiting hours. They tried to sum things up. Miss Dorothy Daw had cancelled her flight, lied to her uncle, changed her destination in the cab, bought no train ticket, but might have taken a train. Or, it might have been her plan to become anonymous and vanish in the city.

Betty said, "She paid the cab. She tipped. Did she give him *all* her change, down to the last penny? And what did she do with her hat? And her other things? Do you get the feeling that this is turning out to be even more peculiar than we thought it was?"

"I get the feeling," said Matt, "that she must have been in bad trouble. I get the feeling that we shouldn't have let them put her picture in the paper. I get the feeling we should have . . . I don't know . . . done *better* by her. If we were going to do anything at all."

Betty stared at his hand on the wheel. She felt invisible, intangible.

"I'm doing the best I can," she murmured rebelliously.

To Matt's surprise, when he came into the hospital, the old man was back. He seemed to be mumbling along in some dream. His brain was sodden. It took Matt ten minutes to convince him that if his daughter had been thirteen years old twenty years ago, then this girl could not be she.

Then there was a woman who said she rented rooms and one of her lodgers had run out without paying. A dizzy little nobody named Natalie Johnson, who hadn't been a blonde at the time but what difference did that make? It turned out that the missing lodger had been two inches taller than the figures given in the newspaper, but the woman was hoping that there could have been a mistake. She couldn't afford to lose the sixty dollars. Matt finally got rid of her. She left as the door was being held open by Leon Daw for Megan Royce.

Mrs. Royce was wearing, over the violet dress, a purple coat cut perfectly square, with huge patch pockets. Her head was high on her long neck, her eyes were bright, she acted as if she were slumming.

Leon Daw said, "St. John Cotter is in touch with the hospital's lawyer. Now, let's get on with this."

Matt took them along to the door of Room 124 upon which the sign hung. He told them to wait. He beckoned the nurse. She came quickly with the necessary garments.

"You will have to wear a gown and mask, Mrs. Royce, and you, too, sir, if you're to go in there."

Megan Royce uttered cries of girlish dismay and began to wiggle rather clumsily out of the purple coat. Matt turned abruptly to Leon Daw. "Have the police been to see you?"

Leon looked at him dumbly and Megan squealed, "Oh, be careful! My bracelet! Here, let me do it myself."

"The police seem to be asking questions," Matt said.

"This is not police business," said Leon coldly.

And Megan cried, "Oh, my hairdo! Oh, *dear!*" The nurse was tying the mask. She finished and turned with other gowns on her arm. Megan's bright eyes were shining over the white lower half of her face. She had her hands to her back hair, as if to adjust the mask to a more stylish position. "I *must* be ready!" she said, gaily. "I feel *terribly* sterile."

"All right," said Matt. "Now you, Mr. Daw."

"I don't need to go in," he said. "I know who she is. I told you."

Matt opened the door to the room. "Mr. Cuneen,"

the nurse said warningly.

"Oh, yes." Matt plunged his arms into the sleeves of the gown she was holding. "Wait a minute, Mrs. Royce," he said sharply, as Megan began to tip forward. She didn't heed. He grabbed his mask and tied it in swift motions as he took long strides after her. She was already standing beside the high bed. He came up beside her and said, "Don't touch her. Step back, please."

She turned her head. The face, blunted by the mask, seemed animal-like. The skin around the bright eyes crinkled. She was laughing at him. "What in the world is the matter with *you?*" she said. "I'm here to look closely and I'm going to do it, aren't I?"

"Look, then," he said grimly. For some reason he took hold of her arm. The arm was thin. It seemed to shudder. The blunt face turned. "Leon," she called out. "Yes, it *is!* It really *is!* Poor dear Dorothy."

The man growled from the doorway, behind. "You better listen to that, Cuneen. You look me in the eye and tell me she *isn't* Dorothy."

But Matt was looking at the sleeping girl. It seemed to him that her face was thinner, her breath was more shallow. He himself could not breathe. It struck him that she might drift away—just softly drift away on a breath, one day. She was all through with the world.

Then Megan Royce spoke sharply, "No, no, darling. You mustn't come in. Not like that."

And Matt turned, with a start. The nurse was trying to step into Leon's way. He was trying to enter. Megan pulled out of Matt's grasp. Matt was suddenly furious. He swung his arm over the woman's shoulders and forced her around. He said harshly, "All right. All right. You've seen. Now, get out of here."

She turned up her eyes, rolling them, showing the whites as if he had frightened her, as Leon Daw bellowed from the doorway, "I won't stand for this overbearing attitude much longer, *you* . . . Cuneen."

86

"And *you,* stay out!" Matt bellowed back.

The woman was rigid under his arm and Matt slipped it lower, to her waist. She again seemed to shudder but she began to walk under his guiding and insistent pressure. Matt took her out of the room, pushing Leon aside, and the nurse slipped quickly behind them to close the door.

(Oh, let her sleep! Let her sleep in peace.)

Leon was dancing in an absolute rage, "I say damn you," he muttered thickly, "and your damned interference. That's my *niece* in there and I want her out of this place and damned fast, too."

Megan Royce had pulled her mask off. "She looked perfectly ghastly. I had no idea . . ." She sounded shaken. "I'm sorry, Mr. Cuneen." She looked him in the eye. "That girl is dying, isn't she?"

Leon said, "Hurry up. I want to talk to this Atwood. And where is that stupid doctor?"

"Why don't you go on ahead, darling?" Megan said. "Don't wait. Perhaps *I* can make Mr. Cuneen believe us."

Leon gave her a hard glare and went down the corridor with bouncing strides. The lady settled her hat and her hairpin, slipped into the purple coat, felt of her back hair once again, smiling brightly at Matt all the while.

"Let's walk a minute. I've realized something. I had better tell you." Her eyes flattered him. "Tell *you,*" they emphasized.

She didn't thank the nurse. The nurse gaped after them, as Megan took Matt's arm and began her swaying walk. Matt went with her to the intersection of two corridors where there was a tiny alcove, lined by an upholstered bench, a place for visitors to wait for other visitors to leave. There was a cylinder of stone, filled to the brim with sand to make an ash-receiver. Megan pulled a cigarette case out of her purple pocket and sat down with a sigh.

"Oh, come, sit down. We can talk here." She held the cigarette towards her lips and waited for him to produce a light.

"I don't know why I hadn't thought of this," she sighed, blowing smoke. "This woman who says that Dorothy is her daughter? Her name is Hopkins?"

"Yes," Matt said.

"Well, of course, that is not the name." Megan crossed her legs and twisted her torso. She seemed to do nothing without tension, and creating a line. "I once had a girl come to model for me. Let me see, it must have been two years ago. As a matter of fact, that is how I met Leon! Isn't that strange? He was there, this day, with one of my patrons. And when this particular girl came out to show a dress he almost fainted in his chair."

Matt sat still, listening to the rise and fall of her voice.

"I remember having quite some trouble persuading him that she was *not* his niece Dorothy. The resemblance, he said, was absolutely uncanny. At that time, I believe Dorothy was supposed to be in Rome—or some such place. But this little blonde girl . . . She wasn't quite tall enough for wearing clothes. I do remember that. I didn't use her long. Now let me see. She had taken the name of Kinsey."

"*Taken* it?" said Matt.

"I suppose she thought that was cute." Megan smirked. "She called herself *Alison* Kinsey, as I remember. Now, don't you guess that *she* must be that woman's daughter? She was—so Leon said—almost a perfect double for Dorothy Daw."

"And was she?" Matt asked. "You've seen them both—so you say."

"Oh, dear. Well, it was a while ago," said Megan. "Yes, of course, she was *very* like. I really don't remember Alison's face in every detail. At that time, of course, I had never seen Dorothy herself. But you

88

must agree that this is the explanation. That poor mixed-up woman, the mother, may even *believe* what she is saying." Megan Royce was smarter than that, her pose implied. Megan Royce—groomed, composed, sophisticated—knew better than to believe very much of anything and weren't people amusing?

"You say Mr. Daw was hard to convince?" said Matt. "Isn't he making the same mistake again?"

"Ah, but not *I!* I studied Dorothy's face, in a very good light, not three days ago."

"If the resemblance made such a great impression," Matt was stubborn, "why hasn't Mr. Daw said a word about it?"

"I *don't* know," she said slowly. "When I spoke of it at lunch, just now, he seemed to have forgotten. You know, two years ago, on the very next day, he and I took the girl, Alison to lunch and I do remember that he said she wasn't really anything like Dorothy. In manner, you see. Or personality. But he and I . . . got on well. He's rather a pet, you know." She smiled at him, perfectly perfidious. She was saying, I would of course have preferred *you*. Her left hand came to touch his sleeve and it said so, too. She seemed to think that she was ageless in allure. But a lock of her dark hair had lost its moorings, perhaps because of the strings of the mask, and it stood away from the right side of the otherwise smooth mass on her head, spoiling the effect, making it ludicrous.

Matt looked down at her claw with its long pointed fingernails. "Your hair is loose," he blurted.

The cigarette fell into the ash-receiver. Both hands flew to her head. She twisted her torso and looked at him sideways. "Don't, *please*," she said, "talk to the Press about what I've told you. Will you promise me?" She was tucking her hair back. She leaned towards him, sending off a cloud of perfume. "Ah, but you will not. You will help us keep this dreadful publicity down. *You* understand that people with any

89

money are so very vulnerable."

Matt couldn't help it. He had leaned away.

She straightened, twisting again at her supple waist. Every move she made was full of muscular tension. "Don't hold success against us," she said, and twisted back again, and smiled. Her right hand was plunging the burning cigarette deep into the sand, with that same exaggerated tension. "Or Leon against me?" she added softly.

Matt said, "I see no point in mentioning this model to the Press—if that's what you want me to say."

She blinked, rebuked and knowing so. "Now, hadn't we better find my angry man before he tears this hospital down?" She rose and he rose and moved politely out of her way.

They started for Atwood's office and met Leon Daw bouncing angrily towards them. He said to Matt, "They tell me they'll have to hear from *you*. Well?"

Matt said steadily, "They'll hear from me."

"Then be quick about it. I'm calling my own doctor, at once."

"Why don't you do that?" said Matt.

Leon said, "If she dies . . ."

And Megan said, "Oh, darling, hush." And then to Matt, "But ought you to take that risk? You are . . . a young man on his way up? Publicity can be so . . . terribly destructive."

Matt said nothing.

They swung away together, faces blank.

Matt, who didn't think a doctor was going to jump in on another doctor's case quite as readily as Leon Daw seemed to imagine, and who knew, besides, that Dr. Prentiss had already called in consultants of high repute, went thoughtfully on to Atwood's office. He felt as if he had just escaped from something . . . spiritual rape, perhaps. He ground his teeth together.

Atwood said to him, "Well? Who is she?"

90

Matt said, "It's stranger than we thought." Atwood listened to Megan's story, as reported, and seemed to find it a relief.

"But if there *is* this startling resemblance, that could very well explain the woman Hopkins. I'm afraid it looks to me as if Leon Daw is in the right."

"If so, he is an oddly forgetful man."

Atwood's face sagged. "You don't agree?"

"Not yet, sir. I haven't seen Mrs. Hopkins."

"And when you do, that will clear your mind?"

"I hope so, sir."

"Go and see the woman, then. And get this over, will you?" Matt began to turn away when Atwood added, "What was that you said on the phone about the police?"

Matt told him. "I'm wondering why they are in the picture. Leon Daw didn't put them into it."

"I wouldn't put it past that woman Hopkins," said Atwood, "to have stirred them up with some wild surmise they would have to investigate. Why don't you get going?"

But Matt turned again. "Tell me, does Dr. Prentiss think she is dying?"

"Not that I know of," said Atwood, "especially since they can't seem to find a damn thing wrong with her."

Chapter Eight

Mrs. Bobbie Hopkins told them, through the door, to go away and not bother her. But when Matt said he represented both his mother and the hospital, she opened up.

"Well, it's about time," she declared. "I guess now you got it through your head I know what I'm talking about."

When Betty was presented, Bobbie nodded with great care. She was looking ravaged and without doubt she was hung over. She had a green turban wound over her hair, her lipstick was on crooked, her skin was grey.

Her small redwood house, perched on a steep bank up in the hills above Hollywood, was cluttered with cheap furniture. There seemed to have been some attempt made at bold solid colors, but the decorator had lost her grip on the décor. The draperies of yellow bamboo sticks were drawn across all daylight, and a lamp with a rose-colored shade was burning in a corner. The air was close and full of smoke and rancid perfume.

When their eyes had adjusted, Betty and Matt saw that there was a young man in the room, a thin nervous young man with dark glasses dominating his long pale face.

"Excuse me, Bobbie," said he. "I got to blow, now."

"Oh? Well. O.K. then, Larry. Listen, don't worry. Nothing bad is going to happen."

"That's right," the young man said. "You just stick up for yourself, see?"

"O.K."

"O.K."

The young man ducked his head and went out the door as if he slithered through a crack.

"A friend of mine," said Bobbie complacently. "Sit down, why don't you? Gads, what a night and a day I've been having. Anybody care for a little schnapps?"

When they didn't, it seemed that she did.

Finally they were settled, more or less cozily.

"I'm telling you," she said, "it's been wild. Mr. and Mrs. Barrington went down there, didn't they?"

"You mean early this morning? Yes, some couple came."

"What do you mean, some couple? Listen, they're my next-door neighbors and they should know Alison. You see her picture, by the way?" The woman picked up a large photograph and handed it to Betty. Matt looked over her shoulder. It was the face of the girl in the hospital, in every feature. Yet it was the face of a person they had never seen. Evidently it was supposed to display the attributes of an actress. The pose of the head. The eyes were trying to smoulder. The mouth was trying to be seductive. The bare shoulder was trying to allure. Poor Alison.

Betty held it for Matt to take, but he did not take it. It made him sad. He glanced at Bobbie. "I have some questions. Your daughter *has* lived here, hasn't she?"

"Well, sure. What do you mean?"

"Who is her dentist?"

"Her what!"

"Her dentist."

"Jeepers," said Bobbie, stricken stupid. "I don't know."

"You don't know the name of your daughter's dentist?"

"Listen, I thought you meant did she live in L.A. I don't say she lived right here, with me. Why, when we first came here, lemme see . . . right after she got out of . . . uh . . . high school that was . . . Well, Alison was eighteen about, and she took an apartment with some kids from the studios. Over in North Hollywood, that was. But they busted up and she had a place by herself, but then the Freeway came through and she hadda move. She . . . uh . . . well . . . moved around, see? I forget. Anyway, then she got this chance to go to Spain. So when she gets back, natch, she's got no place. And that was when she came to me. About two weeks ago."

"How long had she been in Spain?"

"Oh God," said Bobbie, calling on the Deity quite unnecessarily, "it was a year and a half. Well, see, that turned out not to be so great because she kinda lost track of her contacts around this town. I mean, boy, they can forget you ever lived in about six weeks, around this town. And she was real, real tired, see? She had to get some rest. So she just hung around the house, sleeping. . . ."

The woman paused and her face became a little bleak.

"Of course, she's my baby," she said, putting on another voice, another aspect. "And my home is her home, if she needs it."

Matt said, "Has she a California driver's license?"

"What do you mean? Why?"

Betty said, with some asperity, "Because it might have her thumbprint on it."

"Oh. I never thought . . . Yah, but the thing is, Alison don't drive."

"Doesn't *drive!*" said Betty, astonished. "How old is she?"

"She's twenty-three. Well, see, she kinda never

94

bothered." The woman's remark fell very flat.

"Mrs. Hopkins," said Matt sternly, "don't you realize that we have to find some proof of this girl's identity? That you are going to have to give us the right answers?"

"Listen . . . the truth is . . . She don't like this to get around. Her eyes aren't too good." The woman looked up blindly. "Mine, either. But some people can't stand contact lenses. Sensitive, you know?"

"So she couldn't pass the test? Is that it? She couldn't *get* a license?"

"That's right. Listen. I don't want that in the papers." The woman reached quickly for her drink. "People are funny," she announced.

Matt was discovering that he didn't believe a word she said. Betty said, out of the blue, "Does Alison wear lace on her slips?"

The woman goggled. "For God's sake! Certainly. Alison likes nice things."

"You haven't looked at the clothing our girl was wearing, have you?"

"No," said Bobbie. "No. Why should I? Listen, I got problems I never even used yet."

"What was Alison wearing when you last saw her?"

"She didn't show me what slip she had on." The woman was sulking.

"A black dress?"

"No, no. Her green lightweight wool with the jacket." Bobbie was staring at Betty.

"*When* was this?" said Matt, impatient with details of clothing.

"Well, that was last Tuesday night, around seven-thirty, eight o'clock. She came in around five, I guess it was. She didn't say much. She went in her room. I was going out to eat. I mean, there wasn't any reason why I should call her or anything . . ."

"You mean," said Matt, "you weren't going to serve any dinner." He surprised himself. He seemed to

95

know exactly what she was feeling guilty about.

"Oh, Alison liked to snack around," said Bobbie. "Well, then, here she comes all of a sudden with her suitcase."

"A grey suitcase?" asked Betty.

"No, no. It's blue. One of them wardrobes."

"And?" Matt brought her back sternly.

"Well, natch, I want to know what's with *her?* She says she's found a place to stay and she's taking off. She says maybe she has a job. She don't know yet. So I say, 'Well, look, baby, I haven't got any money, you know that.' But she says not to worry about it. She's moving in with a friend, she says."

"Where?"

"She didn't say."

"Who was the friend?"

"Well, she didn't say."

"Male or female?" snapped Matt. "Did she say? Or didn't you ask?" He couldn't imagine what was the matter with him. He was sounding like an elder of the church.

"I didn't ask," said Bobbie sulkily. "Listen, a girl today, she's got her life. I got mine. Such as it is," she added bitterly.

"Did the friend call for her?"

"She walked," said Bobbie. "There's a bus. *I* don't know."

Matt said firmly, "Has your daughter Alison any scar from some old injury? Or," he added, uncontrollably angry, "don't you know that, either?"

The woman drained her glass. "You got the nerve of an elephant, you know that?" she said calmly. "But you also got an idea there. All right. I didn't look when I went down to see her. I didn't think to look. Why would I? So — I should have looked. O.K., Mr. Smarty. Alison got some quack to take off a mole she had on her . . . uh . . . left breast. And I dunno, he kinda butchered the job. So she's got a shiny spot there. It don't tan, see? Alison takes sunbaths in the altogether. She can't afford strap marks—not in her business. But that spot don't tan."

"What is the doctor's name?"

"I don't know," said Bobbie. *"Should* I know?"

"But she has such a mark? You've seen it?"

"Of course I've seen it."

"Well then," said Matt coldly, "I'll have to tell you that the girl in the hospital is *not* your daughter Alison."

(And so be it, and alas.)

"What are you talk . . ." She let her red-smeared mouth hang open.

"She can't be." Matt stood up.

"Now wait a minute . . ."

"Have the police been *here?*" Matt said suddenly.

"What?" The woman was looking terrified.

"Could you answer the question? Have the *police* been here?"

"No. Why should they be? What's going on? Listen, I don't have to sit still for this. And how do *you* know," she howled, "she hasn't got a mark on her left breast, you dirty—"

Matt had to take her by the wrist. Bobbie now began to cry hysterically.

Betty said, "Mrs. Hopkins, don't carry on. Just try to calm down, please. After all, if she *isn't* your daughter, why then you shouldn't cry."

"Oh God, I do the best I can," the woman wailed. "I try to do the best I can. Listen, my"—she gulped in air—"the father," she said, "ran out on me a hundred years ago. What am *I* supposed to do?"

"Did your daughter model for Megan Royce at one time?" asked Matt.

"For who? Listen, I guess she did some modelling. She had to eat. Don't worry. She didn't do nothing dirty. And what have some of those kids got that she hasn't got?" Now Bobbie was fierce. "She should be

on top. She just needs a break. She photographs . . .
Look how she photographs. That stupid director she
had in Spain . . . Oh, I'm telling you, it's rough. It's
rough!" The woman seemed to be drunk now. "I
coulda done all right myself if I'd have had a coupla
breaks. So now look? So now what? *What?* Eh?"

Matt signalled and Betty turned to go.

"Look," said Bobbie, seeming to become suddenly
sober, "maybe I made a mistake. But maybe not.
Right? Listen, she's been away, Alison has. Listen,
maybe the rain in Spain . . . ? What? Who can say?
Maybe that spot don't show anymore. Maybe it was
just going to take time. Couldn't that be, huh? Could
that be?"

"Didn't you know," said Betty gently, "that she was
a double for Dorothy Daw?"

"How should I know anything?" cried Bobbie
Hopkins. "Nobody tells *me* anything. And I got a dis-
tinct feeling I might as well be drunk as the way I
am." She went, like a bee to honey, for her bottle.

Matt opened the door for Betty. There didn't seem
to be anything more that they could say.

When they had gone, Bobbie put the bottle down.
"After dark," she muttered. "So what do *I* know?
Damn'kids!"

In the car Matt said, "Frustrated mama, using the
child? 'She'll get where I never got'? Classic. Do you
think so? Maybe Alison was running away from *that*.
I wouldn't blame her."

But Betty said, "Alison got away, a long time ago.
And our girl can't be Alison, can she?"

"You should have heard Bobbie, howling that she's
a mother." Matt sputtered in a moment. "Doesn't
know the simplest facts about her own child . . ."

"Why blame Bobbie exclusively?" said Betty.
"Maybe Alison doesn't *let* her know."

"Oh, come *on,* Betts. That godawful woman."

"She isn't much like *your* mother."

98

Matt said stiffly, "Shall we stick to the point? Does Bobbie Hopkins know whether Alison's scar still shows? Or does she not? And if not, how can *we* know?"

"You *want* our girl to be Alison, don't you, Matt?"

"Now that," he said, "is idiotic! What's the matter with you?"

"Probably I'm using my feminine intuition."

But he fell silent. He wouldn't quarrel.

Betty held her tongue, but she thought, For just a minute there, he knew I was alive. Oh damn . . . damn . . . damn. . . .

Peg said that Tony Severson had called and left a number. So Matt called it.

"Hey! Hey!" said Tony. "What do you know?"

"You tell me."

"Well, the lieutenant ain't talking. Tate, that is. But something's up and I'll tell you what I bet it is. Don't upset your mama. But he's got a body."

Matt looked into the living-room where his mother sat. "Who has?"

"Lieutenant Clarence Tate of none other than Homicide. So what's he mixing in for, if he hasn't got a body? So one of those two chicks is dead. That's the way I figure. But I'll tell you this. If he has got a body, he hasn't got it here. Not in the morgue. That's for sure. I looked."

"You're not making a lot of sense, Tony."

"But then I got an idea," said Tony softly. "I got this *brilliant* idea. I looked in the newspapers. Hold on to your hat, now. Last Tuesday morning, a certain truck driver—name of Bailly, Sam—he pulls up in Fresno to unload, and lo and behold if there ain't the dead body of a nekkid blonde in the back of his rig. How do you like that? And what's more, the statistics tally pretty good. About twenty-two to twenty-five years of age. Five feet four. Around a hundred and ten. Blonde. Hoo! Hoo!"

"Fresno?"

"So what?" said Tony. "This here very same damn truck left the L.A. area around midnight, Monday."

"Monday!"

"Right. So now you know, don't you? You got Dorothy Daw in your hospital. Because how can she have lunch with Uncle Leon, Tuesday, if she's dead in Fresno at the very same time. So this poor kid, this starlet, this Alison, she must have fallen among evil companions. And there you are. As for friend Tate, so he saw our girl's pitcher in the paper and he's no fool. Fact, he's kinda brass—which he'd better be, if he's going to pussyfoot around the Daw involvement. He was quietly checking that out. Don't worry. He'll be checking out the other one. He'll probably get around to you."

"I see," said Matt, somewhat dazed. "Well, thanks."

"Don't thank *me*. Thank your daily newspaper, buddy. *I* should thank *you*. If I hadn't tailed you guys, I wouldn't have got on to Tate's nose in the pie. Say . . . uh . . . I'd be just as pleased if you didn't spread this around too much. Hey? I'm exclusive, as of now. Got to double-check it. You see that."

"There's only one thing."

"Yeah?"

"Mrs. Hopkins says Alison left her house, lively enough to be carrying a suitcase, on *Tuesday evening.*"

"Well, that's impossible," said Tony cheerfully. "I'm saying the old biddy made a mistake. She's the type that would."

"Is that a fact?" said Matt caustically, and hung up.

He called the hospital. Atwood had gone home. He called the Atwood house. Atwood was out for dinner

100

and the evening. He called Dr. Jon Prentiss. Dr. Prentiss was on a call and his return was unpredictable. He called the L.A. Police Department, and after long waiting and several voices he was told that Lt. Clarence Tate was unavailable until morning.

So Matt gave up and Peg called them to supper.

At first, Peg Cuneen resisted the whole idea of a body, and what must be a murdered body, having anything to do with the case. Tony, she surmised, was off on some wild tangent and only trying to beef up his precious story.

Matt, who couldn't suppose that a police officer was trying to beef up anything, kept silent.

"There isn't any trail for Alison," said Betty. "She walked out of her mother's house, whatever night of the week it was, carrying a blue suitcase and wearing green. How can we follow her?"

Matt shook his head.

"But because of that scar or mark that won't tan (and after all, how could her mother have invented such a thing!) . . . can't we say that our girl isn't Alison?" Peg struggled to be logical.

"We ought to check with whatever 'quack' made the mark," said Matt.

"How can we?" Betty said. "Maybe the police can."

"It seems to me," said Peg, abandoning logic, "that our girl must be Dorothy Daw. You did say Mrs. Hopkins was *very* upset when you told her we don't have Alison. Perhaps she wanted Alison as safe as that, at least." Peg winced.

"*She*," said Matt fiercely, "has a brain the size of a peanut and she operates in such a raggle-taggle alcoholic confusion, I don't *believe* . . ."

He was showing too much fury. He stopped, wary, for some reason, of Betty Prentiss.

But she said quietly in a moment, "We don't know,

that's all. What are we going to do, now?"

"*I'm* going over to the hospital and see whether any half-way decent people have come to identify her," he said, too furiously, and went off. *What's the matter with me?* he wondered.

When he had gone, Peg looked at Betty.

Betty said, "I don't know, Peg." She got up and went to the kitchen window. It wasn't quite dark yet. She could see, between houses, the end of the park and she saw Matt, walking with his head down, taking the path.

"It's a funny thing about identity," she said. "That girl just lies there, sleeping. She hasn't *any.*"

"It's mysterious, I suppose," said Peg lightly, answering the unspoken question. (Why should that be so attractive?)

Betty's eyes began to fill with tears. She told herself to cease and desist such nonsense, and stood waiting for the tears to dry.

Peg got up and began to make a cheerful clinking of the dishes. She was thinking, I don't expect myself to be reasonable all the time, but Matt *does* expect that of himself. He always has, he thinks, been reasonable. He thinks we could all live by our reason, if we only tried. But he isn't being reasonable—he's involved—he's hooked on some dream that he doesn't understand, and he can't admit. And it's making Betty cry.

But there was nothing his mother, of all people, could do about it.

There were no new claimants at the hospital. There had been some phone calls from shy people salving their consciences. A stewardess with whom Dorothy Daw had flown, who did not feel she could help, really, unless the hospital insisted. She'd be back in four days. A fellow starlet to Alison, who hadn't seen Alison for a year and a half and really hadn't known her very well, but who would be glad to do what she ought, although at the moment she had a miserable flu bug.

Matt put the messages in his pocket and forgot them.

The girl lay sleeping.

In the hush, the somehow holy hush, of the little room, Mrs. Marsh said to Matt, "You know, I thought a while ago that she had her eyes open and was just staring. It wasn't *so,* of course, but it scared the *life* out of me, for just a minute."

Matt said, "Well, take it easy."

He wished he could.

Chapter Nine

When it was dark, Bobbie Hopkins left her house. She backed her "transportation" out of the shed and turned down the winding roads. She kept watching her rearview mirror. She took some extra windings, once she reached more level ground. She didn't think she was being followed but she intended to make sure.

Finally, she steered a direct course for her destination and came into one of the lost streets of Los Angeles, a piece only a block long that had been cut off by the Golden State Freeway so that it could only be reached from one side and was hard to find. The houses were small and shabby and forlorn. Bobbie stopped her car in front of one of them and scurried down a walk beside it, heading for the even smaller house at the back of the lot. This was a so-called "rear house," a rental property. Every time Bobbie came here, the loneliness made her shiver. Talk about being hidden away, she thought.

The tiny house, only one room, bath, and kitchenette, stood square, with two small window eyes over which the lids were down. But there was a light.

Bobbie sighed and knocked. Nothing stirred.

"It's only Bobbie," she said into the wood. "Look, honey . . . let me in, huh? It's only Mama."

In a moment, the door cracked and Bobbie made

herself as narrow as she could, slipped in, and the girl closed the door.

"Alison?" said Bobbie, reproachfully.

"Oh, Mom, listen . . . why did you have to come here? Listen, if anybody saw you . . ."

"Don't worry," said Bobbie grimly, "I took care of that. Where's Lilianne?"

The room was barely furnished. There was a day-bed, a table, one straight wooden chair, one that was partially upholstered, a rag rug on the vinyl floor. A closet door stood open; there were only a few garments hanging there. The door to the tiny bathroom stood open. The kitchen was only an alcove. Nobody else was in the place. Bobbie said again, "Where's Lilianne?"

"You ought to know," said the girl sulkily. "I've been scared to death, ever since I read about *you* shooting your mouth off."

"What am I supposed to do?" said Bobbie passionately. "Nobody tells me anything. I thought it was *you*."

"Yeah?" The girl who was wearing a green dress that was much rumpled, shoved at her blonde hair and said, "As long as you're here, you got any cigarettes?"

"Smoking again?"

"You better believe it!" said the girl, and cast herself down on the day-bed.

"O.K." Bobbie fished a package of cigarettes out of her large handbag and threw them at the girl. She sat down in the softer of the two chairs. "So I had to go and make a fool of myself, and now I want to know the reason why. I hope you realize your sister is maybe going to die."

"Naw," said Alison.

"Where did you go? How come you've holed up here? Come on. Give, baby."

"All right, if you want to know. I *better* hide. I maybe know too much."

The girl lit a cigarette and blew out smoke jauntily and then collapsed and began to cry.

105

"Tell Mama," said Bobbie in a moment. *"You're* Mama's girl. You know that, baby?"

"Well, listen"—Alison sat up and mopped her face—"and then you tell me. Somebody called me. She got my number from Central Casting. It's this dame I had a job with once. Megan Royce."

"Yeah, they asked about her."

"Who asked?" The girl was stiff with alarm.

"Never mind. Nothing. I didn't say a word. Go ahead."

"So she says do I want a job and I said I did so I went to her apartment. That was Monday."

"You didn't tell *me.*"

"She told me *not* to tell. It was a funny kind of job, Mom. There's this Dorothy Daw, who looks just like me. Well, she's Miss Rich-Bitch herself."

"Just like you, baby?"

"Oh, *I* knew that, years ago."

"How come *I* didn't get to hear about it?"

"I don't tell you everything," said Alison sullenly. "You mess things up, Mom."

"You better," said Bobbie grimly, "tell me now."

"And so Megan says that Dorothy Daw wants to get away from the newspaper reporters. So she wants me to act like her—you know, stand-in? And all I have to do is have lunch with Megan and Dorothy's uncle on Tuesday. She says that's the first step, and if I get away with it, maybe there'll be more. She says Dorothy is made of money and couldn't care less *what* she pays. And I'll get five hundred bucks, just for Tuesday.

"So why should I complain? So I met her in her apartment Tuesday morning, and she's got an outfit for me to wear and it fits. So I put on this suit . . . you should have seen it. It must have cost three hundred bucks if it cost a nickel, Mom. And a hat that was out of this world. Then she takes me up to this big old mansion which is the uncle's dump. He wasn't there. She takes off. And then I'm supposed to call a cab, see, and take it to the restaurant. So I did. So here was Uncle Leon. Well, I met him once."

"You *did?*"

"Listen, I'm *telling* you. So Megan told me what to say. I can act, you know. Well, we ate lunch and I swear that was all there was to it, as far as I could see. Except afterwards, I had to pull a kind of disappearing act. This uncle-type puts me in a cab and I'm supposed to tell the driver to take me to the railroad station, which he does. Then I got to go to the ladies' room, put on this coat I'm carrying — and it cost plenty, too, you got to believe it — and take off the hat and let my hair hang down. And then all I had to do was put the hat in the suitcase and put the suitcase in one of those lockers, you know? And then walk out of the station and over to Olvera Street. It's not too far. You know? And I walk all the way through Olvera Street from Sunset and when I get to the other side, Megan is there in her car to pick me up.

"Well, that was O.K. And she said I did great. And she takes the key to the locker, you know, and she hauls me back to her place and she takes all Dorothy's clothes back and then she says . . . she's kind of excited . . . she says, 'How would you like to play Dorothy Daw some more?'

"So I said as long as the price was right, why not?

"So that's when she said I'd better move in with her because I'd better not be running around the streets looking too much like myself. She says it's luck I've been in Spain. And better not spoil the luck.

"So — well, she's got this huge place and everything real plushy and what did I have to lose? So I came home, you know, Tuesday? And that's when I packed my stuff and I walked all the way down to the bus and went to her place. And everything was ducky. Oh sure, just ducky!

"So she has a fancy meal sent in, just for me though. *She* went off to have a date with Uncle Leon. And here

I am, watching TV. By myself.

"Then there was this thing on the eleven o'clock news and that's when I began to smell something. Didn't you see it?"

"What?" Bobbie hadn't seen it.

"There was the body of a blonde girl found in a truck, upstate. It was on the local station. The guy gives her measurements and that's when I . . .

"Listen . . . Sure, this Dorothy has got millions and all that . . . but . . . See, at first I didn't think so much about it. But I went to bed and then I got to thinking and I couldn't figure why they'd pay me five hundred bucks for just eating a big fat lunch, like that. And I couldn't figure how the heck what I did was supposed to protect this Dorothy from the newspapers. *I* didn't see anybody from any newspapers. it was just too damned fishy, Mom. You see what I mean?"

"Yeah," said Bobbie. "They were using you."

"Sure they were using me, but for what? I mean, I dunno, but there was this *dead* girl. And what *if* they wanted it to look as if . . . somebody *wasn't* dead?" Alison stared at her mother and added, "Yet."

"Oh, baby," said Bobbie. "Oh, baby."

"Well, Megan comes in and I'm still not asleep. I was so nervous, I got up. And she was as drunk as eighteen goats, Mom. And she needed a nightcap like a hole-in-the-head, but that's what she had. And me, too. I didn't know what to do — what to say. I kept watching her. She was feeling pretty high. She says she's going to marry Uncle Leon, and then she laughs and says maybe *he* doesn't know that, yet, but he will. Then she says, 'You stick to me, kid.' She says, 'There's more gold in them hills than you ever saw in your life.'

"Then I said — I couldn't help it — I said, 'Is Dorothy dead?'

"And she starts looking mean. And she says, 'What makes you say that, dahling?'

"And I said 'I don't know. It just came into my head.'

108

"And she says, 'Well, you just better put your busy little head on the pillow and sleep that off.'

"And I said, "It *is* late, isn't it?' Mom, I was never so scared. I was lying there, just trembling all over.

"And finally it was about five o'clock in the morning and I hadn't even closed one eye. I couldn't stand it. So I got up and sneaked into my clothes and I took my stuff and I could hear her snoring. So I sneaked out. There wasn't anybody around. I walked about two miles. Finally I got a bus and then I . . . didn't want to come to your house because listen, Central Casting has got *your* number. She could find out where it is. She *phoned* there, for Pete's sakes. So I came *here*. And Lilianne let me in."

"She did?" said Bobbie who was licking her lips in agitation.

"Yeah, but you know how *she* is. So I said, 'Look, sister mine, *I* got to stay here. So if you don't like it, why, you go elsewhere. You can go to Alfreda, can't you?'

"And she says, yes, she can. She must. She will.

"And she was looking goofy, as usual. I told her she had better not even mention that she had a twin sister.

"And she said I needed to be alone and think over my past sins. Phooey! Well, so she packed up a couple of things. And I . . . well, you know . . . I can always play Lilianne. And I was scared. So I took her ident out of her handbag. I took *everything* when she wasn't looking. But I gave her money, Mom. I gave her half of my five hundred bucks. You got to admit that was fair enough. I told her she could pay Alfreda board and room out of that.

"So she said some kind of mumbo-jumbo—God bless me, and so on—and she went. *I* didn't know she was sick, Mom, or going to get sick. That's if she *is* sick. She's O.K. in the hospital, if you just keep on . . . I mean . . . not letting *them* get her. Otherwise," the girl wailed, "what am I going to do? Mom, I don't want to be in a mess about a murder. With cops and all. Gee, I mean, they'd make the connection. And if they did, there goes my career. The kiss of death. And you know it. But listen, I don't want to get *myself* murdered, either."

Bobbie said firmly, "They've got to be wondering where you'd run away to. Some dame already called up, twice."

"When?"

"Wednesday morning and Thursday, too. She hints around about a job. Listen, didn't know where you were — don't forget."

"You *bet* you didn't."

"So on Friday, *they* saw the picture, too."

Alison said, "Lilianne isn't talking."

"That's right." Bobbie squirmed. They looked at each other, at first fearfully, and then with thoughtful eyes.

"I got to get out from under," Alison said. "You know that. And you know Lilianne, it doesn't make that much difference."

Bobbie sighed. "You got any schnapps?" she asked suddenly.

"Yeah, I thought it might calm me down, but it didn't. I sneaked over to the liquor store, playing Lilianne. Wait." Alison got up and fetched her mother a bottle.

Bobbie drank from it without even looking at the label.

"Honey," she said at last, "I'd say you oughta go to the cops if you really *knew* anything. But you can't *prove* anything, right? And maybe, you know, you could be wrong. Maybe this Dorothy had already disappeared, see, and — something to do with the money — they needed you to stand in. Maybe they really do think it's Dorothy in the hospital. I coulda let them think so. I might have goofed already, see, on saying it was you."

110

"Oh, no!"

"Well, you know your mole? If I'd have looked, in the hospital. Never crossed my head that was Lilianne. Jeepers, I never see her anymore—year in and year out. I practically forgot about her. She never . . . Well, you know how *that* is."

"You told, huh? You told how to tell us apart?" The girl was frightened and angry.

"No, no. Nobody even knows there *is* any Lilianne. Listen, why should I tell the world I got a nut for a daughter? I *never* do that. It's not good for your career. What I say—so let *them* think it is Dorothy Daw in that bed. I mean, you know—you could be wrong."

"I can't go very far on two hundred and forty-two bucks," said Alison, "or I'd been long gone."

"*I* think," said Bobbie briskly, "we got to know more. Lie low, baby. Nobody's going to find you here."

"If I don't go crazy," Alison said.

"One thing. You don't have to worry about Larry."

"What *about* Larry?" The girl jerked her head up.

"Oh, he wants no part of it," Bobbie said. "He comes crawling to me. He says I don't have to tell that he was ever married to you. His new wife might have a fit if she, you know, made the connection. He was pitiful, I'm telling you. He says not to drag him into it. Let him alone and he'll let us alone. And that's all about that."

"He *better* keep still. Why don't we let *the whole thing* alone? Huh? For a while?"

"If they did anything to Dorothy, then they got to say *she's* Dorothy." Bobbie wiped the bottle's mouth with a nervous finger.

"Maybe Lilianne is really sick, this time. What do the doctors say?" Alison was breathless and eager.

"What do *they* know?" said Bobbie. She braced up. "Somebody says the cops are snooping around. Maybe *they'll* find out what's up."

"Sure they will. Who knows, huh? Maybe it was some bum, or a sex-fiend. I mean, poor Dorothy, huh,

Mom?"

"I don't see how you'd be in any trouble if they do find out in the end," Bobbie said. "After all, you did a job and then you got scared and ran out on this Megan. But you don't really *know a thing*. Do you, baby?"

"I sure don't," said Alison dismally. Then she said, righteously, "I just felt nervous, because I wouldn't want to do anything dishonest."

"That's right, baby." They were both bright-eyed, and pious, in decision.

"Well," said Alison, "look, if the cops should get them for whatever they did, couldn't I say it was *Lilianne* who played the stand-in? That way I'd get out from under the whole thing."

Her mother looked dubious.

"I mean, maybe Lilianne is never going to wake up this time. Well, we can't do anything about that. I mean, she'd have the best of care, but if that's no good . . . I could say I went on a little trip or something and then when I'd come back . . . There might be publicity but it wouldn't be bad publicity. Mom, if it comes out that Larry and me did three months' time for you-know-what, *I'm* cooked forever!"

"*Sssh*. They won't make the connection. It was under a different name."

"I know. I know. Oh God, if Lilianne *dies* and they think it's me—then the whole thing dies!"

"You could even," Bobbie said, musingly, "get a driver's license."

Bobbie took out her lipstick. She began to paint her mouth, contorting it violently. She spoke in the midst of this performance. "Lilianne always thought that I was a devil and drove your saintly father out. Some saint, eh? So why didn't he ever come back and take her with him? He coulda had her, for all of me." She put the red paint away and said piously, "I did the best I could, for both of you. It wasn't easy."

"Listen, Mom, I was always on your side, wasn't I?"

112

"That's right, baby." Bobbie stared at her daughter. "I guess we can get along," she pronounced. She got up to go. "Well, I'm glad at least I know what's going on."

Alison said coaxingly, "Don't be mad at me."

So Bobbie embraced her, briefly.

Alison said tearfully, "You're tops, Mom. I mean, honest. Wait."

Bobbie had cracked the door. "Nobody's around," she said.

"No, I mean . . . if anybody does show up, here, I'm going to be Lilianne. I'm Lilianne."

Her mother didn't answer. She went away.

Leon Daw was walking back and forth in his den, a large room at the back of his house, with sliding glass doors to a patio. The glass was covered with heavy draperies now.

He said, "I wish I had your nerves, believe me. What if that kid wakes up? Don't you ever think of that?"

"She probably won't," said Megan Royce, who was sitting in a chair beside the cold fireplace, nursing a long drink. Her lean feet, in her very high-heeled shoes, were placed arrogantly.

"Probably! *Probably!*" stormed Leon. "Why didn't you tell me she had this damned mother?"

"How did I know she had a mother? Or that the mother was around? They'll give you the girl. You'll see. And then what?"

"You're so right," he snarled. "And then what?"

"Could we bring her here?"

"I don't know. I don't know. I wish you hadn't messed in, with your *brilliant* ideas."

"You do?" she said sweetly. "And what were you going to do if I hadn't? Maybe I shouldn't have 'messed in,' as you put it. Maybe I should have walked in on you, choking your darling niece to *death,* up in her bedroom, on Monday noon, and maybe I should have

113

turned right around and walked out and called the police?"

"I didn't—" Leon rubbed his face. "You know damned well I didn't mean to. It was just that she was going to wrap up the whole thing! Give the whole fortune to this damned medical missionary, or whatever he is, and *drop* me. Just *drop* me. At my age! *Out*. Just *out*. When I could have chiselled, here and there, for years. And never did! And never did! She'd made a date with St. John Cotter. She was going through with it. She wouldn't *listen*."

"Possibly, she thought it was her money," said Megan frostily.

"It was my job, my living, my income! I didn't inherit. She got it *all*. Certainly it was *her* money. But she was absolutely maddening. She never knew anybody else was alive, except little Dorothy. She didn't *understand* money. I could have stolen a million or two. And never did."

"Oh, I don't blame you for being annoyed," said Megan.

"I'm *not* a murderer. I'm an honest man. I never meant her to die. You know that."

"I do?" said Megan, smiling.

"Just don't get ideas now," he snapped. "You're just as guilty as I am, now. You unmade her date with Cotter. You made the reservation to San Francisco. You cancelled it."

"Haven't I," said Megan, "been the busy little bee? That's what I wanted to explain to you. Oh, I don't mind," said Megan, shifting angularly, "but I *am* a little weary of holding your nerves together. You've muffed too much, already. You chickened out on getting her ready. Who had to fix her fingerprints? You chickened out on driving her down to the ocean. Oh no, you had to put her away in that damned truck. And don't think they won't know where *that* happened. The driver knows where he parked and where he ever left it.

And where it could have been done. Don't kid yourself, darling. She's been found. The police have already come sniffing around. So what *would* you do, if you didn't have a perfect alibi? If you weren't seen, lunching with your dear little, rich little, niece at Nickey's, a whole day after that corpse got to be one?"

"All right," he said sullenly.

"Who remembered that she had a double?" Megan went on relentlessly. "You didn't even remember *that* until I did. And who knew exactly how to get hold of this Alison? And who conned her into the act? And who stage-managed that whole scene, and did it damned well, too?"

"Nag. Nag," he said. "And she ran out on you?"

"She's sleeping, now," said Megan, "and not talking in her sleep. And when, by the way, do we fly to Vegas and get married?"

"Soon. Soon."

"All right, then. Listen. I think I'm going to clinch our identification."

Leon turned on her viciously. "You were going to get dear little Alison dead this afternoon. And chickened out. Didn't you, darling?"

"How could I know I'd have to get into that stupid gown? Even then, I had the stuff ready. And that was better done than you can imagine. I had it in my hair."

He goggled at her.

"I came close," she said.

"Close. Close," he mocked.

"If I had more sense than to do what I couldn't get away with doing, you ought to be glad. Because what *I* do, *you* do, and don't forget it. It works both ways." Her eyes blazed. "Now, will you listen to me or not?"

"Go ahead," he said sulkily.

"I happen to have the key."

"What key?"

"To the locker. Where Dorothy's suitcase is, right now."

"So."

"So I'm going to use it, to prove that girl *is* Dorothy."

"You are?"

"I'm going to get myself up a bit, and go rent a room from Mrs. Cuneen."

"You can't do that!" He was aghast.

"Of course not. But I can look at a room, can't I?"

"I think you're crazy. You've done enough."

"I thought you were worried." He didn't answer. "I thought you wanted to get her away, somewhere else, where you would have the chance to—shall I say—watch over her? I'm sure you'd find a way to do better than I did. At murder. After all, you've had more experience."

"Ah, lay off." He groaned and fell into a chair. "Lay off, will you?" And then bitterly, "Maybe she'll die a natural death."

"That would be ideal," said Megan calmly. "If you've got nerve enough to wait for it."

"We're back to nerve?" he said angrily. *"Your* nerves were pretty wracked, for two days. After *you* let her get away. We still don't know why she ran out or where she's been or what she's said. You talk about nerve! I did *my* share. When we saw her picture, *I* went and did something about that. *I* was the one who stood up to the mother. You didn't even know there was a mother. I was the one who held on to my nerves and bulled my way through that one."

"Good for you," she said. "Hold on some more. I told you I'd fix it, with the key. So you'll get her. And when you do, why then you'll have her, won't you?"

The man said thickly, "Don't leave me."

"All right," she said with sudden energy. "What is ideal, darling? That she dies while she is still in *that* hospital, under *their* auspices. Isn't that so? What if I figure how to make that happen, when we *both* have a perfect alibi."

"When?" he said.

116

"Tomorrow. All you have to do is marry me."

At the hospital, in the dim deserted lobby, Matt was talking to Mr. Atwood. "I'm sorry about your party, sir, but I thought you'd better know that Megan Royce was planning to poison the patient in Room 124 this afternoon."

Atwood's eyes were hard in his bloodhound's face.

"Look at this," Matt had a small tray from the lab in his hands. On it lay an ordinary glass eyedropper. "Nicotine," he said. "It was in the ash-receiver. That thing full of sand, where the corridors intersect, where Megan Royce and I sat down to talk. Megan Royce put this thing in that sand because she hadn't been able to use it and because I scared her. She was afraid I'd see it. It was in her hair."

"*Did* you see it in her hair?"

"No, sir."

"Then what convinces you of all this?" Atwood was very cool.

"The whole thing!" cried Matt. "Her antics. Something about her, when she was in the room. I took her arm. I dragged her away. I didn't know why, then. I could just feel—some excitement. I can't explain it."

"And can't prove it, can you?" Atwood was searching Matt's face.

"And then there was her tension. The way she sat, moved, watched, reacted. The way she panicked. The way she pushed her cigarette deep into the sand. That's when she got rid of this. I'm positive."

"But you didn't *see* her do it?"

"All right, there *is* no proof. But I'll tell you now—and anybody else who wants to know. I won't release that girl to Leon Daw and Megan Royce."

"You may have to," said Atwood. "St. John Cotter is making legal noises."

"Let him. I'll raise the question."

"Any visitor, to any patient, or any one of an assortment of hospital personnel, could have put that thing

117

where it was found."

Matt said, "Theoretically."

"How was she going to administer it? Pour it in an ear, like Hamlet's father?"

"I only say she had it ready. She *intended*—"

"You can't know an intention. Have you questioned everybody," Atwood snapped, "who was on the floor, at any time, all day?"

"No, I have not. Will you get in touch with the Police Department about this?"

"I don't think we had better make an unfounded accusation in a very serious matter."

Matt despaired. The world was sluggish. He couldn't make it move. "Then what *are* you going to do about it?"

Atwood answered with a question. "The girl is all right, I take it?"

"So far. But if I didn't trust Selma Marsh, for the night, I'd sit at the door myself."

Atwood said slowly, "Even if it were true that somebody had a wild impractical plan to poison one of our patients, that somebody did not succeed. Did not, in fact, really try."

"Didn't succeed, *this* time." Matt felt wild.

"Let me warn you, very seriously, not to mention this idea to the Press." Atwood kept looking at him solemnly.

Matt said furiously, "I'll mention it to the police then. I'll get in touch with a Lieutenant Clarence Tate the first thing in the morning. He'll be in touch with you."

Matt sailed, fuming, along the park path. Nicotine, the gardener's poison. Easy to come by. It *might* have killed her. He didn't know how. But he did know that Megan Royce had put the poison in the sand. He could see her doing it. Had not seen her at the time. Could see it, now. Plain as plain.

He had been some time at the hospital, in the lab—

pouncing on the discovery, rousting out Atwood. So it was late. The whole world slept. He couldn't rouse it. The house, when he let himself in, was quiet. His mother had obviously gone to bed.

He didn't hesitate long. He went upstairs, fast, and tapped on Betty's door. When she put on her light and appeared, looking tousled and alarmed, he made her come sit on the top step with him and he told her.

"So there's murder in it," he said. "There's a connection with that murdered body. There's danger all right."

"M-Matt?" Betty's teeth chattered and she hugged herself against the chill that she was feeling. "We know our girl's not Alison. Alison must be the one in the truck. I don't want to sound like Tony, but what if somebody was hired to kill Dorothy Daw, and got her double instead? And what if Dorothy caught on to that? And that was her reason to run away?"

"Who is somebody? Who did the hiring? It's a hypothesis," he agreed grudgingly.

Betty began to shiver so violently that he put his arm around her and held tight. She buried her face in his shoulder.

"It's a police matter, now," he said, with grim satisfaction. "*They* won't get her."

"They?"

"Uncle Leon and Megan-baby. Listen, Betts, this is strange. But it seems to me that I *knew* it. Uncle Leon wanted, in the worst way, for me to tell him she would die. How did I *know* that? I didn't realize, then . . . but now I'm sure I did know it. I felt it. In the air."

"People do sense things," said Betty, muffled against him. "It's called intuition."

"Is that right?" said Matt vaguely.

She sat straight suddenly. "*Some* people sense things, *sometimes*." In the dim light her eyes seemed to glitter. "Not all. Not always."

"Well, it's a police matter, now," he repeated.

119

"Oh, sure," she said, in a minute.

"I guess we ought to put in a little sack-time," he said, as if he were a kind big brother.

"Sweet dreams, eh?" she said tremulously.

"I had to tell somebody. Hey, listen, don't worry too much. We won't let them get her." He kissed her lightly on her cheek and helped her up.

She stood there in her robe, her face bare of make-up, looking both younger and older than usual. Tears were making the glitter in her eyes.

"Go on," he said. "Get to bed. Don't feel so bad. Forget it."

Her mouth pulled in a strange expression. She said nothing, but turned away.

"Good night," he said kindly.

He went downstairs, feeling a little guilty for having wakened and worried her.

Betty put herself, robe and all, very deliberately into her bed. She turned off the light and said aloud, *"Forget it!"*

Chapter Ten

It was nine o'clock on Sunday morning when Matt finally reached Lieutenant Tate on the telephone. Matt told his story and stated his case for an attempted poisoning as quietly and as lucidly as he could. He did not want to sound a calamity howler or a conclusion jumper. But his facts were undeniably feeble. The voice on the other end of the wire listened to his account without excitement. Then Lieutenant Tate said, with no more ado, that he would meet Matt at the hospital at about noon, the earliest he could make it.

Peg tried to herd her son back to the breakfast table, but he couldn't sit down. He drank another cup of coffee and left the house.

Betty Prentiss, at the top of the stairs when he went out the front door, did not call greetings. She saw the top of his head go by. She let him go.

When she came down, Peg gave her a good morning and by a glance prescribed a quiet Sunday for them both. The morning dragged.

After church, just after lunchtime, Tony Severson arrived. "Good day. Good day. What's new?" He had found them in the kitchen.

Betty shrugged and Peg said, "Do you want some lunch?"

"I see it before me." Tony took a slice of bread and

121

began to butter it vigorously. "Where's Matt?" He looked around suspiciously.

"He's been gone all morning."

"Huh?" Tony placed a chair in his favorite position and straddled it. "What's he after? Am I missing something?" He was highly intuitive. His lively eyes watched them as he munched on the bread.

"How do we know what you're missing when we don't know what you know?" said Betty crossly. The Press was not to be told about the poison. (The Press was not to be told that Matt was probably on guard, like some idiot knight on a white horse.)

"I don't know whether I'm glad I know what I know, or not," said Tony. "How complicated can it get? O.K. Now hear this. I've been digging. I went for the vital statistics. I won't bore you with my methods. But I happen to know this chap in Yuma. So I got this phone call. Fact number one, Alison Hopkins got married, aged sixteen, to a fella name Larry Wimberholtz. Divorce quickly followed—"

"*Larry!*" said Betty.

"Why? Why?" Tony pounced.

"When we saw Bobbie Hopkins yesterday, there was a Larry there. She said he was a friend of hers."

"Larry *Wimberholtz?*"

"Larry somebody. She didn't introduce him."

"Here, eh? In the area? Hereabouts? Well, well." Tony folded his hands on the chair back and put his chin on them. His tongue reached for a crumb.

"What difference does it make?" said Betty tiredly.

"I dunno. Those are funny people, those Hopkins. They hide stuff under rocks. Fact number two is going to rock the both of you, angels. It's got *me* dizzy. Now hear this. Alison Hopkins has got a twin sister. Identical. Can't tell them apart. No death certificate for this twin, either. Not there. Not here. Now what? Now we only got *three* girls who all look alike."

"I don't believe it," Peg said.

"Oh, you got to believe there *was* this twin. Seems Mom Hopkins and the girls took off for L.A., five years ago. (Pa, he'd taken off long ago.) So they came for the usual. Fame and fortune in Hollywood. And, as usual, it wasn't growing on the palm trees. What I want to know is how come the neighbors don't seem to know anything about a twin sister? Why did I have to find out about *her* from Yuma? So I high-tailed it up to Bobbie's dump, at the crack of the A.M. And I braced her. I hammered on the door and I hollered and made a big nuisance and pretty soon, there she is. And Bobbie in the morning, um-boy! Well, so, anyhow . . . I ask her politely how I can get in touch with her other daughter.

"So our Bobbie looks like she's going to fall down. She lets out a whisky breath and she says she won't say. And she says, with some agitation, that nobody can make her say. And she says her other daughter is a religious. How about that? And she says she, Bobbie, respects religion, which is more than a heathen like me knows how to do. And nobody is going to disturb her holy daughter, the one who is out of this world. And she starts to heave and holler so I got to take my foot out of the door. Especially since who pulls up in car? Lieutenant Tate of Homicide, that's who.

"And Bobbie finds out he's from the police and starts hollering that he has got to protect her from me. So he not only won't talk, he won't let me talk. He boots me down the hill. But what's he doing there, you know? And how do you like this twin angle? Oh wow . . . if *I* could find this twin before anybody else gets on to her . . . But I dunno about tangling with the Church, see? You know any good Catholic who could give me a line on how to find out about a nun? Or even if it's possible?"

"The twin sister is a nun?" said Peg wonderingly.

"What else?" said Tony. "Isn't that what a religious means? And if she looks as good as the kid in the hospital, oh wow! A nun, an heiress, and a movie starlet . . . and all of them beeyootiful blondes. I got, here, an embarrassment of riches."

The two women were looking stunned. "I don't understand any of it anymore," said Peg.

"What's the twin's name?" asked Betty.

"I don't have to tell *you* everything, either." Tony looked coy and got off the chair. "I'm going to tell you one more thing. There has been absolutely no hanky-panky with the Daw money." Tony put his finger beside his nose. "The paper knows! Hey, where did Matt go?"

"To the hospital, I believe," said Peg.

"Did she wake up? Or did she die? What? What?" Peg shook her head and then put it between her hands.

Tony said in a moment, "I got a feeling you two are holding out on me. Is that neighborly? O.K., I'll go get it out of Matt."

"Matt is meeting this police lieutenant," Betty said crisply. "You'll have to wait."

"Is *that* what you think?" said Tony, grinning wide. Then he was off.

When the turbulence of his leaving had left the kitchen air, Peg said softly, "Poor Matt."

Betty excused herself and went upstairs, not even helping with the dishes. She had nothing important to do upstairs, but she didn't want to admit that she knew what Peg meant. The girl in the hospital would turn out to be the nun. It fitted, somehow. It felt right. But then — she wasn't, somehow, real at all! Betty didn't want Peg to notice the streak of human meanness that made her glad, although ashamed to be.

124

Upstairs, the front bedroom stood open, the bed changed and spread, the room clean and bare. The belongings of the girl had been taken to the hospital because Peg had been pestered by people who wanted to photograph them. So it was as if the girl had never been there.

Betty closed her own door. She sat on her bed. The house was very quiet. Against the silence a hard truth rang. Poor Matt? But what difference would it make to poor Betty Prentiss, who had something to do upstairs after all.

For-get it.

She had sat in his arms last night on the top step. A living waking longing body of a girl who was no nun. He hadn't noticed. Therefore, he never would. So snap out of it, she told herself savagely. Skip it. *Forget it!*

After a while, she heard voices. Peg was coming up with somebody. A female. Betty lay low. Somebody to look at the room, she supposed. She was in no state to pop out and be introduced to a stranger. She hoped Peg wouldn't knock. After a while, she began to trust that Peg would not. She guessed Peg knew how it was with Betty. Which was humiliating, too. Skip it, she told herself. Wipe it out. OUT.

Then she heard Peg saying, rather crisply, outside her door, "I have another roomer, a very nice girl who teaches. Betty Prentiss is her name."

There was silence. Then, Betty could hear Peg's voice diminishing, going down the stairs. The other voice was silent. Betty hoped this meant that whoever it was had not taken the front room. It was better to be up here alone for a while. When you found yourself in the classical position of being in love with a man who didn't notice you were alive and got no messages from your living, waking flesh — that was a position to get *out* of. Alone. The best you could.

125

* * *

Lieutenant Clarence Tate, who appeared at the hospital, as he had promised, a few minutes before noon, was a quiet man, medium tall, with a seamed coarse-grained face over which a great deal of time seemed to have passed without having affected the middle-aged sturdiness of his body. Time had turned the face into a mask. Tate was not in the habit of giving much away by an expression.

He had seen the sleeping girl, taken her fingerprints efficiently and without comment. Now he sat in Atwood's office, listening.

He listened to Matt, to Dr. Prentiss, to Mr. Atwood. When they had nothing left but questions, he began to speak. "Here are some photographs, taken in Fresno. Photographs are tricky, as I guess you know. But the body found in a truck in Fresno on Tuesday morning, with the neck broken, seems to be a ringer for the girl you have here. Look and see."

They looked at the pictures. They were brutally clear. It was very much the same fair face. The hair was cut short. That was the second most obvious difference. Matt winced to see the primary difference. The girl in the pictures was not sleeping, but dead. Dead. Dead.

The truck, Tate told them, was carrying cartons of wooden toys. The driver, Bailly, had loaded in Los Angeles and driven directly to a hamburger joint on San Fernando Road, where he parked the truck, on Monday night, from about eleven-thirty to midnight. He was inside, having a meal and bracing himself for the night run with four cups of coffee. Now that he had begun to speak, the lieutenant went along with apparent candor in an easy flow, as one among his peers.

"Now, they interrogated this Bailly in Fresno, on

126

Tuesday. On Wednesday, a police officer from Fresno came on down and I cooperated with him, checking out what the driver had testified about his actions in this area. By Wednesday night, it seemed pretty plain that he had told the truth. Which didn't get us very far."

Tate reached for the photographs and put them away as he went on talking. "The hamburger place has a big parking lot where nobody saw a thing. The truck was in a slot nearest an alley. Nobody lives on the alley. But the counterman knows the driver and says he was there, at that time, eating, just as he said. My colleague went on up the line, checking every stop the driver says he made, but it turned out that he had stopped only very briefly, at country corners. So it began to look as if the body was put into his truck while it waited in that parking lot, on San Fernando Road, on Monday night. Which put it up to us to try for an identification of the victim, as having come from around here.

"Which identification, by the way, somebody wanted to prevent. Not a stitch of clothing. And the fingertips of the deceased were crisscrossed with small cuts, probably from a razor blade. We are also inclined to think that the hair was cut short after death."

"How *can* you identify?" Atwood inquired.

"We are checking out Missing Persons. Circulating dental charts. Of course, that takes time."

"And our girl's fingerprints?" Atwood looked hopeful.

The lieutenant sighed, for lay ignorance. "If we find your girl's prints some place, we can assume she left them there. But unless we've got her prints on file, that won't tell us who she is."

Atwood groaned softly. Dr. Prentiss said, "She is the other one."

127

"Probably so." Tate nodded. "I saw the news photo Friday morning. And the resemblance. But *she* wasn't the one I was after—not being dead, you see. But as soon as I heard there'd been two identifications of your girl, it looked as if our dead girl had to be the other one. Either Dorothy Daw or Alison Hopkins. And the case comes down here."

He looked stern.

"On Saturday morning, checking up on the Daw girl, I showed these photographs to Leon Daw, who wouldn't have any part of them. I checked on where the Daw girl was last seen."

"You saw Leon Daw on *Saturday?*" Matt broke in. "What time, sir?"

"Why?"

"Because he didn't mention that. To me, I mean. Not at all."

Tate's face did not change. He waited for Matt to go on and when Matt did not, the lieutenant continued his own account.

"Dorothy Daw dropped out of sight, Tuesday, midday, at the Union Railroad Station. By then, our girl was already in the morgue in Fresno, so it seemed clear that out dead girl isn't Dorothy. So, I went after Hopkins."

The lieutenant paused and looked at them sombrely. "I waited for today, because the body was transferred to us and arrived last night. Early this morning, on the strength of her reaction to these photographs, I was able to take Mrs. Bobbie Hopkins to see the deceased. So I can tell you that Mrs. Hopkins definitely identifies our girl, the dead girl, as her daughter Alison."

"Wait a minute!" Matt felt outraged.

"That's right," said Tate severely. "She fell apart quite a bit, but she made a positive identification. So . . ."

128

There was an intrusion. Tony Severson knocked and squeezed into the room, pleading himself as a messenger from, and a personal friend of, Mrs. Cuneen. Tate accepted Dr. Prentiss' acceptance, only warning Tony to listen off the record. But whatever message Tony had proposed to deliver was temporarily lost in the shuffle.

Because Matt lunged forward. "Did Bobbie Hopkins look for a scar or a mark?" he demanded.

Tate's deadpan turned to him. "What scar is this?"

Matt burst into an account of the mark that would not tan.

"The dead girl has a nice easy tan, all right," Tate said thoughtfully. "Mrs. Hopkins didn't mention any particular mark."

"Is there any mark? Or *marks?*"

"Other marks?"

Matt recognized his own technique. Tate wasn't going to be forthcoming on the subject of marks. "Mrs. Hopkins didn't even look?" he cried.

"No."

"Then the woman is crazy. She identified *this* girl, *our* girl, as her daughter Alison, on Friday. She practically fell apart then, about being a mother. Yesterday she told me about a mark on Alison that this girl, our girl, does *not* have. I told her so and she argued with me. Now, she identifies your body as Alison and didn't even mention the mark that might prove it. O.K. Either she doesn't know what she's saying or doesn't care. She doesn't make sense at all. Don't you know that she says Alison left her house, alive and well, on *Tuesday evening?* How could Alison be dead in a truck on Monday night? There's something wrong here."

Tate said, "She was pretty hysterical. Took it hard. She admitted to me it might have been *Monday* night that Alison left her. I don't know that I'd call Mrs.

129

Hopkins the most reliable witness in the world."

"Then *you* don't believe that identification either," cried Matt.

Tate didn't answer. Prentiss said thoughtfully, "Still—what you call the mark indicates that *we* haven't got Alison. Surely you can inspect the victim for such a mark."

Tate nodded glumly, his face giving nothing away.

But now Tony pushed forward. "Excuse me, gents. Did you know that Alison has a twin sister? Identical. Who is some kind of nun."

Tate turned to stare at him. Tony bubbled out his news, but he had the knack of attracting a scolding. The lieutenant turned very cold. How had it happened that Mr. Severson had not given his information to the police? Tony said, "I'm *giving* it. I'm *giving* it." But the lieutenant grew colder. Why had he not given it early this morning, in Mrs. Hopkins' driveway? "You weren't in the mood," said Tony, and the lieutenant was not amused. Mr. Severson had better mend his ways and had better be sure to remember that what he had just heard in this room was off the record and not to be broadcast. Furthermore, Mr. Severson had better go now, unless Mr. Severson had anything more to say that would pertain.

Mr. Severson had. Did the police know that Alison Hopkins had once been married to a Larry Wimberholtz? And did the police know that there was a reason to believe this man was now in the area?

The police did not say whether the police had known. The police put Tony out.

After he had gone, Atwood said impatiently what all of them were thinking. *Three* girls, all alike, were simply too many. Furthermore, it meant that they still did not know which one of them lay asleep in Room 124.

Matt said hotly that if they didn't want two out of

130

three dead, they had better protect the one they had. An eyedropper full of poison, found so near the room of a girl whose double had already been murdered, justified in Matt's opinion a round-the-clock police protection.

But the police officer did not offer any. He said that he would prefer, and it was a hard word as he said it, that the girl not be let out of this hospital until Tate gave his permission.

Atwood was much relieved by this pronouncement. He shook the lieutenant's hand heartily and announced that the hospital would keep her, and would protect her, for its own sake. He would hire two guards, one to replace the policeman who could no longer be spared for the lobby, to keep the Press out. And the other to stand guard at the door of the girl's room. He would move her, in fact, to a different room and its location would not be given out at all. The guard would wear a gown and enter the room whenever anyone else did. Atwood had every confidence in the Police Department. He felt sure that the lieutenant would clear up the whole affair, very soon. Meantime, the lieutenant could rely on the hospital.

Tate permitted a wintry smile to widen his mouth and said that he would now visit the Cuneen house, if Mr. Cuneen was ready.

Dr. Prentiss, nodding general approval, went off about his business. Matt walked through the park with the policeman, trying to feel happier about the whole thing. But he was deeply depressed.

Tate said, "You'd rather Alison wasn't the dead one, eh?"

"It's nothing to do with what *I'd* rather." Matt felt shocked.

"Probability says your girl is this religious twin. That is, until we find out the twin is dead, long ago. Or tucked away in some convent. Or also

131

recently vaccinated."

"Vaccinated? Oh, I see. Our girl has no scar, of any kind. Yours has?"

Tate wasn't saying what scars his girl might have. "Everybody gets vaccinated. The scar could vanish with the years?"

"I guess so."

"Within *three* years?"

"Three?"

"Looks like your girl shouldn't be Dorothy. And shouldn't be Alison, either. Alison just got back from Spain. So those two would have to have been vaccinated within the last three years. That's the law. Otherwise, they don't get back into the United States." In a moment, the lieutenant asked the sky, "But does a vaccination *always* leave a scar?"

"I don't know," said Matt miserably.

"I'm not so sure your girl isn't Alison."

"Why is that, sir?" said Matt quickly, his heart jumping. "I don't know why that is. You get hunches. This is quite a bit like the old shell game."

"Pardon?"

"My job is to find out which walnut shell the dead girl is under."

"That involves finding out which girl is in the hospital and where the third one is. If any."

"Seems so. Why don't we get a clue from the name she gave, I wonder? What was it again?"

"Olin, Dolan, Tollin, Bowlen."

"You didn't publicize that?"

"No, sir. It couldn't help. And people by any of those names would have been pestered."

"And besides, you didn't like your mother looking like a fool."

Matt suddenly felt as if he were less than half the other man's age.

132

Chapter Eleven

Lieutenant Tate listened respectfully to Peg's tale of the girl's arrival, which was told with the glibness of practice now. As she went, she quite obviously decided that she liked and trusted the man. Tate's face could not change much but his voice seemed to soften.

When they all three went upstairs, Betty came out of her room, was introduced, and told her portion of the story with precision and calm. Matt tried to wink congratulations at her, but her eyes wouldn't meet his.

They all four went into the front bedroom. Tate had the grey suitcase with him, destined for the police lab. He set it down and asked if the room had been occupied since the girl's departure.

Peg said, "No, sir. Let me see — I think three people have come, because of my For Rent sign. A woman was here today. Fortunately, she didn't want the room. I wasn't exactly drawn to her, either."

Tate was quick, "You weren't drawn to this girl, then?"

"Not really," Peg answered frankly. She went on defensively, "But you see, she looked so exhausted. She needed to lie down and rest, I thought. Everybody is somebody." Peg began to sputter as if this were an argument. "That girl is *somebody*. *Somebody* has to notice. It's my house."

"You apologising, ma'am, for a good heart?" the lieutenant said. "Don't do it. In my business, I meet too many people with scar tissue beating in there."

Um—boy—the philosopher, thought Matt and glanced to see whether his contemporary was beginning to be amused. But Betty was just standing there, detached and unresponsive.

The lieutenant asked to what degree the room had been tidied. He looked into the closet, along the floor, along the edges where the mattress met the bedstead, at which point Peg said, mischievously, that she always turned a mattress.

He said he wasn't surprised and began to open the dresser drawers.

Betty leaned on the doorjamb, watching rather dreamily. She wasn't feeling a thing, she told herself. Matt was a nice boy, the son of old friends. She wouldn't see very much of him in the years to come. She would go home in a day or two, get a part-time job of some kind that would be interesting for the summer, or perhaps plan a few little excursions to interesting places. Next year, she would live elsewhere. Take an apartment. She wouldn't be here.

Tate said, "What is this?" He had a key in his hand, a medium-sized key with a flat round head.

"Why, I don't know," said Peg. "Let me see."

He let her see. "It was down in the top drawer, under the paper. Not yours, Mrs. Cuneen?"

"No. I don't think so. I can't imagine . . ."

"When did you line those drawers, ma'am?"

"Why, soon after the last girl left me. That was . . . let me see . . . the end of April."

Betty said, "I'm afraid that hasn't anything to do

134

with the girl in the hospital. I looked in those drawers myself and I would have found it."

"Perhaps not. It was hidden."

"But I'm rather sure. It wasn't there on Wednesday."

"You searched the whole room, did you, Miss Prentiss?"

"*We* did," Matt said. "Betty and I."

"Uh huh. Two people searching can fail to overlap."

Betty protested no further.

"This may not mean anything," the lieutenant said with the key in his open hand. "But since you don't claim it, Mrs. Cuneen, why don't I run down whatever it is the key *to?*"

"Can you really do that?" Peg gasped.

"We can have a good try," he told her comfortingly.

At point of departure, the lieutenant had a word of warning. "I understand," he said, "that you young people were trying to follow some trails?"

"Yes, sir."

"I think you had best leave that to us, now."

"I see," said Matt a bit stiffly. "Fortunately, the hospital is taking steps."

Tate said sternly, "A personal conviction doesn't count in court."

"So I understand, sir."

"Your girl was not poisoned. Nor was anybody else. Are you prepared to accuse this Mrs. Royce of attempted murder? How will you back that up?"

"I am personally convinced of it," Matt said, quietly. "I have no way of proving it. I am stating it, to you."

Tate said mildly, "We'll see what we can do, of course."

135

And he went away.

Peg was aglow. She had liked him. She was sure he'd get to the bottom of the whole thing. Hadn't they liked him, too?

Matt said he thought Tate was a bit of a sentimental old coot. Didn't Betty?

Betty said, "It doesn't matter whether we *like* him. It's in his hands now. I hope he gets it straightened around pretty soon. After all, I do have to pack up and toot off home, one of these days."

"Oh, Betty," said Peg brightly. "I'll hate seeing you go but you ought to have a little fun during the vacation."

They went off together into the kitchen with a curious jauntiness.

Matt stood in his mother's living-room, feeling abandoned. He thought his mother was being awful damn quick to shake off all the responsibility she had been taking so seriously. And Betty was welching on a handshake, wasn't she? Didn't that count anymore?

Matt remained, he felt, responsible, at least to a degree. For instance, he had to go over to the hospital in a little while to see what nuts this day would bring.

He might as well go now. He pounded back through the park, feeling put-upon and disgruntled.

There was a new guard already at the big front doors of the hospital, a man in a plain suit who wanted to know who Matt was. Matt was privileged and could prove it. When he was inside, it didn't take him long to find out where they had moved her. There was a guard sitting on a straight hard

136

chair beside the door of 208. There were gowns hanging there. Matt didn't go in; he had no reasonable reason. He looked at her through the open door.

She slept as sweetly as before.

No one had come to see her. No nuts for Matt to interview. But he remembered something. Speaking of nuts—*He had an idea*. He went racing home again.

In Room 124, the patient lay dozing. Nobody was coming to see her during *these* visiting hours. They had only just put her in here. They'd gone home, to sigh with relief, no doubt. She dozed defensively. Then she sensed a presence, opened her eyes, and stared into the startled face of an ugly oldish woman who was leaning over the bed.

The patient heaved herself up. The ugly woman in the raincoat stepped back so as not to be hit by the patient's knobby old forehead rising so abruptly from the pillow. "Say, who are *you?*" the patient demanded.

But the intruder turned and ran away, without explanation or apology.

The patient in Room 124 put her hard old thumb on the call button. When the nurse came, she had her bed cranked up and sat glaring at the wall, thinking hard thoughts about her daughters-in-law. It didn't occur to her to mention a visitor-to-somebody-else who must have made a mistake.

The ugly woman in the raincoat left her car at the Lockheed Airport's parking lot. Carrying the big brown paper bag, wearing the old coat, the flat shoes, the scarf on her head, with the five-ninety-eight nylon wig hanging down around her old and ugly face, she boarded a plane.

137

Tony Severson had an idea. It was brilliantly simple.

Tony had been finding himself in a miserable position. His own story was getting away from him. All more or less obvious channels of information were being opened up by foxier men than he. For another thing, in view of the Daw millions, and a dragon named St. John Cotter, the powers-that-were on Tony's paper kept dampening Tony down. They wouldn't, for instance, go for any ingenious theorizing about the identity of a dead girl in a truck. All *that* would open up, sooner or later, through the police. Open up for everybody. But it was part of *his* story! Had to be. And what could Tony do about it?

Tony had felt that he must make the most of his private inside track, his acquaintance, through Betty Prentiss, with the Cuneens. It was paying off, he felt, but he had been stymied. Until, inspired, he had looked through the Los Angeles area telephone books. So brilliantly, so simply.

He parked in front of the tract house. Sunday. Good. The householder wouldn't be at work, then. Pleased with himself, Tony rang the doorbell. He had devised a strategy.

"Mr. Larry Wimberholtz?" said he, politely, to the slim pale young man who opened the door.

"That's right."

"My name is Severson. I . . . er . . . happened to be in touch with a fellow I know in Yuma . . ." Tony trailed off questioningly and watched like a fox. He saw the face change and soften with a mention of the old home town. Yup. This was the man, all right. Uncommon name. Luckily.

"Is that so?" said the young man. "Somebody

138

who knows me, was it!"

"Somebody who knows you were once married to Alison Hopkins."

At this, the young man took a step backwards and a look of horror came over his face. Tony's imagination took wing.

"And now she's dead," he said. "I guess that's too bad. Right, Larry?"

"What do you mean, dead?" the man said belligerently.

"That's what her mom says. Murdered. Naked, in a truck in Fresno." Tony's ideas were burning bright. "You want your side of it in the papers, too, don't you, Larry? Listen, the cops aren't far behind me. So why don't you tell me about it, Larry? Maybe you won't get to talk, see, later on."

The man screamed like a woman. "Get away."

Tony winced as the door hit the soft toe of his suede shoe and the end of his nose. The door wooshed firmly shut. He was outside. He rang the bell five times. Nothing happened. So Tony went out to his car and sat there a while. Nothing happened. He was in a state of wild excitement. It occurred to him that the cops might not be right behind him, after all. Wasn't it his duty to tell them about this ex-husband? This big fat suspect that Tony had turned up, single-handed? Tony started his car and roared away. Let him run, he thought. Makes a good story better!

Inside the house, Larry Wimberholtz wept in his wife's arms. "Damn her! Damn her! That damn' Bobbie! She *told* them. She said she wouldn't. Listen, honey, I didn't want any part of this. I didn't want to get mixed up with that old mess. Now, I can lose my job. It's not *right*. I begged her. I said . . ."

139

"I think I heard his car."

"Go and look, Dolores honey, would you?"

When she came back, he said, "I'm getting out. I'm not going through the mill for that damned Alison. Not anymore. Listen, I never talk about it, Dolores. It was a bad time in my life. I've got a right to forget. I paid my debt. I wish I'd *never* got mixed up.

"Listen, in those days my dad was still alive and in the chips and I was going to a private school, see, and I had this car. This real neat car. Well, I made a date with this cute girl who was in this girls' school, you know. Lilianne, her name was. A kind of quiet girl, real nice. I mean I had respect for her. So I asked her out again the next Saturday night and when I came by for her, this girl comes running out of the house. So we go to the show and I was having, you know, a nice time. But afterwards when we park . . . I'm telling you, I was never so surprised in my life.

"I was a kind of innocent kid, Dolores. I really was. I mean that. Two days later, I found out it was her twin. It was *Alison,* that second date. Seems like she used to do that all the time. Play she was her sister. Any time her sister looked like having anything Alison wanted. Like my real neat car.

"Seemed like everybody knew all about them, except me. Couldn't tell them apart. That's one reason they went to separate schools. Alison, she was the wildest kook in the public high school. And the other one, the nice one, she didn't have a chance. So there was this woman, ran the girls' school, was taking an interest, trying to help, I guess.

"But *I* didn't know. *I* didn't know a damned thing. So what did *I* do? Damned idiot, *I* stuck up for Alison. I said it was love. We ran away and got

140

married. You see . . . uh . . . you see . . . uh . . .
she was pregnant."

"I knew you were married before," Dolores said
softly.

"Yes, but . . . well, but . . . well, you know my
dad died, and there wasn't anything, and my mom
had to go to work and Alison . . ."

"You got divorced."

"Yes, but . . . Oh, Dolores, she just about
wrecked me forever. The things! She smashed up
my car. She lost her license. She . . . did worse than
that. I was innocent, but they wouldn't believe it.
We . . . she . . ."

"Don't tell me," Dolores said. "It's O.K. It's
O.K."

"Now look!" He wept. *"Now* she's got herself
murdered. Isn't that what he said? Believe me, I'm
not surprised. But I'm not going to get mixed up in
it. I can't stand . . . You know I only feel better if
everything's quiet. You know how I am."

"I can say you're out of town, Larry."

"Would you? I'm out of town, you can say. On
business. Then they can't arrest me. Let them find
out who did it and I can come back when they do.
Because I didn't do anything, but I can't stand going through all that. . . . I'm a damn coward. All
right. I know it."

"It'll be O.K., Larry," said his wife. "I don't want
you to get mixed up in it. They can't make me say
anything. You can go somewhere and just be
quiet . . ."

"Honey, get your mom to come and stay with
you?"

"I will. Hurry."

He kissed her. He whimpered like a kitten. She
was nineteen years old, and heavy with his child,

and stronger than a lioness. She packed his suitcase.

When the plane landed in Las Vegas, the woman in the raincoat went into the ladies' room.

A cab picked up a little later the smart-looking woman in the yellow knit and took her into town. She walked two blocks on her high thin heels. Leon Daw opened the door of his car for her and she got in, sighing. "Don't talk about it," said Megan. "It's not wise."

(There hadn't been a way in the world to do it. There was no way in the world she could have done what she had meant to do. But she need not say so.)

"We drove over just for the ceremony," Leon told the man who married them. "Driving back tomorrow."

"You're not gambling, then?" the man said.

But the bride was. She continued to say nothing.

Betty Prentiss was sitting in Peg's living-room, doing her mending. She hated to mend. It was just the thing to do when you felt too numb and miserable to do anything else. Matt was in the front hall, on the telephone. He'd been on the phone all afternoon, and now again.

Peg came in and said, "What *is* he doing?"

"He's trying to locate a woman named Alfreda," Betty said drearily. "She's one of the people who came to the hospital and said she knew the girl. She's some kind of religious nut, Matt thinks. A cult leader, maybe. Now, Matt thinks that could have been what Bobbie Hopkins meant."

"And not a nun?" said Peg softly. Her bright eyes

knew everything.

Betty felt herself flush. "I give up," she said boldly.

"I know," said Peg. She sighed and sat down and let her hands fall idle. She wouldn't go, she thought, to her meetings tomorrow. She had left the church supper early. She could not answer all the questions — over and over and over.

Matt left the phone and came into the living-room, too restless to stand still. "Nothing," he told them. "I've tried every religious editor in town. I've also been trying to find out what court she could have been in. She said she'd had to be in court on Friday. But that's hopeless. Sunday night. And all I know is that she calls herself Alfreda and wears a robe. Alfreda Jones? Smith? It was a good idea while it lasted."

"You think our girl could be this twin sister?" Peg was calm.

"I think this Alfreda may at least know where the twin sister can be found."

"Won't the police find her, dear?"

"Maybe," said Matt gloomily. "One thing, though, this character Alfreda did say she was coming back to the hospital. Maybe she'll be there at seven-thirty."

"I'm going with you," Peg said.

"Why, Ma?"

"Because I want to see our girl, how she is."

"She's the same," he said painfully. "I thought you didn't feel responsible any more."

"I'd still like to see her," Peg said. "She's beginning to seem unreal."

"Oh, she's there," murmured Betty. She looked up with her head down, her old look.

Matt paced. "Don't give me any of your dark

143

looks, Betts," he burst impatiently. "Give me a bright idea, why don't you?"

She flushed and lifted her head, abandoning her "look" forever.

He smiled suddenly and fell into a chair. "Don't worry, eh? That's the good word, I guess."

Betty said, in a moment, as if she reluctantly brought her mind to the problem, "I think we should have gone back to the restaurant."

"Why?"

"We didn't talk to the hat-check girl or the waiter."

"Does that matter?"

"We don't know whether it matters," she answered patiently.

"The one in the restaurant was Dorothy Daw. But there is *still* no trail between here and the railroad station. In between, Dorothy could have . . ."

He gave it up. It was suddenly absurd. His girl, with or without a vaccination, must be Dorothy Daw. Running away. Needing something? He brooded.

The phone rang and Matt leaped to answer it.

Tate said, "Cuneen? We went right *to* the key. It was easy."

"Is that so, sir?"

"Thought your mother would be interested."

"Yes, do you want her?"

"I can tell *you*. The key fits a locker at the Union Railroad Station. They'd stored the contents, after twenty-four hours. But the contents were — one white suitcase with initials D.D. Inside, there's a lot of expensive clothing, a small hat with orange feathers, and Dorothy Daw's passport."

"I see," said Matt.

"You can tell your mother I'm inclined to believe

her ex-roomer is Dorothy Daw, all right. The dead girl is Alison Hopkins."

"I see. Complete with mark, is she?"

Tate evaded answering the question. "There's this. Alison's ex-husband has taken off for parts unknown. So, as of now, it looks like two entirely separate stories."

"That's . . . pretty hard to believe, isn't it?"

"Oh, you can believe it, if you try," said Tate dryly. "This Severson is a personal friend of your family, is he?" Tate brushed on.

"You might say so."

"If you've got any influence, tell him to keep out, will you? We could have had this Wimberholtz easy, if Severson hadn't flushed him out and scared him away."

"But you'll find this Wimberholtz, I suppose?"

"Oh, sure," said Tate carelessly. "Give your mother my regards, will you please?"

"Yes, sir. Thanks for calling. *Wait*. She's Dorothy Daw, if you say so." Matt was tense. "That means Leon Daw gets to claim her? How about the poison attempt?"

"Her own uncle," said Tate, "should be able to protect her."

"You mean you *can't?*"

"You give me proof, or take the chance of making a charge, I'll get after Mrs. Royce. If not, then Leon Daw will have to take care."

"That's what I'm afraid of," said Matt, cautiously.

Tate did not speak for an instant. Then he said, "There's a lot of pressure on, in a lot of ways. Publicity is a pressure. He may leave her in your hospital. May think that's wise."

"I see." Matt's spirits were both rising and falling

145

in confusion. The policeman half believed in the poison? The policeman couldn't do anything about the poison?

"Let me catch this ex-hsuband," said Tate, "and I'll tell you more. Or, let your doctors cure your patient. That would help some."

He hung up.

Betty said, "I don't see how I *could* have missed that key."

"Well, you must have, dear," said Peg, who was feeling more cheerful. "The suitcase went into the station with Dorothy Daw. How could anyone else have put it into the locker? How in the world else could that key have got here, unless *she* put it in the dresser drawer?"

"Two separate stories!" fumed Matt. "Naw! I don't believe it. I'll bet you Tate doesn't believe it, either. How is that *possible?* Three girls, who all look exactly alike, and at least two of them turn up missing at the very same time?"

"And one dead on Monday night," said Betty, "although neither of the missing two *was* missing until Tuesday."

Matt blinked at her. "Unless Bobbie Hopkins made a mistake."

Peg said, in her wisdom, "You *can't* believe all of it. Somebody must have made a mistake, somewhere."

Chapter Twelve

The bell pinged, the front door opened. In popped Tony.

For one who had been practically scalped by Lieutenant Tate, he was looking healthy. "Ex-husband on the lam! How do you like that? Poor little Alison fell among her angry ex. Happens every day. Probably there was something wrong with the divorce. He's married again, you know."

Tony sat down. "I'm pooped," he announced cheerfully. "We still got to find out, is our sleeping beauty Dorothy Daw? Or some religious, *née* Lilianne?"

"Oh, we know, now," Peg said. Matt wished he could stop her but did not try.

Tony listened to the story of the locker key. "Oh wow!" he said. "That's going to be a feather in the department's hat. An orange feather, hey? I got to go, *get* that." He got up. "Oh say, some scoop came in from . . . what's its name, now? . . . town, name of Entebbe, Uganda. Guess what? Dorothy Daw got religion. Seems she fell like a ton for some guy who is some kind of junior Schweitzer. Noble young doctor, name of Harness, George. Slaving away to save lives in the jungle. (Do they have jungles? Aw, they gotta have jungles.) Well, seems Dorothy hung around about a year making eyes at this bird, but he's dedicated, *he* is. *He* don't want to marry the Daw millions and sit on his duff on some yacht. Poor little rich girl who couldn't buy love. How do you like that for a heartbreaker?"

Matt was furious. By a superhuman effort, he kept his mouth shut. But Tony leered at him and said, "Hey, Matt, you're a noble young scientist yourself. So what's to stop the inevitable consequences? Ah! At last, she opens her beautiful eyes. The mists clear. What does she see? The face of poor-but-honest compassion."

Matt said with his teeth clenched, "If you don't want a bust in the mouth, shut it fast."

"I'm only kidding," said Tony, with round eyes. "For Pete's sake, Matt! Hey, Mrs. Cuneen, wasn't I only kidding?"

"Maybe you had better get along, Tony," said Peg gently.

"Hey, Betts, how's about a date? Let's you and me go hash this whole thing over without getting into a *fight*. We could, eh, doll? Gadzooks!" Tony was righteously indignant.

"I," said Betty quietly, "am going to wash my hair."

"Well! What man," said Tony, "has got a chance against *that* glamorous prospect? O.K. O.K. O.K. I know when I'm not wanted." And off he went.

Matt said, when he had gone, "I'm afraid I'm fed up to here with Tony. If you really want to come, Peg . . ."

"Give me a minute to get ready." Peg got up, sampled the passions in the air, and left the room.

Matt walked up and down three times. Betty stabbed herself with the needle and sucked her finger. He had forgotten she was there.

"What's the matter with me?" he said aloud.

"You don't want her to be Dorothy Daw, that's all."

Matt hadn't expected an answer. "What's the difference what I want? Will you tell me that?" He turned on her.

"There's a difference to you, I suppose. You don't want her to be a nun, either."

"I'll tell you what I *don't* want," he said angrily. "I don't want her to get killed off by Megan Royce. *That* buzzard in female form . . ."

"You're awfully sure." Betty had her head up.

"*That* bright-plumaged bird-of-prey!" he raved. "Then there's that chicken-headed Bobbie Hopkins. *Why* won't she say where the twin is? *If* there is one? I wish I could locate jolly old Alfreda. There's another female for you. A real nut! A juggernaut-nut!"

"What do you want her to be, Matt?" asked Betty, calmly.

"Who?"

"The sleeping one."

"*Want* her to be? I don't *want* her to be anybody." He choked and stopped speaking.

"Not even in a dream?"

"A dream?" He was shocked and astonished. "You mean I've got *designs?*"

"No, I don't mean sexy designs. I mean another kind of dream. A dream of fair woman." Betty was wide-eyed.

"Tell me more," he said, relaxing suddenly and sitting down on the sofa. He had a feeling that something was going to break open and he was feeling desperate enough to be glad of it.

"She's so beautiful. She's so helpless. She's so empty."

"Empty?"

"Her spirit isn't there," said Betty solemnly.

He looked at her as if she had gone mad.

But Betty went on recklessly. "So you can dream it's anything you want."

"So *that's* what I'm doing? Dreaming?"

149

"Aren't you? Don't you want to? Doesn't everybody?" She wasn't looking at him. The sleeve of the blouse she was mending was a blur in her lap. "Of course, nobody wants to admit it today."

"It sounds a little . . . uh . . . medieval," Matt said, taking care to speak dryly.

"It's a little impossible . . . to dream about today's woman." Betty was bitter. "Providing she's awake and walking around, that is."

Matt was rocked. "Honey, women are supposed to be people today," he chided, as gently as he could.

"Oh, sure, they've established that. At great expense."

"What's the matter with *you?*" he asked her lightly. (He was afraid he knew.)

"I'm mourning the myth," she said. (Because what did it matter what she said to him?) "I took a course once. The triple goddess. Maybe you haven't heard?"

He didn't say anything.

"Birth, love and death," said Betty. "Mother, bride and wise old crone."

"Must have been quite a course you took," he muttered, threshing.

"It's the only way you'd even hear of such a thing today." She looked straight at him, brilliant-eyed.

"Oh, come on. Everybody's got a mother, for instance."

"Kids get born, I will admit. And raised by the book *and* run to the psychiatrist. It's the husbands who get mothers. The mother-wife, to watch over his little ego and patch it up, from time to time. She reads magazines, today, to find out how to do that."

"Oh, I don't know." Matt stretched out on the sofa where he need not look at her. "There's brides."

"Brides! Ho! Right away *she* has 'my marriage' to analyze and she starts to figure how to express herself, *though* married."

"Wow," said Matt.

"So who can blame you if you can't dream . . . much?" she said.

"What's this about old crones?" He was keeping it light, he hoped.

"Oh, it goes all the way. All the way," said Betty in despair. "Where are the wise old women, the magical ones?"

"Witches, eh? You mean like Megan-baby? Or Bobbie Hopkins?"

"Where are the *good* ones," Betty rushed on, "that used to be handy with potions and cryptic advices. Now they're like your darling mother, and she'll be one of the best of them. 'Hands off,' says Peg. 'I'll be me and you be you.' My mother, too. They don't tell. We don't ask. Or else, they're sweet little old ladies in rest homes, where nobody listens to a word they say."

She was crying—for the destiny of woman? Matt felt like crawling into the upholstery. He didn't know how to stop her. He rolled over and said, "Don't do that, Betts, please? Look, why don't we . . ."

"So how can you dream of fair woman?" She wept. *"Who* gets dreamed about, unless she's one of those sex-symbol celebrities. *Her* you dream about, sex-wise."

"Why, sure," he said, amiably.

"But what you *get,*" Betty threw down her sewing, "if you're bourgeois and respectable, is the jolly old suburban pal with the station wagon and the Cub Scouts. Of course, sometimes a woman teaches school. . . ."

Betty sprang up. "Poor Matt. Don't look so pale. Fear not. I'm going home as soon as this mess is over and I'm not needed, even to provide a car. Excuse me for blasting off?"

"Well, sure." He squirmed. He was flummoxed. He said, "But you're not making too much sense to me,

Betts. Are you mad at *me?*"

"Sure I am," she flashed. "You're a man, aren't you? I'm mad at *all* men, let me tell you. What have *I* got to dream about? Somebody should make a survey. Suppose I want a bridegroom, to cherish me. A *man, with whom* to have a marriage and make children. I may even need, and deserve, a part-time father-figure for the days when *I'll* feel like an ornery little girl. Suppose I want to grow up and be wise, because I've *had* a life?"

"Well, look . . ." he said awkwardly.

"Oh, I'm civilized. Why, I'm one of eighty-two million female college graduates. I'll conform. I know. I'm going to settle for the first reasonably neat and clean young organization man that I can find. And that's what today's woman, good old Betty Prentiss, is going to do. What else?"

He knew what she was saying, now. He started to say that he was sorry but he couldn't say that.

"Don't *bother* me," she said fiercely. "I'm going upstairs to cry. Release my tensions. I'm entitled. Hysteria? Pertaining to women?" She danced away.

She'd done it. She'd let everything out. That tore it. It was finished. She went upstairs and sat down quietly and did not cry at all.

And if he didn't understand a word of it, she thought, what do I want with *him?*

Peg came bustling and found Matt standing in the middle of the floor. She took one look at him and said smoothly, "It's after seven-thirty. Shall we walk?" All the way across the park, in the dim evening, she kept chattering along about nothing much. How could she help him? What could she tell him?

Matt stubbed his toe on the hospital steps. He wished he could ask her. But you don't ask your *mother* what to do about a girl who wishes you felt what you do not feel. Or what to do about yourself,

152

when she'd made you feel like a heel, and you weren't. And you didn't mean to be.

There was nobody in the lobby, seeking to see the sleeping girl.

Up on the second floor, Mrs. Marsh was no longer on special duty. Matt and his mother and the tall guard went, in their gowns, inside the room where she lay sleeping. Peg's head inclined with solicitude. Matt couldn't see her face. No one could see his face, either.

So Matt looked at the sleeping one and held his breath. Full woman—but young and so fair. (What are you, what are you—that you trouble me?)

He didn't speak and neither did his mother. When she touched his arm, signalling that she was ready to go, he turned away obediently. The tall guard in his mask and gown let them go first.

The man pulled down his mask in the corridor and said, "It's sure peaceful in there."

Matt looked at him, startled. The man had spoken as if he were dreaming.

Peg trudged home beside Matt, thinking that her son had become enchanted. Enchanted as ever was. Who could break the spell? Not she.

"I thought you'd never come back," said Alison to her mother that same night. "Where the hell have you been? I can't put my face out the door, you know. What's going on? I'm practically climbing the walls."

Bobbie's girdle squeaked as she sat down. "I *dunno* what's going on, I'm telling you, baby. *I* been climbing the walls, too. I been trying to raise a little dough. Yah, my fair-weather friends! I was thinking you ought to get away on a little trip." Bobbie's face

153

twisted as if she were going to cry.

"Suits me," said Alison. "You bring cigarettes? Because if you didn't you can go get some."

"I brought them. Here." Bobbie fished a carton out of her voluminous straw bag.

"Gee, thanks, Mom."

"You got enough food? I brought this and that."

"I don't feel like eating much. There's stuff around. No butter."

"I forgot butter."

"Who cares? Listen, Mom, what's up, huh? How's Lilianne?"

"I don't go down there. It's in the papers. She's just the same." Bobbie wriggled. "But listen, Ally, you were right." Bobbie lit a cigarette. "I got a lot to tell you."

Alison jumped to fill a glass for her, avid to please, to get the news.

Bobbie told her about the body in the morgue. "You don't know what I been through. I had to go see her." Bobbie's voice went into a squeak. *"She's mine,"* wailed Bobbie.

Alison frowned at her as Bobbie began to cry in earnest. "I never told you," she sobbed, out of control. "I didn't *ever* tell. But I had a baby I gave up, one time. A year and a half before you and Lilianne was born. Me and your daddy, see, wasn't married at the time. My God, I was only fifteen years old. So they sent me back east, to Aunt Milly, in New Jersey. And I gave my little baby up. So later on when Charley and me—"

"When he got you pregnant *again*," said Alison nastily, *"next* time, you got married. Well? So what?"

"So I never did know what became of my first little baby girl. Now I know, Ally. Now, I know. Dorothy Daw was your own sister. Your own sister." Bobbie howled.

Alison said, *"Go on!"* But she believed it.

"Baby, I can't help it." Bobbie sobbed. "Gee, it hit me terrible! But I said she was you. I mean, I said it was you, so you'd be O.K., anyhow."

"Are you out of your mind, Mom?" Alison's face was rumpled angrily. "Why did you say it was *me,* for God's sakes!"

"Well, if you're dead, who's going to try to kill you?" Bobbie began to pull whatever there was of herself together.

Now Alison began to wail. "How stupid can you get, Mom? They killed this Dorothy, whoever she was. So they got to know she wasn't me. You've just messed everything up worse."

"I don't see it that way," said Bobbie stiffly.

"You don't see, period." Her daughter was sitting with her legs apart. She looked shrewd and vulgar. "Now what? You're trying to raise money. So you dig up a little dough, what does it buy me? Plastic surgery? What am I supposed to do with my life, now that I'm dead?"

Bobbie said, "They're looking for Larry. The cops are. He ran out."

"Too bad for him," said Alison. "So what *about* that?"

"Well, listen, baby, it gives us a little time."

"Time for what? For *what?*" The girl screamed frustration.

"O.K. I'll go to the cops, if that's what you want. I'll tell them it's Lilianne in the hospital, and they'll have you, so now they'll believe the dead one is Dorothy. And that gets Mr. Leon Daw in the soup, that does. He thinks he's going to get all the money. Oh, sure. When her real mother and her real sister aren't going to get one cent. But I guess I've got to go to the cops and tell them the whole bit."

"What makes you think they're going to believe

what *you* say?" said Alison viciously. "First, you say it's me in the hospital. Now you say it's me that's dead."

"They're going to believe you're alive if they see you alive."

"I don't want to be seen."

"Baby, listen now, you got to do *something*."

"Sure. Drop dead."

"I'll go to the cops," said Bobbie, looking pious. "I guess that's the right thing to do."

"And they'll put me in jail," cried Alison, "when I didn't do a thing and I suppose that's right? What I can't get through your head, I *helped* them. I didn't mean to. I didn't know what I was doing. But I *helped* them. For five hundred lousy bucks, I got myself mixed up in a murder."

"The cops will believe you didn't know about it."

"Oh, come *on*. I've got a record." Alison fell on her face. "You know what's got to come out. You know that's the end. Better I murdered eighteen people than beat up one baby. The kiss of death! I can't put it all on Larry. I *tried* that already."

"What else can I do?" said Bobbie. "Of course maybe I'm crazy—but I did think of something."

"I'll *bet* you did."

"Why couldn't you be Dorothy Daw?"

"What?"

"Well, listen now for a minute. She was your sister. You got some right. Why can't you show up and say you lost your memory or something like that?"

"Because I couldn't get away with it. Because I haven't lost all my marbles yet, like you."

"But don't you see, baby, they'll absolutely have to help you."

"They would, eh?"

"Sure. *They* got to have her alive. Why do you think they took you to lunch? Why do you think they

156

keep on saying Lilianne is Dorothy? *They* know she isn't. You said that yourself."

"Yeah."

"So I go, I say the sick girl is Lilianne."

"And everybody's going to believe you, right off the bat."

"And *you* say you're Dorothy Daw. They'll be *glad* to hear it."

"And how do I live?"

"Pretty high on the hog," said Bobbie slyly, "I should think, wouldn't you? They couldn't *do* anything. You'd have them in a bind."

"Mom, I'm so scared," wept Alison. "I feel like screaming, all day and all night. They *killed* her. They *did* it. Then they made me into their alibi. If I show my little toe, the cops put me inside. Or else *they* get rid of *me*. Why can't you see that?"

"Well, I'm only saying—not if there was to be a deal."

"I won't do it. I'd be *helping* them again. I'm not going to be mixed up in a murder."

"Looks to me," said her mother coldly, "like you *are*."

"Don't try and get smart, please, Mom?" Alison pleaded. "Just let them keep thinking it's me in the hospital. Let it alone. As long as they think that, they're not looking, anyhow."

"Yes, but we haven't got any money," said Bobbie. "And *they* got it. I mean, let's face it. You might not get to be a star."

Alison looked at her sourly.

"So, say they'd go for it. Say you'd show up and guarantee to play you're Dorothy. For a couple of weeks, maybe. I mean, talk to the Press and all that. Put them in the clear, but good. So, then you can take a big old trip. That's what Dorothy always does. And say I'd meet you some place, like Paris. They'd pay

157

off big, see? And you and me could kinda travel."

"You've got it figured, haven't you?" the girl said sulkily. "Mom, I hate to tell you how nutty you are."

"You can act," her mother said.

"Sure. Sure. But I'll never get to be a star."

"Listen, I can handle them. I can feel them out, can't I? I don't have to say one word about where you are."

"You better keep still in eighteen languages," snapped the girl. "Don't say *anything*. Or I'll run out. I'm warning you. I'll kill myself!"

"Oh, you wouldn't do that," said Bobbie.

But the girl was suddenly limp and staring at the floor. "O.K., I guess that's it. I got to go to the cops. I guess that's the way it has to be. So I go, and that's the end. And I go down the drain."

"You're safe here," said Bobbie. "Wait a while, why don't you? Huh, baby? You can take it, for a little while longer."

"Maybe I'll get cancer," said Alison and whammed the carton of cigarettes on the day-bed and began to howl.

When Bobbie left the little house she took her old car racketing along dark streets, turning and twisting. Finally she judged herself in the clear and headed home.

She unlocked her door and listened to the silence of her house. She poured herself an enormous drink. She sat down, kicked off her shoes, and drank it all, thoughtfully, steadily.

At midnight, she got up and went to the telephone. Her finger, with its cracked red polish, hesitated over the dial. Suddenly it pounced and dialled vigorously.

Clicks and whirs. A voice sad, "This is a recording. Mr. Leon Daw is not here at this time. Will you leave a message? Speak slowly into your telephone when you hear the buzzer."

But Bobbie stood still, biting her lips.

The voice said, "This a recording. Mr. Leon Daw is not here at this time. Will you leave a message? Speak slowly into your telephone when you hear the buzzer."

Bobbie gathered breath.

"Mr. Daw, this is Mrs. Bobbie Hopkins. I have something to say to you, of mutual interest. I guess *you* don't believe all you read in the papers, either. Call me, in regard to my daughter and your niece. That's all for now. But you'd better," she wound up breathlessly.

She hung up and went for her bottle.

Chapter Thirteen

On Monday morning the paper had it, about the key and the suitcase. The girl asleep in the hospital was now presumed (by authorities, it said) to be Dorothy Daw, the tenth richest girl in the world. There was a drippy feature about poor little rich Dorothy, living simply nearby and doing good in a small hospital in a far-off country. A photograph of a lonely-looking, but fairly modern structure with the figure of a man standing before it gave very little information about its subject. There was a pseudoscientific article on sleeping sickness. There was a note saying that Leon Daw was unavailable for comment, he having driven out of the city with an unidentified female companion.

Under another headline — Ex-HUBBY SOUGHT — there was news of the identification of the naked body of a blonde by her mother, Mrs. Bobbie Hopkins, who was prostrated and unavailable for comment. Mrs. Dolores Wimberholtz was under a doctor's care and could not be reached.

The stories were tied together by a page of photographs. The top three-quarters of the page ran assorted pictures of Dorothy, at all ages. Across the bottom ran the theatrical picture of Alison and the original shot of the girl in the hospital. All the faces on the page were alike, and also unlike.

There was no mention of a third girl, a religious

twin. Or, of course, poison.

Matt passed the paper along to Betty, who had come down in her right mind, as pleasantly friendly as ever. It was as if she had never said all that bitter stuff. Matt felt grateful for a comfortable surface and took care to be as pleasantly friendly as ever. But warily.

Then Betty announced that she had gone out with Tony after all, to a late supper at Nickey's. "Dutch," she added with her old quick smile. She had spoken to the hat-check girl and the waiter, Russ Morgan.

"Anything?" Matt came to attention.

"I don't know, Matt. I doubt it. The hat-check girl knew from nothing."

"But what?"

"I couldn't ask the waiter much. He had to keep coming and going. So I just asked him if he had happened to overhear anything that the girl had talked about. I finally came right out and asked if she had said anything to do with Africa. He said, Yes, come to think of it, she had. They had talked about hunting animals. The other lady wanted to know if Miss Daw had ever seen a lion. Oh yes, she had seen lots of them. And Tigers too." Betty went right on. "Also, they did talk about some show."

"Show?" Matt knotted his brow.

"Some TV series that was a big flop. That's what the waiter said."

Betty, who had been wondering why she had gone at all unless it was conscience, watched him with a flicker of amusement.

Matt said, "You know, if true, that's peculiar. A *show?*"

"Maybe they get American TV in Uganda."

Matt grunted skeptically.

"Tony didn't notice, either," Betty said.

"What?"

"They don't have tigers in Africa."

Matt sat still, while his mind raced. Then the se-

161

quence of his reasoning lifted him off the chair.

"O.K. Then the girl in the restaurant was *not* Dorothy Daw. The girl who put the suitcase in the locker, who brought the key to our house, who is in the hospital now is NOT Miss Dorothy Daw."

Betty began to squirm and shake her head. "Unless she was just putting Megan on."

"Huh?"

"I'm afraid it can't mean very much. She could have been tempted. It could have been sly. I wouldn't blame her."

"But listen, Betts—"

"You can't *count* on it." Betty was severe.

Peg said, "Oh, leave it to Lieutenant Tate, children. Please, don't just go around and around."

Peg felt and looked tired. She wished they wouldn't go around again. She had cancelled her engagements. She couldn't face the questions with the same old answers. Yes, she had felt responsible. No, she was not able to say whether the girl would get well. Yes, it was very strange. She had hoped to be able to say that from now on, the girl was Dorothy. But the young people were going around again. (Meanwhile, Matt was enchanted. Betty was going to be lost to them.) Peg worried about Matt. She worried about Betty. She worried about money, as a matter of fact.

Betty was saying, "I think so too, Peg. Lieutenant Tate is in a much better position to find out stuff than we are."

Matt had been pushed back into his chair by the reasonable caution of his womenfolk when Dr. Jon Prentiss appeared.

Peg put him before a second breakfast while he told them the consensus. The girl's condition might well be emotional. A psychological coma. Oh, yes, these could happen. This judgment was not, and could not be, absolute. But it was strongly suspected, at the moment. If so, it was more important than ever to know her history. And —

Matt said, with excitement, "Wait a minute! That's what *she* implied."

"Who implied?"

"This nut! This Alfreda. She came around, dressed in a robe. She said she knew our girl. Said she was a protégée. Maybe she was right. There *is* a twin, supposed to be religious — whatever that means."

"You aren't talking about Dr. Ruth A. Dienst?"

"What's that, sir?"

"Calls herself plain Alfreda, so I've been told. Why, she's a renegade from the profession. Runs some kind of temple school. A kind of cult, I suppose. A more-or-less faith-healing theory as I understand it, which I don't suppose I do."

"A *temple?* Where is this place?"

"Why, right up the hill," the doctor said.

"What hill, sir?"

"There's a road up this side." The doctor was pointing to the east. "You go up to the end of this street and the road takes off, a little to your right."

"A *temple?*"

"It used to be somebody's house. Colonial, with white pillars. She's got some fancy nameplate on it. I knew her slightly, years ago."

Matt sat a moment with his mouth fallen open. Then he said, "Our girl is the twin. I mean," he corrected, "there's a great probability that she is."

"How do you figure?"

"Because there has never been any explanation of how she happened to be on *our* street and see the sign on *our* lawn. Until now. O.K. *This* house is on the way to this temple."

"That depends," the doctor said. "There's a better road, up the other side of the hill, you know. Isn't there a higher probability that our girl is Dorothy Daw?"

"Not if Dorothy was *not* the girl in the restaurant. Or the cab. Or the railroad station."

163

The doctor scowled. "Who *was* that, if not Dorothy?"

"That was our girl."

"The twin?"

"The alibi."

"So . . . you are calling Leon Daw a liar, a deceiver, and a murderer?"

"And nothing loath," said Matt, rather gaily.

Dr. Prentiss viewed him with obvious alarm.

Matt kept talking. The doctor volunteered no comment on the waiter's remarks.

"Are there tigers in Africa?" Matt demanded.

"I wouldn't have the faintest idea." The doctor was cold.

"I'm going up to this temple."

The doctor said, "I'm afraid Ruth Dienst has become a bit of a fringe character. Great waste of training."

Something in his eye was saying to Matt, *"Watch it. Don't get out of line. Don't let yourself veer towards the fringes, mind you. Don't waste your training."*

Betty said, "I'll go with him, Uncle Jon. We'll take my car."

Then Matt said, out of nowhere, *"Lilianne!"*

"What?"

"Lilianne! That's what Tony said, didn't he? And that's what this Alfreda called her."

Dr. Jon said, "Humph." His stern eye yielded to reason and he nodded.

Matt drove off in high spirits. Betty beside him was good old Betty again. He was darned glad to have her back. "This is it," he said to her.

"It looks as if," she agreed cheerfully.

They bore to the right, at the end of the street, upon a steep and winding narrow road that could not be the best way up this hill. It brought them to a wider road along the ridge-top where there was only one house that could be described as Colonial, with white pillars.

The building looked somehow insecure. As they got out of the car, they realized that it seemed to teeter on a brink. There was very little land between it and a precipice.

There was a small sign on one of the pillars. Gold on black, it read, THE TEMPLE OF HEALTH THROUGH ART. They went up on the pillared porch. There was no button to push, but a big brass knocker of Oriental design was centered in the door. Matt used it, vigorously.

When the door opened, there stood the tall woman, in her white robe, with the purple cord around her ample waist. "Mr. Cuneen," she said not uncordially. "And who is this?" Her head with its home-made haircut bent graciously.

Betty felt the weight of the woman's gaze as Matt made the introduction. Alfreda's eyes were dark brown, soft, and powerfully intent. "You may come in." She led them through a kind of foyer, rather shallow, running along the house to parallel the whole width of the outside porch, and pierced by arches so that it only introduced them to a large room with a wall of glass at the far end.

"It won't fall down," the woman said. "See here."

She led them across the big and almost empty room, which was furnished only with a grand piano and its bench, and a dozen large bright-colored floor cushions, towards the glass, which showed nothing but the sky until they were close enough to look directly down.

A dizzying sixty feet below, there was a supermarket, its new roof bright. The white lines on the parking lot were fresh and sharp. When the land had been cut back, Alfreda told them, there had been a land-slip. Her building had been condemned and closed. But she had hired engineers and geologists to go into the problem and her temple could, and would, be saved by sinking cassons and building a retaining wall. The market chain was going to have to pay for the work, since she had gone to court and won her case. In the meantime, however, she could not hold her classes.

Matt drew back from the glass and looked around. "What kind of classes, Dr. Dienst? What is this place?"

The woman smiled. "I use only the one simple name now," she said. "Alfreda will do. Why, this is a place for people who need it. Come, sit down." She seemed pleased to see them, as if she had been a little lonely.

There was nowhere to sit in this room, except on the floor cushions. The huge woman led them back to the foyer, to the right, through a small room, where ordinary chairs were lined up on two walls and a green file cabinet stood against another. Beyond this, there was another small square room, with a desk, and bookshelves, and two fairly comfortable visitors' chairs. It perfectly resembled a doctor's office.

Alfreda enthroned herself behind the desk. "You have come about Lilianne Kraus?"

Matt said, "About the girl in the hospital. Tell me, could her last name have ever been Hopkins?"

"She might have used her mother's name," said Alfreda calmly. "She prefers Kraus, which is her father's."

"O.K.," said Matt. "That does it. I'm afraid it's too complicated to go into thoroughly. All I need to say is that since there is still a question of her identity—"

"There should not be," said Alfreda, in her booming voice. "I told you who she was. I told you, some days ago."

Matt gaped. Betty said, "You know this Lilianne very well, do you, ma'am?"

"Certainly. Lilianne is very close to me. I permit her to come here, every day, to act more or less as my receptionist. I cannot, of course, permit *anyone* to live here. But Lilianne makes herself more or less useful—that is, when we are functioning. I have known her very well for at least four, perhaps five years."

"How do you know our girl is not Lilianne's twin sister?" Matt asked. "Or didn't you know she had one?"

"I knew," said Alfreda loftily. "Certainly."

"Have you ever seen Alison Hopkins?"

"Oh, yes. Some years ago."

"Can you tell them apart? Is there a mark?"

The woman's brows rose and gave her an expression of tolerant amusement. "My protégées sunbathe in the nude, that's true," she said, "but we are not nudists, here. Didn't you ask me about a mark or a scar, on Friday morning?"

"On Friday morning," Matt said, rather hotly, "you told me she was Lilianne. And now it's Monday."

"I do not break the Sabbath," Alfreda said.

"Will you come down there now, please? I'll take you to see her."

"She still sleeps?" the woman said placidly.

"Yes. Yes. Will you come?"

"Not now."

"Miss . . . Doctor . . ." Matt sputtered.

"The contractor has promised to be here, some time today," Alfreda said, "I cannot leave."

"You say you are so close to this girl. Don't you realize she has got to be identified? She may be claimed by Leon Daw."

The woman was an immovable mass. "No one of that name has a right to claim her. Do you understand that I may not bring her here, at this time? It is not permitted."

"You don't have to 'bring' her anywhere. All you have to do is make them believe, down there, that she *isn't* Dorothy Daw. That is, *if* she isn't. Maybe you don't know what you are talking about. How come other people haven't been around to say she's this Lilianne?"

The woman pitied him with her look. "Because I have taken care to explain to *my* people, that I have the matter in hand. It is wiser to keep her where she is—"

"All right!" Matt shouted. "But you've got to come down and swear—"

167

"I do not swear. I have told you, very simply — yea or nay — who she is."

"Tell the hospital."

"I have told the hospital."

"Come down there. Please?"

The more he begged the more immovable she seemed.

"Why not?" he demanded.

Alfreda shook her head. "You do not listen."

"I sure as hell con't understand you at all." Matt was furious.

"Quite obviously," said Alfreda condescendingly, "you are not even trying. But I have said that I will come soon. Perhaps as soon as tomorrow."

"I thought you were a doctor." The sentence condemned her.

"Who told you so, please?" Alfreda spoke with an air of adult patience towards a child in a tantrum.

"Dr. Jon Prentiss. He says he once knew you."

"Prentiss? A relation?" The big head turned.

"My uncle," said Betty. She was thinking. Why, she is vain, enormously vain. She has power. She *likes* power. Matt isn't approaching her in the right way. He can't tell her what to do.

Alfreda now graciously told Matt what to do. "Then please notify Dr. Prentiss, or the hospital, or whoever *can* receive such a message, that I shall try to be in tomorrow to straighten the matter out."

Matt sat glowering.

Betty inserted herself as oil on the waters. "I realize that you must be very busy, ma'am. You treat patients here, do you?"

"In a way," the woman said. "I prefer to say that I show them how to be healed. I came to a point, you see, where I could afford to do what I am really obliged to do. A point where I could no longer limit myself to orthodoxy. I don't practice medicine, in the ordinary sense." Her eyes flickered to Matt. "We are a group. We

168

gather. This is for women. All ages of women. Although men, I am quite sure, could also benefit, I feel that to teach men, too, would be even more easily misunderstood." She flashed a cold smile. "Now then, we paint and read poetry. We dance. We use color therapy. Perhaps you don't realize that I can change the light. We are, of course, religiously oriented, although not conventionally. There is a kind of healing that operates on the soul. This is, to a degree, experimental . . ."

"But do you make money?" Matt said edgily.

"My fees are as modest as I can afford," Alfreda said, stiffly.

"Oh well. The girl in the hospital is a *poor* soul," he said with insulting emphasis. "She has two hundred and fifty dollars, period, almost all of which she now owes the hospital." He got up and walked out of the room.

If Alfreda was offended she showed it only by a movement of one massive eyebrow.

Betty said apologetically, "Oh, I'm sorry. Please try to understand that he is just so concerned for the sleeping girl . . ."

"Yes," said Alfreda. "I'm sorry."

Betty had a sense that the woman was seeing right through her. "Do you read the newspaper, ma'am?" she asked quickly.

"Not often. Someone called Lilianne's picture to my attention."

"Then maybe you haven't read that Alison Hopkins is supposed to have been murdered?"

Alfreda said, with such calm as to seem perfectly cruel, "That is the way that Alison was going. I never held much hope for her. Or for her mother. They are locked to the material in a romantic sort of way that is inevitably destructive."

Betty said with a gasp, "Don't you try to help everybody?"

"I can help the blind," said Alfreda, "but not the ones who will not see. Now," she became brisk, "you must believe that I know what I am doing."

"But do you know what *we* are trying to do?" said Betty. "You see one girl has been murdered. We don't know but what it was a mistake. Maybe the same persons now want to murder *this* girl."

"In the hospital?" said Alfreda with pity.

"It might be."

"You *do* read the newspapers, don't you?" said Alfreda. "I should imagine that the number of people murdered by *mistake* is very small. Killed, yes. Now, my dear, I have said what I will do. I shall come tomorrow. By daylight. I do not walk by night."

"May I come to-morrow, then, and drive you there, ma'am?" said Betty.

"Thank you," said the woman remotely. "That won't be necessary." She became very still.

Betty realized she had better not move or speak.

Finally the woman sighed. "The twins are identical in the body," she said. "I was wondering about a mistake. As I have reason to do, perhaps. But I do not believe that Lilianne is dead. I am too close to her spirit. I should be able to sense if it has departed."

"We are pretty sure," said Betty, quickly following, "that it can't be Alison, in the hospital, because of a certain mark."

"Do you put your faith in such things?" said Alfreda with a tilt of her head. Her gaze became a blow. "*You* are not a happy spirit, Miss Prentiss. You are not in tune, are you?"

Betty said with asperity, "I'm afraid that I don't expect to be happy, all twenty-four hours of every day." She got up. "Are you thinking that *I* ought to come to your classes?"

The woman was really monstrous. It was hard not to be angry with her.

"Not in your present mood," said Alfreda flatly.

Then with a sudden change of manner, she became crisp. "Surely even by your lights, you can see that I must be here. They are coming to discuss and arrange for the future of my house. I must have it put in order. Many people depend on me. I am not understood, Miss Prentiss, by some people. Particularly by people like your young man. Therefore, I take care to break no man-made laws that I need not break. This house was condemned and I cannot have my people here until this work is done. It will do no harm if Lilianne sleeps on, for one more day. Or several."

"I hope you are right," Betty said soberly. "I hope you are *not* making a mistake."

She started for the door. The woman did not move. Her eyes were baleful. Betty could read her mind: *"I do not make mistakes, you poor crawling creature."* Alfreda was offended.

Matt was standing in the foyer and when Betty came, he took her arm and swung her towards the door to the porch. They went out, unushered and with no fare-wells.

Matt was seething. He whisked them down the hill at a perilous speed. Once on the level, he said, "Get out the map."

"O.K." Betty gasped relief that they were safely down. "I'll say it for you. She is not only a nut of the purest ray serene but some kind of *monster!*"

"But *does* she know what she is talking about? That's what we are going to find out."

"What do you mean?"

"We are going to find out, because I snooped in that file cabinet. There was an address for Lilianne Kraus."

"Oh, Matt, good for you!"

"So we go there. If Lilianne is missing, that's one thing."

(And if she isn't, that's another, thought Betty.

171

That's Dorothy Daw.)

"That's a witch?" he said in a moment. "Alfreda? One of your magical ones?"

Betty swallowed hard and looked out the window. "I'd be glad if you skipped all that. Just kindly forget it? I'm agreeing with you that Alfreda is sure weird. She was trying to get a message, telepathically or somehow. Was Lilianne's spirit departed? she was asking."

"And what did the Devil tell her?" said Matt bitterly.

"He didn't think so."

"Whew!" Matt let out a long whistling breath. He quoted an address. Betty began to hunt in the map for Opal Street.

Chapter Fourteen

Even with the help of the detailed map, it took time to find the short left-over piece of street. 438½ would mean a rear house. They found 438, parked the car, and started along the path beside the shabby and deserted-looking frame house on the front of the lot.

"If her mother said she was out of the world," said Betty, "she could have been thinking of *this* place."

But Matt had eyes, ears, nose, fixed ahead upon the little shack they were approaching. "What do I smell?"

Betty could smell burned wood and was about to say so, when he gestured for quiet and tapped on the door. A female voice said, at once, "Miz Gibbs?" Then the door opened and there she stood.

It was the girl in the hospital. It was the same face. But it was different. It was not asleep. These eyes were open. Large and grey, they glistened in a way that was not entirely pleasing. The skin had the same soft tan, or perhaps a shade deeper. It was bare of make-up. The blonde hair was hanging down around the face. It was not exactly the same color. The color was more evenly pale yellow.

The girl stepped back, as if disconcerted by the sight of strangers. She said in a clear voice, high in her throat, almost a child's voice. "Oh, *I'm* sorry. I thought it was the lady down the street."

Matt was stricken dumb. So Betty spoke. "Miss Kraus?"

173

"Yes?"

"May we come in?"

"Oh. Yes, if you want to. There was a fire here last night. I'm sorry."

The girl stepped backward. She was wrapped in a long cotton garment of faded blue-and-white print and on her feet she wore white ankle socks and no shoes. She stepped as softly as a kitten. Her mouth was holding a meaningless smile. Her glistening eyes seemed to ask for kindness.

"I could smell it," said Betty. Now she could see the scorching on the wooden wall, and the charred spot in the ceiling. The frame of a day-bed, stripped of any bedding, stood near the scorching. "In the *night?*" she said. "How did it happen? Weren't you lucky?"

"I am a friend to fire and to wind," the girl said in that childish voice. "They will never hurt me."

"Are you Lilianne?" said Betty bluntly.

The girl's large eyes turned in glistening innocence. "My name is Lilianne Kraus." She did not ask them who they were. She stood there in her white socks, holding the wrapper close, waiting passively for what they would do or say next.

"We have just seen Alfreda," said Matt, in an unnatural voice that had just recovered the power to speak at all.

"Oh, yes." The girl showed no surprise.

He began to speak, as if to a child. "My name is Matthew Cuneen. This is Betty Prentiss. We came about the girl in the hospital who looks just like you."

This girl said, "My mother told me that if I didn't go out, nobody would bother me." But her hands crept up to her throat.

"You live here? And work for Alfreda?" Betty asked.

"Sometimes I do. Alfreda is a very good person. I don't like to work where there are too many people. Men, I mean." The girl looked down at her feet. She

174

kicked the long garment to cover them. "Do you want to sit down?" she said vaguely.

Matt said, "The girl in the hospital *must* be your twin sister Alison. She is *very* ill. She won't wake up."

The girl tilted her head as if she couldn't quite hear what he was saying.

"You didn't know that?" He hammered away. "Would you come to see her? You would know for sure if she is your sister."

"I never see my sister anymore," she said in that childish piping. "It is better if I never do. She was my *doppelgänger*. Everything she did, I was guilty for. So I had to get out of her shadow." The girl spoke as if she had been taught the speech and kept smiling at something over their heads.

"Don't you care for your sister, at all?" Matt said.

"Oh, no." She kept smiling. "Alison went with the world. I had to let her go. I was told to let her go. My mother, too. I can't hope for them."

(This was an echo of Alfreda, as Betty recognized.)

"But you have seen your mother recently?" Matt pressed.

"I think so. She came . . . one time. Maybe two times." The girl looked vague.

Betty said, "Is there a way to tell you apart? Your mother told us there was a mark."

"She had a mark," the girl said, in a moment. "But she let a doctor take it away." Her eyes rounded. "You shouldn't do that. If God gives you a mark, then you should keep it."

"But did the doctor leave another kind of mark?" It was like talking to a four-year-old. Matt was dumb again. Betty kept pressing.

The girl gazed over both their heads. "She came and laughed at me, one time. She showed me where the mark was gone. She said, now, not even Mama could tell the difference." Her shoulders began to shake.

"Your mother says it can still be seen."

175

The girl didn't answer. She rolled her head to one side, her eyes the other way.

"Would you put on a dress and let us take you to the hospital?"

"Oh, no." She shrank back.

"Please?"

"Oh, no, I can't go. There would be doctors."

"You needn't see anybody but the girl who might be your sister."

"There would be doctors and nurses," she said, seeming to panic. "I don't like doctors and nurses. I don't like hospitals. I can't go. I mustn't go. Alfreda says I don't have to go."

Matt said in weary disgust, "All right, Betts. We might as well get out of here."

But Betty said stubbornly, "Let me stay with her, alone. Maybe she'll show me where the mark should be."

The girl clutched the wrapper tightly and her eyes began to roll. "You are of the world? And the *flesh?*" Her voice spiralled upward.

"Let her alone," Matt said. "Just let her alone."

They went out into the air and breathed deeply. The little room had reeked.

"Nutty as a fruitcake," said Matt. "A real weirdie. *That's* Tony's nun?" Pain flashed across his face. "She turns my stomach." He hurried towards the car, impelling Betty with a hand on her elbow. "What the *hell* is the *matter* with people? Nobody gives a damn about anybody else. Not even the so-called 'religiously oriented'."

Betty didn't speak.

He put her into the car and ran around it and bounced behind the wheel. "I'll tell you one thing. Alfreda didn't know what she was talking about. Which doesn't surprise me much. Still . . . now listen . . . it seems to me that it's absolutely impossible for Dorothy Daw to look that much like Lilianne Hopkins-Kraus.

How could she? So our girl has got to be Alison. She's just about got to be, Betts. Now that we've seen them both."

"What about the scar thing?"

"That's only according to Bobbie. Bobbie doesn't know what she's talking about either."

"But if . . . if *we've* got Alison, how come Bobbie says that Alison is the dead girl?"

"Who knows why Bobbie says anything? I do not understand *that* witch, let me proclaim!"

Matt slammed the little car around corners.

Betty said "O.K. Lilianne was also nutty enough to drive you nuts. Why take it out on a defenseless Chevrolet?"

"Sorry." Matt took hold of his temper.

"Do you see what I see?" he asked in moment. "If you throw out Bobbie's erratic carryings-on, and stop believing a word *she* says, and if you take into account tigers—Isn't the plot unthickening?"

"Maybe," Betty admitted.

"Then what?" He wanted her to state it.

"Then," she said, "the dead girl is Dorothy. The girl in the restaurant was Alison and we've got Alison."

"Ah ha! And who knew there was a double? Megan knew. She told me. I told you."

"I remember."

"So now, Leon Daw and Megan-baby, *they know* it's Alison we've got in the hospital. And they *can't afford* for Alison to wake up and talk. That's why Megan tried to get at her. Doesn't it follow?"

"It seems to," said Betty unhappily.

"What's the matter? You got some female intuition our girl has to be Dorothy?"

"I don't know what I intuit," said Betty, taking no offense. "I wish I did, because it makes me, although female, pretty darned miserable not to believe *something.*"

"Me, too," he said, rather contritely. "Me, too,

177

Betts. But now I can figure a theory that at least hangs together. Megan and Uncle Leon hire Alison to impersonate dear Dorothy, after they've knocked off the original, sometime before Monday midnight. But Alison, instead of flying to San Francisco or whatever she was supposed to do, fixes to disappear. And up and falls ill. This puts them in a panic. They have to get their clutches on her. She might give the whole thing away. So they get to Bobbie Hopkins. Maybe they buy her off. I wouldn't put it past her. She obliges them and says the dead one is Alison. Now they can get the real Alison."

"To do what to the real Alison?" said Betty shrewdly. "And Bobbie, mother-to-Alison, is going along with that?"

"Betts," said Matt, "that dame is not only what you could call a real bad witch, but brainless, besides. Maybe they're telling her Alison can go on playing the little rich girl and Bobbie gets in on the perks. Bobbie would have no more sense than to fall for that. She doesn't know they already tried to poison Alison, in the meantime. *I'm* the one who knows that."

"But what are we going to do, Matt? This is a pretty tall tale. It sounds like Tony Severson in his riper moods. It's . . . awful fringy, Matt."

"We're going to the hospital," Matt said. "Don't ask *me* what we're going to do there."

What they did was tell the tall tale, to which Mr. Atwood listened patiently.

Then he began his questions. "Tell me this. Why did Alison's ex-husband run away?"

"I don't know, sir," Matt said.

"And why, if this girl Alison was hired, as you suggest, to play the part of Dorothy Daw, didn't she continue to play it?"

"I don't know."

"Why did she leave the suitcase, and the clothing that belonged to Dorothy Daw, in a locker at the station? How did she get to your mother's house, in old clothes?"

"I don't know."

"Why did her mother tell you about a scar or mark if it doesn't exist?"

"Why did her sister tell us it doesn't exist if it does?" Matt countered. "Has the body of the dead girl got such a mark?"

"I haven't heard. I can call Tate."

"And if it has *not?*" Matt was keen.

Atwood shook his head. "On the other hand, if it *has,* then Alison is dead." Atwood couldn't reach Lieutenant Tate on the telephone. He hung up, defeated, and said to Matt, "Leon Daw is in Las Vegas, so his lawyer tells me. He and Mrs. Royce drove over yesterday, to get married."

Matt grunted.

"So I suppose we hold everything, until he's back, at least."

"You don't think what the waiter said indicates doubt about the girl in the restaurant?"

"It may or may not," said Atwood. "It is not against the law to imply, for fun, that there are tigers in Africa."

"Talk about a TV show?" Matt kept on pressing. "*Alison* would be likely to know about show business."

"In Spain?" said Atwood.

"Why not? *She* would know the trade gossip."

"So might anybody. You know, I am a little surprised," said Atwood, leaning back. "I don't think your head is quite clear, Cuneen. Look what you are going on. Something you 'sensed' about Mrs. Royce. A possibly kidding remark that Miss Prentiss heard, second-hand. On such bases you accuse Leon Daw of murder, Mrs. Hopkins of lying for a bribe about the death of her own daughter, and you suggest that an innocent man is running away from the police who wish to question him about the death of his ex-wife."

179

Matt said, "One girl *was* murdered."

"And perhaps when Lieutenant Tate catches the run-away husband, he will turn out to have had an innocent reason. It is all very well to spin theories. What we shall *do* is continue to care for our patient, which is our business, as long as she *is* our patient." Atwood lifted all his flesh in a smile and nodded dismissal.

Matt and Betty went out into the corridor.

Betty said, "Would you let me see her, Matt?"

"It's not hours. But come on."

So they went up to the second floor and endured the ceremony of mask and gown. The tall guardian went with them. They stood like spectres around the high bed.

She slept in peace. Her breath came softly.

Betty said, "Will you let me make sure there is no mark?"

"Go ahead," said Matt gruffly and then to the guard who was shifting his feet, "It's O.K."

So Betty, very gently, took the blanket down and tugged at the short hospital coat while the men stared at each other. Betty said, "No. Nothing," and covered the girl again. "May I turn her hand, please?"

"I guess so." Matt didn't know what was in Betty's mind but he had, he discovered, a basic faith in Betty Prentiss, that she would do no harm.

Betty took up the girl's right hand. Young and fair was its flesh. It looked unused. She turned it in both her own, looking closely at the fingers. "Is she right-handed?"

"How can we tell?"

Betty took up the left hand. It was as limp and as warm and as spotless as the other. When Betty put it gently down, the girl stirred. Her head rolled. Her mouth firmed a moment. Then it relaxed. She slept.

Three pairs of lungs took air again. Matt said,

180

"Come on. Come on." He was dragging Betty away. In the corridor she saw the sweat on his forehead as he tore off the gown.

"I was only w-wondering," she stammered, "whether she is a s-smoker. Even in that awful stench, at Lilianne's house—"

"Oh, no, no, no," he groaned. "Don't remind me of Lilianne. She made me *so sick!*"

Betty trotted fast, because he was taking steps too long for her.

It was a long Monday afternoon. Matt went dutifully back to the hospital to check for visitors, but there were none. At Peg's house, there was no news. Not even Tony came bounding in. TV news made no mention of the hunt for Larry Wimberholtz or, indeed, had any new developments in the matter to report.

Matt ranged the house like caged lion. She wasn't Lilianne. She probably wasn't Alison. If she was Dorothy, how could she be saved?

Leon Daw and his wife Megan came driving home at eight P.M. Three newsmen were waiting for them. Leon introduced his bride with the proper pride of a bridegroom. Megan was properly starry-eyed. Leon said that he was very very glad to know that the identity of his niece was now established beyond question. He was sorry, of course, for poor Mrs. Hopkins. But he would be removing Dorothy Daw from Cooper Memorial as soon as possible. No doubt tomorrow, in the morning. Very sorry—he would not care to say where. No stone would be left unturned to speed her recovery. He was much upset by her condition and very anxious to have his own doctors on the case. He now thanked the Press for its fair treatment, but hoped that his niece could have the peace and quiet she must have. She was, he said, too young and beautiful to die.

Yes. He and the then Mrs. Royce had driven to Vegas yesterday, leaving late in the morning. He had needed the-woman-he-loved. The newlyweds then hurried into the Spanish house.

The rooms were chilly, this June evening. Leon punched the furnace button. Megan drifted, in her yellow knit, to the bar. Her slim hips swayed.

He rolled his eyes at her, sat down and called the hospital. A voice told him that the girl's condition was unchanged. So Leon sighed.

He took his drink from Megan's wifely hand.

"Better this way?" she said. "That . . . *was* dangerous."

"Not very, was it?" he said, with a sneer.

But her eyes were steady and he looked away. He began to make brisk phone calls. He called St. John Cotter. When he hung up he said, "The pressure is on," and Megan's brows flew.

He called Dr. Jon Prentiss and was sharp. He would have an ambulance at the hospital door by nine o'clock on Tuesday morning. He expected to remove his niece, Dorothy Daw, to seclusion and the care of other physicians. He had the right and he intended to exercise it. He had no complaint to make against Dr. Prentiss, none at all; nevertheless, he would expect the doctor to have made the necessary arrangements for her release and to have secured all necessary permissions. Very well. Very glad.

He hung up. He said nothing.

Silent, in victory, they toasted each other.

After a while, Leon turned on the tape recording of his calls. They were monotonous. Then, the voice of Bobbie Hopkins came on. The listeners were galvanized.

Chapter Fifteen

It was after evening visiting hours. (All quiet at the hospital.) Peg was saying, in her living-room, and sadly, "I just can't make myself *believe* in Mrs. Hopkins."

"You are a dear sweet innocent lady," said Betty.

"Oh, am I?" said Peg tartly. "I'd like to see her myself. I never have, you know. *I'd* like to talk to her."

"Why not?" said Matt. He raised his brows at Betty. "Why don't we take Peg up there? Maybe that's not such a bad idea. She's a wise old woman."

Betty said, as if *she* were his mother, "It's better than watching you try to sit still. So, Peg, do you want to?"

There was a light behind the bamboo blinds at Bobbie's house. She didn't open the door, at first. Her voice cooed through the wood to find out who was there.

"It's Matt Cuneen, Mrs. Hopkins. I've brought my mother to see you."

"Oh, for pity's sake!" Bobbie opened up.

She was dressed in a basic black silk and wore several strands of phony pearls. Her hair had been retouched and was carefully arranged. Her face was heavily made up. In the pinkish light, Bobbie looked no more than in her ripe thirties. She reeked of perfume.

"Oh, Mrs. Cuneen," she gushed. "It's so good of you to come. I'm not really seeing people. I'm in mourning."

Peg said, "Im very sorry about your daughter."

"Yes," Bobbie sighed, "yes, it isn't easy. But I'm so sorry I worried *you*, and all. Can I fix you a cup of coffee? Or something stronger?" Her brows were aching sweet.

Matt could feel his stomach turning. Poor daughters, he thought. Lilianne, driven into drivelling. Poor Alison, the other daughter . . .

Peg, graciously declining refreshment, sat down. He and Betty did so, too, and let Peg do the talking.

"You had twin daughters, Mrs. Hopkins?" said Peg, who wasn't wasting time.

Bobbie's brows lost a little sweetness. "I don't talk about my other daughter," she said, bridling. "I don't see her any more. She's a kind of recluse. She was always a little bit different. I had her to the psychiatrists. Well, it never seemed right to me, but they tell me it's better for her to live by herself. So that's that."

Matt opened his mouth but his mother spoke.

"Is their father dead, then?"

"I wouldn't know," said Bobbie, martyred. "When the children were very small, he just went away. So I got the divorce. And that's that, too."

"And you brought them up by yourself?" Peg was willing to sympathize.

"I did the best I could," said Bobbie. She took a clean handkerchief with a lace edge from her cuff and didn't quite touch her painted eyes. "Maybe I'll travel," she sighed. "I've always wanted to travel. I'm not getting any younger. But there was Alison, you see. It was her ambition to become a motion-picture actress. Well, you know, Mrs. Cuneen, a mother ought to keep an eye on. That's a tough racket for a young girl."

"I'm sure it is," Peg.

"Poor baby," said Bobbie, "poor poor baby." Her face twisted.

"What a bad time you must have had," said Peg.

"First, to think it was your daughter in the hospital . . ."

Bobbie had clasped her hands. "Honest to God, Mrs. Cuneen, when I saw it was my own little girl and what they done to her, and her throat, and her five little fingers . . ." Her mask had detached. A haggard tormented woman looked out from behind it.

"Are you all alone here?" Peg said, with compassionate alarm.

"All alone. Oh, yes. Well, that is, I'm expecting a friend. Fact is" — Bobbie darted little sideways glances; she was pulling herself back together — "I wouldn't want you to feel I was putting you out, since you were so good as to come, but I have things to get ready."

"Well, of course," said Peg generously. She rose.

Matt rose and said, "We saw your daughter Lilianne."

Bobbie who was standing, too, gave him a shocked glare. "You did! How did you find her?"

"We found her," Matt said. *"She* doesn't seem to think that her sister's mark shows very much. Or at all."

Bobbie's glare was frozen into her eyes.

"Have you changed your mind about that?" Matt asked her. "Was there ever such a mark?" In all innocence, he wanted a fact.

But Bobbie's real color came up under the cosmetics. "Look, I'm sorry. I didn't want Lilianne to be bothered. She's got to be let alone. It's not good for her to be bothered. You sent any newspaper reporters on her, listen, I . . ."

"No, no. We haven't," Betty said quickly.

"You had no right," cried Bobbie. "You had no right. And I think you'd better get out of my house. I'm sorry. I thought you came in a decent Christian spirit. I guess I was all wrong. Me and my girls are none of your business. You let us alone, you hear me? I'm surprised, Mrs. Cuneen. I am surprised. This son of yours, he's got no respect or his girl friend, either. So who expects them to

185

have any? But you're old enough to know better. I suppose you came around to see what kind of freak I am. Is that right? Well, you can take your . . . kindness and you know what you can do with it."

Peg bent her head and went out the door that Matt was holding open. Betty said, "Excuse me," and walked past the furious woman to follow Peg and catch her arm.

Matt stood holding the door, looking at Bobbie Hopkins. He felt detached. He thought, She doesn't know what it's all about any more. She goes the way the wind blows. Her brain is pickled. Her mind's a ragbag. Her heart's scar tissue. Her children would have to run away. What would she want now? What could she *get?*

"How much," he said quite calmly, feeling no malice, "were you paid to identify the body?"

"How *much!*" she yelled. "How *much!* Now, that does it! Get out! *Get out!*" she howled. She picked up a magazine and hurled it at him in a futile flutter.

Matt got out.

When they were on their way down out of the hills Peg said, "She was right, you know. We did come to see what kind of freak she was."

"Granted," her son said. "We are miserable sinners." His tone was not as saucy as it might have been. "So," he coaxed, "what kind of freak do you think she is?"

Peg had her hands to her heart. "I can't imagine," she said in a moment, "how I would behave, if *I* were to see a child of mine, mutilated in a morgue."

"She saw a child of *hers?*" Matt was listening hard.

"Of course she did. She *suffers.* We shouldn't have come. We didn't come to help her, and we can't help her."

Peg had spoken.

They drove home in chastened silence. When they came into the house, the phone was ringing. Peg took the call. Matt and Betty heard her say . . . "Yes, I do agree, Jon. . . . Yes . . . I think it *must* be so . . . All right . . . Good night."

She hung up and said to them, "Dr. Jon wants the girl released to Leon Daw. The police are leaving it up to the hospital. The hospital's lawyer so advised. Jon thinks she's Dorothy. And I agree."

She then bade their stunned faces a sad good night.

Matt came out of shock and said to Betty, "Don't worry. I'll talk them out of it in the morning."

"Will you?" Betty was feeling sad and far away.

"Megan Royce was ready to poison our girl. It doesn't matter whether they think she's Dorothy—"

"Oh, Matt. If Peg is willing to let her go—"

"You, too?" he said stiffly.

"Oh, I'm willing." She'd been willing, for a long time.

"How odd of me, then, to prefer that she doesn't get murdered."

"Oh, Matt."

"Oh, Matt, what?" He was, in frustration, asking for war.

"It just isn't your responsibility, all alone."

"What difference does that make," he said tensely, "whether I'm alone or not?"

"I'm only trying to say that you can't—"

"Can't stop Leon Daw and Megan Royce from taking her away? The funny part of it is, I'll bet I can."

"No."

"I signed her into the hospital. My name is on the papers. I can refuse to relinquish my responsibility. I can say I'm not convinced of her identity. Which is the truth. I can tell the newspapers about the poison and stir them up. Oh, I can get into the headlines. 'Budding biologist refuses to give up tenth-richest girl. Suspects plot against her life'."

"You can ruin yourself," she said firmly.

"Sure. Lawsuits. Sensational publicity, unbecoming to a serious scientist. I'll say she's Alison."

"Matt, you have no proof."

187

"Tigers?" he challenged.

"Don't be so damned *silly!*" she shouted at him.

"There's the point about the vaccination," he said steadily. "That's reasonable."

"Maybe Dorothy is immune."

"Then show me some certification of that. How do we know Alison isn't immune?"

"Why won't you admit she could be Dorothy? And if she is, where's the motive? There wasn't any hanky-panky with the Daw money."

"You don't know that. You can't be sure."

"I don't have to know it or not know it. The police should know it. It's none of my business. Why is it yours? You'll have to let her go."

"I may be the only one who *doesn't* have to."

Betty got up and started for the hall. She felt stiff and cold. She turned to face him. "Shall I tell you why you've *never* wanted her to be Dorothy?"

"Go ahead." He gave her a smouldering look.

"Because Leon Daw has the money and the power to take her away, where you can't find her. Then you couldn't go and moon over her any more."

Matt said icily, "Thanks a lot."

"You never caught yourself rationalizing?" she cried. "You never, never did? You think that isn't possible? You think you know — you always know — exactly what your own motives are?"

He was infuriated by such condescension. "Why do *you* want me to let her go, for instance?"

Betty turned and walked stiffly into the hall. She stood there, looking up the stairs. Then she said to him, "I don't want you to ruin yourself. I am, also, just as jealous as hell. What's the difference? You're going to protect your lady fair — with the whole rest of your life."

"I don't have to be madly in love with her to prefer that she doesn't get murdered," he shouted.

"I know," she said forlornly. "But you absolutely have to dream, don't you?" She went stiffly up the stairs.

188

Matt stood there. Well! If Betty Prentiss had been dreaming — and he knew what — she had better dream again. On the other hand, he could oblige. He could fix her girlish dreams with a little coming-true in bed that would show her what. . . . His brain began to take note of his body's state, and his wish to punish, and the way he raged to do it. Betty *Prentiss!* Oh, for the love of . . . what? What was the *matter* with him?

He waited it out. Guessing he'd have to . . . he had better . . . let the girl go. Forget it. Forget *what?* Just — forget it.

Bobbie Hopkins had smoothed down her feathers as best she could. No harm done. Not really. Damn kids. That Cuneen kid . . . Skip it. Skip it.

She hesitated over the glasses in her cupboard and chose two of the smallest ones. She put them on a tray and got down the liqueur. It was awfully sweet, but she felt it would be elegant. While she was at it, she had a good slug of straight whiskey from the bottle. Not too much. She must have her wits at the ready.

She couldn't sit still. She stood at the edge of the window from which she could see the road and peered along the edge of the blind. "He won't be late," she said aloud. "He knows better than that."

But he surprised her. She was watching the road, where she could just see bare pavement. The walking shadow slipped almost up to her front door before she knew it.

"Mr. Daw? Do come in." She was flustered.

"Mrs. Hopkins?" He was polite. He stepped in and looked all around, quickly. Then his gaze returned to her face.

Bobbie had composed it into what she intended to be a poised and sophisticated, but slightly menacing smile. "Won't you . . . sit down?"

"Thank you."

"May I pour you a little sip?" She spoke too fast. Her bangles jangled.

Leon sat down on the couch in the spot where the spring was busted. Bobbie, who was less sure of herself than she wanted to be, drank down her portion of the fiery sweetness much too fast. Leon Daw held the little glass in his fingers daintily and somehow distastefully. Finally he said, "I am at a loss, Mrs. Hopkins. What did you wish to see me about?"

Bobbie took her heart in her mouth and said, "About money."

"You wanted to talk to me about money?" he purred. "Does that mean you want me to give you some?"

"As a matter of fact," said Bobbie, with a jerk, "I wanted to talk about my daughter Alison, who may be, you know, in a position to do you . . ." she became arch . . . *"another* favor?" She tilted the empty glass to her lips. Her tongue licked at the sweetness left on the rim.

The man said, "Are you sure you want to talk to me about money, with a witness to overhear you?"

"What?" Bobbie was badly startled. "Where?"

"Do you mind if I make sure?"

Bobbie had no chance to say whether she minded. He got up and went swiftly into the next room. She sat there, stunned, realizing that he was searching the house for an eavesdropper. She didn't follow him. She leaned over and poured herself some more of the liqueur. She needed it. She felt shaky. Because this had got to mean that she did have some purchase on him. Which had got to mean that what had been, in her mind, a not quite solid dream, an excitement, a stab in obscurity, an "if" and a "maybe," was acquiring substance.

He had gone through the dark middle room. He must be in the bedrooms, looking in the bathroom, probably into the closets. He'd come around by the kitchen, where the dishes hadn't been washed. Oh well, the hell with his impression of her housekeeping. Bobbie drank and put down the sticky glass.

He might be going to go for it! Then Bobbie Hopkins would get to see Paris, and Rome, too, and all those places. For real! Imagine that! Her ignorant jumble of impressions of foreign cities was whirling in her mind when his thumbs came up under her jaws and she felt terrible throbbing and her hands went up, her hands trying for his face, her nails for his eyes, but she couldn't . . .

The hill roads were poorly lighted. He was a shadow along the verge. His car was parked a little way into the next road down, under a bank of ivy and geraniums. He had taken care to point it downhill. Leon got in, let off the brake. It coasted without a sound. He went softly softly winding down.

Megan was reading a book. She had on purple velvet hostess trousers and a flowered silk blouse. She unhooked the earpieces of her harlequin glasses with the rhinestone rims and watched him cross quickly to the bar.

He didn't speak but drank thirstily, not bothering with ice.

In a moment she said lightly, "Letters all written, darling?"

"I'm caught up now," he said shortly and filled his glass again, taking ice cubes out of the little ice maker this time. He took it over to his chair and sat down.

Watching his face, she said, "I heard your typewriter going like mad upstairs. Didn't I?"

Leon's smallish mouth was wet. He opened it and closed it. Finally he said, "I've ordered the ambulance for nine o'clock tomorrow morning. It's a ten-mile ride. I wonder if you'd like to ride with Dorothy?"

"Of course," said Megan. "I'd be glad to, darling.

191

After all, supposing the moving were to wake her up. She knows me. She wouldn't be frightened and cry out, if I were there."

Something in her drawl annoyed him. "I don't like the new rules," he said sulkily. "Why do we have to live as if this place were bugged?"

"*This* place." Megan sighed. "I prefer modern. We should build. There is a lot in Bel Aire. Fifty thousand for the land alone, but a fabulous view—"

"For God's sake," he burst, "don't go shopping, *yet*."

She closed her eyes. "Darling," she said wearily, "don't try to be smarter than I am, do you mind? After all, you have a cleaning woman. Best we don't have to remember what day she's around. I would rather—if you don't mind—talk as if this, and every other place, were always bugged."

He said, in a moment, "When we get Dorothy into the private suite it will be possible to be with her a great deal of the time."

"I know. In case she would wake. Oh, I do think one of us ought to be with her most of the time. But not quite *every* moment, of course."

His eyes seemed to bulge. "She may not live, you realize?"

"She may," said Megan, "just slip away, very quietly, in her sleep. Poor child."

She got up and went to the bar. With her back to him, Megan said, "And what will Mrs. Hopkins say then, I wonder?"

"Nothing," said Leon.

Megan did not turn. She mixed herself a drink. She made it strong.

Chapter Sixteen

Before it was light, a figure slipped along Bobbie Hopkins' path. It tapped on her door. It slithered around the quiet house. It tapped on windows. It sniffed, stiffened, peered, panicked, let out a small moaning sound, ran.

An hour later, and it was beginning to be light, the same figure slouched beside the frame house on the front lot on Opal Street and tapped on the door of 438½, at the rear.

"Who is it?"

"Larry. Larry Wimberholtz. Let me in, would you, Lilianne? I got to tell you something. You got to let me in."

The door wagged finally. The girl was wearing the old print wrapper. The early light fell on her bare face. Her eyes glistened. "Why, Larry," she said in that childish voice, "I haven't seen you for such a long time. How are you?"

"Oh, Lilianne," he said, "listen. Close the door." He slunk within and she closed the door. "I don't know what to do," he said. "I got to tell you. Something's happened to your mom. Something bad, Lilianne. There's a terrible stink of gas and she's lying on the kitchen floor and I think she's passed away. Maybe you'll want to call somebody. *I* can't call anybody. I never thought she'd do a thing like that. I guess Alison

. . . I guess your mom just couldn't take it, the way Alison went and all —"

The girl said, "Balls!"

He was so startled that both of his feet left the floor for an instant. "Alison?" he said incredulously.

"What are you talking about?" the girl said fiercely. The childish voice was gone. The whole face had turned shrewish with the voice. "What *happened* to Mom? Come on. Spit it out."

He said, "L-l-listen. I thought maybe she'd let me stay a couple of days. I can't *stand* those ratty hotel rooms. I mean, Bobbie got me mixed up in this and I was going to make her take me in. But listen, it's true. The gas is pouring out of someplace and she's *in* there. I could just see . . . The oven door was open. It was switched on. She's on the floor, wearing her pearl beads. Her face . . . Well, she had her eyes open. She's dead. Dead as a . . . dead —"

"Well, *she* never did it!" said Alison. "Believe me, *she* never did it. Oh, that poor fool woman! I know what she did. I told her, Larry. Listen, I told her a thousand times . . ."

"What are you . . .? What is . . .? Where's Lilianne? *Oh,*" he said with a thud of knowledge.

"She's in the hospital and what am *I* going to do?" wailed Alison. "What am I going to *do?* My God, Bobbie probably told them! How do I know she didn't tell them where I am? Maybe they're coming after me. Larry, you got a car? My God, I've got to get out of here."

She was tearing things out of the closet, throwing them into the blue suitcase on the floor of the closet. She dropped the wrapper and stood naked before him. Neither of them seemed to notice it. She began to climb into her panties. She hooked her bra. "I'll pack my own stuff," she was chattering, "I can wear Lilianne's junk. Maybe Bobbie didn't tell them. If anybody comes here, they don't have to know I've even been. I got to go

194

someplace. Larry, listen, would your wife mind . . .?"

Larry was sitting holding the edge of the chair with both hands. "No," he squeaked. "Not her. I won't *let* her. What you better do is go to the cops. You don't have to say anything about—"

"Don't be an idiot all your life!" The girl was wiggling into her slip. She emerged and bent for her stockings. "How can I say that? Not *me*, brother. *You* didn't go to the cops, did you?"

"No," he groaned.

"O.K. There's going to be *something* to show that Bobbie didn't do it herself. The cops are smart enough for that. So let them figure out who did two murders. But not three, don't forget. Not *me, too!*"

"Yes, but I mean—"

"You want me to get killed? Do you, Larry? Really? Do you?"

"No," he said reluctantly.

"All right then. I can play Lilianne. I even fooled you, just now. I ought to be able to play Lilianne. I had enough practice. So why should Dorothy's uncle and Megan Royce kill *Lilianne?*"

"Say, why don't you go up to that nutty Alfreda's place?" he said. "You could fool her and hang around her place. Huh, Alison? Why not, Alison?"

The girl was pulling her hair down around her face. She snatched at her coat and her handbag.

"I got *some* money. I got all Lilianne's I.D. stuff. Her wallet and all. I can walk like her, if I have to. I mean, I can mooch along and nobody will even look at me. So come on. Let's get out of here."

But standing over him, dressed and ready, fierce and dominant, she pushed at her hair. "Listen, Larry, you think about *this*. Never mind that old jail bit. Is it going to do you any good if the cops find out *you* were up at Bobbies? Maybe they'd figure you had a mad on her. I mean, they want to see you already. I mean, how are you going to explain that, huh? I'm not going to say

195

one word and you can believe me. That's if you'll take me where I want to go and then forget it. So it's a deal or it's no deal." She was full of threat and storm.

Larry had no power. He stood. "I've got my car," he said feebly. "Where do you want to go, Alison?"

"You mean Lilianne."

"Lilianne?"

"I want to go back to Yuma," she said in the different voice, the childish treble. "I want to go back and see dear old Miss Gray. I can pay the bus. Will you take me to the bus station, please, Larry?"

He said in a squeal, "I'm not going near any bus station."

"Then just to the corner? I can take a bus to the bus station. Can't I, Larry?"

"Hurry up," he said nervously and picked up her suitcase.

They crept down the walk. Alison shivered in the open air. The streets were stirring only a little; only a few early workers were abroad. In the car, she combed a hank of hair down over her left cheek with nervous fingers. She fished in the handbag for a handkerchief. When the car stopped, about a mile from the little house, at a business intersection where no shop was yet open, she got out, handkerchief to her mouth.

"Where will you be?" he said thickly.

"Oh, I'll be wherever dear Miss Gray tells me to be," she said, in Lilianne's voice. "I'll be all right, once I'm back in Yuma. I'll be out of it."

"You want me to drive you to Yuma?" he said suddenly.

"Oh, no. Thank you very much."

"You don't care where I go, do you?" he said bitterly. "Like hell or something?"

"Oh, shut up," said Alison-as-Alison, "and take off, you damn fool. The bus is coming."

Larry stepped on his accelerator and went off, a little too fast.

She watched him turn the corner. The bus came, stopped, wooshed its door at her. She stepped backwards and shook her head. The bus went on.

Alison began to walk. Her heels hit the sidewalk too noisily. She tried to walk on her toes. It was going to be a long walk and uphill too. But she had to make it. She had to get lost, but she wasn't going to dear old Miss Gray. Dear old Miss Gray would put her in the loony bin. Put Lilianne, that is.

"Oh, honey, you're home!" cried Dolores Wimberholtz.

He held her warmth and let his bones shake. "It's O.K. It's O.K. The car's in the garage. Nobody saw me."

"They've been around and been around," she told him, "but maybe they won't come around any more. If they do, you can just keep in the back room. Can't you? Please? Larry, I missed you."

"It doesn't matter too much any more. I'm not going to have too much trouble. I'm not going to be charged with murdering old Alison. She just happens to be alive."

"Oh," said Dolores with delicious relief, "that's wonderful! Oh, Larry, why don't you call up the police, right now?"

"Well," he said uneasily, "not now. Not yet. I don't feel like it. I been so miserable, honey, so lonesome — I missed you."

"*Ssh,*" she said. "You don't have to do it this minute. Let me fix you some hot breakfast. I didn't say *one word*. I did what I told you. I just sat tight."

"That's right," he said. "That's right. We'll just sit tight. If anybody wants to bother us — O.K. That's time enough. Besides, probably she isn't going to fool Miss Gray."

"Who's that?"

"Lilianne's old teacher. Runs this school. Used to try and help her."

"Oh, that's where Alison is?"

"That's where she's going."

"You can tell the police that."

"Sure. Any time," said Larry. "So *we're* all right."

Dolores said, "Of course! Of course, we are!" very vehemently, because she wasn't quite sure that they were.

Alfreda, uprooted so early in the morning, sat behind her desk in an ordinary blue quilted bathrobe and a pink nightgown. The girl in the other chair would not look at her. She kept her head bowed and her hair half over her face. "I knew you'd help me," she said, "I know you won't let them bother me. I was told."

Alfreda's mouth went wry. "I will help you if I can," she intoned, "but I hope you are not imagining that you can fool me."

Now the girl's face came up with a look of terror. She began to weep violently. She slid to the chair's edge. She reached out blindly over the desk. She wept and implored.

Alfreda said in brisk tones, "Well, you are a mess, aren't you, Alison?"

"I don't know how I got in such a mess," the girl sobbed. "I don't know what to do. My mother is dead and she didn't do it herself. I might as well die, too, and get it over. If somebody doesn't help me . . . I didn't mean to fool you . . ."

"You couldn't have done that. I am very very close to your sister, in ways you cannot understand."

"Ah," Alison beat her forehead on the desk. "Just help me, why don't you?"

"I must dress," said Alfreda, rising. "You must weep. We shall see."

Alison, with her head on the desk, sobbed in dimin-

198

uendo. She began to listen intently. The temple was a silent place. She could hear nothing. She had lifted her head and lit a nervous cigarette, when the big woman came back, treading softly, wearing her white robe.

The girl looked up at her. Alfreda said nothing but the girl, responding to her wordless suggestion, blurted, "What shall I do with it? I'm sorry." Alfreda smiled and pushed a small empty vase across the desk. Alison stubbed out her cigarette against its inside.

"Have you touched bottom?" said Alfreda. "Are you quite sure that you must have help? That you can no longer help yourself?"

The girl whimpered.

"You have come to me? You are putting yourself in my hands? Very well. I shall, of course, give you sanctuary and I shall show you how to be healed. But you must, first, accept your position. Completely. You are afraid. Afraid of the police, afraid of the newspapers, afraid of the light, afraid that the sins of your younger days will be known, afraid that you will have no career, afraid that you have been used by criminals, afraid that they will be afraid of you—"

"I don't know *anything*," Alison wept, "I couldn't tell the police anything, not anything, really. I'm just afraid . . ."

"Afraid of death? So very much afraid of death that you long to die?" The big woman was almost chanting. "So all your ways have led you into fear. You have come to an end. Your mind and body. They rattle and jangle and you have no peace. You have no resources. You need to be told what to do to be saved. Very well, my dear. Very well. You must sink down, deliberately. You must let everything fall away. You must rest deeply, deeply. Sink. Fall. I will attend to the circumstances that trouble you. I will protect you from the world. There is time now—time to give up, to sink down, to rest and be healed. You must let go of everything and be nothing. You may sleep."

Lt. Clarence Tate said to Tony Severson, "Who let you in?"

Tony was holding his nose. "Is it safe in here?" he said nasally.

Tate said, "Beat it. Who said you could mess around in that desk?"

"Yah look," said Tony, letting go of his nose. "Lookit here!" He had Bobbie's little black book in his hand and he flipped the pages. "Lilianne. 438½ Opal Street. You know who that is?"

"Let me guess," the lieutenant said sourly.

"That's the twin sister."

"Give me that, and beat it." Tate snatched the book.

"Can I quote you it was suicide?" said Tony, backing away.

"You can't quote me, period," said Tate, "Vamoose."

Tate went back into the orderly confusion of the kitchen, where the smell of gas was even stronger. "Wonder it didn't blow up," he growled. "The neighbor's got a good nose on her, I'd say." There was a sheeted mound on the floor, still. A man was dusting the handles of the gas stove with powder. "Looks like I won't get a thing," he announced cheerfully.

Tate grunted. "What do you say, Doc?"

The man he addressed said, "Somebody took a good hold on her throat. I'll say that. Blacked her out, no doubt of it. But she was breathing afterwards."

"Breathing in the gas, eh?"

"That's right. So whoever took her by the neck, didn't do her any good." The doctor had some curiosity. "Any supsects?"

"A couple," said Tate. "One or two. Or three."

"Don't I see by the papers you're after her ex-son-in-law?"

"I'm pretty hot after *him,*" said Tate.

200

He went back into the living-room. The fingerprint man was now working on the solitary liqueur glass. "Looks like hers and hers alone."

"Drinking alone?" said Tate thoughtfully. *"That stuff?"*

He went back into the kitchen and opened the cupboards, found the shelf where the glasses were kept, looked closely at the five little ones. Four were dusty. One was shining.

Chapter Seventeen

Betty, having steeled herself, said as she came to the breakfast table, "Good morning, I hope. Matt, I'm sorry I screamed at you last night. I won't do it again."

"That's O.K., Betts, forget it. I was probably talking like a jackass. Good morning." They exchanged narrow smiles.

Peg kept her peace. They would have to patch things up by themselves, if patching were possible. At least the mysterious girl would be gone, very soon — whatever wrack she left behind her. Matt had telephoned the hospital and reported that Leon Daw was sending an ambulance for her at nine o'clock. Matt seemed to have accepted this.

At eight-thirty, the phone rang. Peg took up the kitchen extension. Matt saw his mother stagger and jumped to put a supporting hand on her back and snatch the instrument.

It was Tony Severson. Very excited. Bobbie Hopkins found dead! Suspicion of murder! Lieutenant Tate in charge! Larry Wimberholtz suspect and wanted! Tony knew they would want to know.

Matt hung up and said, "O.K. That does it."

"Oh, poor woman," wailed his mother. "I wonder . . . I wonder . . . could we have—"

"Now, listen, Peg." He was stern. "One thing for sure *it's not your fault*. And you hear that, Peg. Now, I'm going over to the hospital and no matter what I have to do, I'm going to stop them from taking *her*."

"Oh, Matt—"

"Nope. There's too much going on that nobody understands. You never mind, Ma. I know you've washed your hands and so has Betty. But I can't. And it doesn't matter why, either."

"This is terrible. All this is terrible," Peg said with control, "about the Hopkins family. But what does it change for us? We still know that the girl who fell asleep upstairs must be Dorothy Daw. And Mr. Daw and his new wife, they *are* her people. Nobody else claims her. Poor Bobbie Hopkins gave her up, and whatever you think, you can't change her mind again. And if what Leon Daw wants to do is simply take her to *another* hospital, how can we object to that?"

"I object," Matt said, "I say she *isn't* Dorothy. I say they are *not* her people, I can say, if I have to, that they are a couple of murderers. Twice over."

"Twice! You can't mean *they* murdered Bobbie Hopkins! Matt, if you say that and it isn't true—"

"And if it *is* true, and I *don't* say it?"

Mother and son faced each other and the impasse. Betty said, "Isn't it a police matter, really?"

Matt turned on her. "So when they kill her, too, we can shrug that off. Blame the police?"

"When all you have is an intuition . . ." Betty began. She felt frightened.

"We should talk to Lieutenant Tate," said Peg. "Yes. We ought to do that much. I do agree."

"First, I have to stop them from taking her. The time's too close."

"What will you do, Matt?"

"Oh, I don't know," said Matt, with a killing glance at Betty Prentiss. "Maybe I'll jump up and down and scream. Or be pious. Or flirt with some nurses, use my sex appeal. I may cry. Because why in hell can't *I* have an intuition?" he roared.

Betty was furious all over again. She said, "Before you make too much of a fool of yourself, may I remind you that there is somebody who claims her?"

"Who?"

"Alfreda."

"The great healer? The witch-woman? She hasn't even checked to see if Lilianne was missing from Opal Street. She hasn't even seen our girl, yet."

"Exactly," snapped Betty.

Matt stared at her. "But we know she's wrong. We talked to Lilianne."

"*Did* we?" said Betty.

And Peg cut in, "But she's right, Matt. This Alfreda must be allowed to see her. Now, that's fair. And that's the way to hold things up . . . until the police might . . . until things are clearer."

"Might work at that," Matt said, suddenly calm. "Alfreda is so sublimely sure of herself, she could upset the little old applecart by sheer bulk *and* gall. O.K. I'll go up to the temple and drag Alfreda down in two seconds flat."

"No, no," said Peg. "You go to the hospital and tell them they will have to wait. You can say I said so. I'm responsible. I'll go up to the temple. Betty has been there and seen this woman. Betty will go with me."

"Betty doesn't want anything to do with it," said Matt. "It's none of her business."

Betty was on her feet, white with anger. "Perfectly true!" she said. "That damned beautiful *nothing,* on the hospital bed, means absolutely nothing to me. But I'll take your mother anywhere she wants to go."

"Do that," said Matt. "Thank you."

Ten minutes later, Betty and Peg stood on the temple's porch and Betty wielded the brass knocker insistently. The sun was high now. From this eminence, the view was wide. They could see the life of the city flowing in its veins, but the sounds of traffic were afar.

Alfreda opened the door, at last, and faced them —

tall, white-robed, heavy of presence.

"I am Mrs. Cuneen," Peg said briskly. "You know Betty Prentiss. We have come to take you to Cooper Memorial Hospital, right away. It is very important."

"So I understand," said Alfreda gravely.

But Peg's impetus carried her on. "They plan to take the girl away but we say she mustn't be let go, quite yet. Mrs. Hopkins has been . . . is dead."

"And you are afraid?" said Alfreda kindly. "Very well."

She stepped backward, leaving the door open.

"I will come in one moment." Alfreda went off to their left, Peg stared in at the odd room beyond the shallow foyer. Betty took in a deep breath. They heard no sound. Peg seemed to be sensing the aura of this place and resenting it with every fibre.

Alfreda returned in the moment she had promised, having fetched a white robe, a simple garment like her own, which she carried on her arm. Now she simply stepped upon the porch, did something to the edge of the door, closed it firmly behind her. Betty seemed to hear the lock engage.

"When I am in residence," Alfreda said, "my door is never locked." Betty wondered how this woman could be such a monster of conceit, and also, half a mind-reader.

Alfreda got into Betty's car, causing it to sag. Peg got in behind. Betty ran around to be the chauffeur. She said, "We need you pretty desperately."

"You do, indeed," Alfreda boomed. "And so does Lilianne."

Betty didn't want to bring this stubborn conviction into question by mentioning the girl on Opal Street. She took the car winding slowly down the steep road, with due caution. But Peg said, "What makes you so sure, Doctor?" In her voice, Betty could hear her distaste for this woman's personality.

Alfreda said, "I suppose I shall have to wake her up,

205

to be believed by lay persons."

"And why not?" snapped Peg. "Why should you be believed?"

"Because," said Alfreda with insulting patience, "I know, as you evidently do not, that Lilianne has fallen into just such prolonged sleeps before. She is my protégée Lilianne Kraus. I have said so, several times."

The car ran on level ground. Betty scooted for the turn around the little park. But Peg said, "Betty, please drop me at home. This is where I get off."

Betty felt astonished but she had no time to wonder. She did as she was asked, and then turned two sides of the park and swooped into a parking space next to a big black sedan she had seen before.

"Leon Daw is here," she told Alfreda.

"No matter. So am I."

Alfreda stalked majestically into the lobby with Betty, beside her, feeling as if she were a tug attending an ocean liner.

Leon Daw, natty in pale grey this morning, was standing beside Megan Royce, who was crisp in black and white. Matt was there facing them, between them and the corridors, with his feet planted hard.

The liner loosed itself from guidance and Alfreda sailed towards the group. She was a force. Megan braced herself and began a kind of glittering. She became like a knife, but Alfreda was a soft mass that could not be wounded.

"I am Alfreda. I have come for Lilianne Kraus."

Leon's mouth began to work like the mouth of a hungry fish. He seemed to recognize Betty. "*We* are waiting for Dr. Prentiss," he snapped. "Where is he? Why this delay?"

"Lilianne Kraus is my protégée," boomed Alfreda.

Megan said, "Well, my goodness, we have no interest in a Lilianne Kraus."

"Indeed, you have not," said Alfreda severely, "and you must stop insisting that she is Dorothy Daw." She turned on Matt. "Now, take me to see her."

"To see whom?" Leon shouted. "Now, wait a minute. Who *is* this? What is she *talking* about?" He was shouting at Matt. "Is this what you were waiting for?"

"This is Dr. Dienst," said Matt. "Lilianne Kraus is an identical twin to Alison Hopkins."

They staggered. They both staggered away from Alfreda, who stood like a tower, patient and powerful, and more or less benign.

"So I'm sure," said Matt, "you'll understand that Dr. Dienst must be allowed to see our girl before we can let you take her away."

"Twin?" squeaked Megan.

"No!" shouted Leon. "You will not let her see the girl. Are you crazy? I have it arranged. The ambulance is waiting. You can't . . . Dr. Prentiss! Dr. Prentiss!"

The doctor was coming towards them with his hand extended, but not to Leon. "Good morning, Dr. Dienst," he said, "I'm Dr. Prentiss. How are you?"

"Very well, Doctor," said Alfreda. "I have come to put an end to this confusion."

Leon was making strange gobbling sounds.

Dr. Prentiss said, "Excuse me a minute, Mr. Daw." Then to Alfreda he said, with a touch of asperity, "You seem very sure that you can do so. This girl has been here since Wednesday last, and you haven't yet seen her."

"I telephoned here, on Friday last," said Alfreda, "and told someone, whom I presumed was able to transmit a message, that you had Lilianne Kraus here. Had you paid attention, there would have been no confusion whatsoever."

"But you didn't come."

"She didn't come," said Leon Daw in an echo. "What has this . . . what . . ."

"Hush, darling," said Megan. "Wait."

"I came," said Alfreda, "on Saturday as this young man can tell you and should have told you. I was then

207

informed of certain rules. I then stated my own obligations. I had urgent problems, at the time. The new supermarket on Parsons Street cut ground away from my hill and my temple was condemned. I was involved with the saving of my home and property. Now, as for Lilianne, I said, on Saturday morning, that I would return. I *have* returned. Are you reproaching me?" This was, she implied, perfectly preposterous.

"I am questioning your pronouncement that this girl is Lilianne Kraus," said Dr. Prentiss. "Especially since I believe these young people have spoken to Lilianne, in the meantime."

Leon Daw was gobbling again. Megan took a tight grasp on his arm.

"An exchange of identities," said Alfreda comfortably. "There is a pattern for it. Lilianne was the 'father's girl,' you see. That's why she kept *his* name. But when he left, she was prey to the more dominant personalities of the mother and the sister. The girl, Alison, began very young the practice of stealing her twin's identity whenever she chose. Which was an evil thing to do. A great evil. It has boomeranged, of course, upon Alison."

"Alison is dead," said Megan thinly.

"Not at all," said Alfreda. "Not at all." She distributed her force between Megan and Leon. "You people *may* only be confused," she said. "I don't say otherwise. But certainly you must now agree that if both twins are alive, the other girl, the dead girl, must be your Dorothy Daw."

"But that . . . that is perfectly *foolish!*" Megan was shrill.

Alfreda said, "No, that is simple arithmetic." She turned to Dr. Jon. "I must discover a bit about how Lilianne fell into this particular spell."

Dr. Prentiss stepped aside, as if to usher her, and Alfreda began to move. Leon Daw made a clawing gesture as if to catch at her, but Megan caught at his hand.

Her high voice scratched. "Some fanatic," it said cuttingly.

"What is she *doing?*" Leon was ready to claw at Matt. "What is she going to *do?*"

Betty said, "She is going to wake up Lilianne."

It was Matt Cuneen who staggered. He gave Betty a strange look and turned to hurry after Dr. Prentiss and Alfreda.

Betty said, "Why don't you wait? Excuse me?" She went after Matt. When the corridor began, she turned to look back and saw Megan silhouetted against the light — a sharp scribbling in black and white. A witch? A wicked one?

Megan got Leon out the door and away from all other ears. "All right," she said. "Calm down. The truth is, we don't give a damn about any twin. She can't hurt anything."

"Oh, you *are* bright!" he raved. "You *are* brilliant! You are *so* smart. And where *is* our little Alison? In the meantime?"

"Shh shh."

Tony Severson was bounding towards them.

Leon whirled and started for the parking lot. But Tony jumped nimbly into his path. "Mr. Daw? Excuse me. Have you heard that Bobbie Hopkins is dead?" Tony was pleased to be bringing news. "Murdered," he added, beaming.

Megan was able to gasp appropriately. Leon simply stared at him.

"They found her this morning," Tony babbled on. "How about that? Any comment?"

"Why should I *comment?*" shouted Leon. He pushed around Tony, who goggled.

"Oh, poor woman," said Megan. "Oh, please excuse us? We have had an upset."

"Why? Why? What's up?"

Megan collided with Leon, now, as he stopped and turned. "You tell *me,*" shouted Leon. "Did Alison

209

Hopkins have a twin sister?"

"Huh? Oh, yah, sure. Some kind of religious. Not a nun, though. Kind of hermit. Lives all by herself in a little old shack."

"Where?"

"What do you mean, where?" Tony was alert, "Why?"

"Leon, dear, it's not good for you to go on like this." Megan began to pat and push at the man. "Please, darling, go to the car. Try not to think. It's too upsetting."

"What is? What?" Tony persisted.

But Leon was striding off and Megan was now in Tony's path. "Oh, there is some dreadful woman, in a white *thing,* and they are letting her see Dorothy. She says that Dorothy is this twin. It seems so *mad!*"

"Yah, that can't be," said Tony flatly.

"Can't?" Megan was on the tip of one toe.

"Nope. Because I just been around there. Four thirty-eight and a half Opal Street. Well, she's either not there right now, or else not answering the door. See, the cops came by, the neighbors said, and she didn't let *them* in, either. Probably she's not crazy about cops. But the point is, I talked to this couple up the street and she *was* there, all right, last Sunday night. Had a little bitty fire in her shack. This fellow, he made with the garden hose and saved the joint. Well, they tell me this kid never hobnobs, just holes up all the time like a scared rabbit, a real recluse and all that. But the fire kinda smoked her out (ha, hah) so I got witnesses that Lilianne was right here on Opal Street Sunday night. So how could she be in this hospital since Wednesday?"

Megan said, "How indeed?" She stared at him. She licked her lip.

"Say," said Tony abruptly, his eyes bright, his ears ready to wag, "was Dorothy Daw an adopted child?"

Megan gasped and said, "Yes. I . . . I think *so.*"

"Did she know?" Tony was excited.

210

But Megan put her hand on his arm and cried, "Oh, I *must* go. I *must* get him home. It isn't good for his blood pressure to be so dangerously upset and confused. Please. Maybe you could call me, a little later? If you and I . . . are beginning to think the same thing?" Her eyes were making themselves worshipful.

Tony responded by hunching himself up and beginning to spout. "Alison's dead as a doornail. So if Lilianne is here in the hospital, then you got to start asking yourself who was almost burned up on Opal Street."

"Ah, don't," said Megan tenderly. "Don't say it. Leon mustn't hear. He's had enough. Don't you see? Of course you do, mister . . ."

"Severson, Tony." Tony was like a bud, opening to sun and rain. Practically nobody worshipped him.

"Severson. She must be hiding from her own uncle. And we don't know why. Oh please, would *you* call me? Maybe you would go with me, to see her, to find out? I know you are on a newspaper, but how marvellous if we could—just you and I—find her alive and safe and not even ill. If I could only find her, she might talk to *me*. And let us in. You do think she is there? Four thirty-eight and a half did you say? Opal Street, was it? You do think so?"

"I think she probably is there," said Tony, furrowing his brow to a look of wisdom. "I didn't bust into the place."

"Then—oh please—before you broadcast anything, call me? In about an hour? *I* won't say a word to anyone else at all."

"It kinda depends," said Tony, shifting his weight, "on the real truth about the one here. Whether she *is* Lilianne."

"I know. But you could find out what this Alfreda does about that? And let me know? And then . . .?"

"I'll see what I can do," said Tony. "If that's a deal. If it's *my story,* Mrs. Royce."

"Mrs. Daw," she said, her voice lingering regretfully. (She would have preferred him, of course.) "But *of course* it is *your* story! I knew you would help me." She smiled at him thinly and ran towards the parking lot on her spindly heels.

Tony bounded up the steps of the hospital and the strong arm of the guard crossed his path. "No Press," the man said. "They've got sick people here."

In the car, Megan was sharp. "Stop panicking, or this is a mess. Pull yourself together. I've got the street number. We'd better go there now."

"In broad daylight?" Leon said. "Oh, you *are* cute!"

"I'll tell you the cute thing to do. Buy Alison out. You should have bought Bobbie Hopkins."

"Too late."

"No, I don't think so. Alison's hiding. Did that fat woman in the *thing*, make any accusations? She'd seen Alison. So Alison's *not* talking. Not yet. Why shouldn't we get to her and pay her enough?"

"She won't play."

"Why not? Why not, Leon? Bobbie thought she would play. Don't be stupid, now. We can't afford it. How could Bobbie have been trying to get money out of you unless she knew Alison would go along?"

"Bobbie's dead."

"Alison doesn't have to know what happened. You jumped too fast. You should have listened to Bobbie, long enough to find out about the twin. *She* must have known that. Ah, you don't understand. You had better just listen."

"I'm not a murderer!" he shouted.

"Oh, darling, who said murder? Stop at a gas station. Get us a street map. This Alison is a cheap little would-be movie queen who has no more brains than her mother before her. I can handle her."

"You did a great job of it before." Leon had revived

enough to snarl at her. "What did you say that made Alison run out on you?"

"Not a thing. I told you. Stop the car. Let me drive. Get out, if you want to."

"Oh, no."

"All right," said Megan. "Sooner or later, Alison will have to talk. To the police, for instance. Is that what you really want? *Listen* to me. The way it is now, Alison is officially dead. Her own mother said so. All we need is the alibi. That's all we ever needed. Let them figure out how Dorothy couldn't be dead on Monday, and lunching with us on Tuesday. Listen! Listen!" she screamed in his ear. "Alison is awake. She'll have to listen. We can make her play the part of Dorothy. For a while. For a while. Oh, get out of the car and go hide your silly head while I do this."

The car kept trundling along.

"All right," said Megan. "Then you can go down alone. I am appalled. I am appalled." Her voice became her normal affected drawl. "Why, that luncheon was, to me, only a harmless little deception to throw the Press off poor dear Dorothy's track. *I* thought the girl in the hospital was Dorothy. How should I doubt you? You are an honest man. But I cannot say, in any conscience, that I knew where you were, at all, last Sunday night. Although I do remember . . . something about a phone call on your tape? Oh, I have been a *fool!*"

Leon wrenched at the wheel and turned into a gas station.

Chapter Eighteen

"I was trained," Alfreda was saying, "in medicine, as you know. I am very well read in psychiatry. Let me say, gentlemen, that Lilianne's state is, in my opinion, emotional. I have the advantage of knowing that, in her history, there have been other incidents of prolonged comas emotionally induced."

They were gathered in Atwood's office. The men were listening respectfully to Alfreda, who sat enthroned.

"We seem to have come to much the same conclusion," said Dr. Prentiss, "without benefit of history. Now tell me, why do you assume that you can wake her?"

"There is a spiritual rapport you may not understand," said Alfreda complacently. "She can sense my presence. She can be reached by me, who will not in any way frighten her and in whom she has great faith. Of course, as I said, I should know all I can about the circumstances."

Nut or no nut, Alfreda had an orderly mind when she chose. She began to ask questions and very soon picked out Betty as the one present who had seen and spoken to the girl before she fell asleep on Wednesday.

So Alfreda caused Betty to be pushed into the centre of the room, and proceeded to extract the whole story in minute detail. "I want to put your mind back in time, to that morning, Miss Prentiss. Play it all back. Hear it again. Give me the sound. Every syllable."

Betty stumbled along, but as she went she began, under the spell of Alfreda's powerful and demanding attention, to hear it all again with astonishing clarity.

"Peg said to her, 'And what is your name, please?' The girl said, 'My name is . . .' " Betty broke off quoting, "Dolan or something like it. Olin. Tollin. *Tollin!* That was *it!*"

"I understand," said Alfreda benignly. "Go on."

"So Peg said, 'And your first name, Miss Dolan?' And the girl just nodded. She didn't answer. Peg couldn't very well insist. Anyway, she didn't. You see, the girl looked fatigued enough to fall down. We didn't understand."

"How should you have understood?" said Alfreda comfortingly. "Now then, what next?"

"Wait a minute," said Dr. Prentiss. "Explain, please."

"Why, Lilianne spoke the truth. 'My name is stolen'," quoted Alfreda. "*I* would have recognized what she meant to tell, because *I* knew that her twin was in the habit of stealing her name, her reputation, and her place in the world."

Atwood had tented his fingers. He groaned softly.

"Is that clear? Then go on, Miss Prentiss," Alfreda commanded.

So Betty went on. Quoting herself, she thought that her words, out of time, place, and mood, sounded idiotic. 'Well, I'm off to the wars. I'll see you later, probably. Gosh, you look as if you could sleep for a week'." Betty made a gesture of *"finis."*

Alfreda sighed. "Very helpful," she said. "Now that was the last word said to her?"

"That was it. As far as I know."

"What is the day of the week, today?"

"Today is Tuesday," said Atwood, after a stunned moment.

"And she fell asleep on Wednesday, last. The week is almost up, then."

"You mean to say—"

"It was a suggestion," said Alfreda, "that may have appealed to her."

"Oh, no," moaned Betty softly.

"Why, I can imagine that it fell in well," said Alfreda. "Lilianne was presented with a situation to which she had no solution. I feel sure that her sister must have appeared and simply stolen her place and selfhood and put her out. So Lilianne, quite naturally, went looking for me. She had no one else. She is much too shy, has been too often wounded, to go willingly to strangers. I was her"—the woman hesitated and chose a word—"*mentor,* you see, and the one in the world who would immediately understand what her sister had done to her, once again. But the temple, having been condemned, was closed on that day. I was not there. She could not find me."

"So she found Mrs. Cuneen's sign," said Betty excitedly. "Dr. Dienst, does Lilianne smoke?"

Alfreda looked at her with hauteur.

"Does *Alison?*" Betty was on the edge of her chair.

"Alison shall give that filthiness up," said Alfreda. "Now, gentlemen, there are reasons why I would rather not wake Lilianne, just now, this morning."

"The other day—" Betty was following her own thoughts.

Matt shushed her fiercely.

"Since, when I do awaken her," pronounced Alfreda, "as I have told you before, then I must take her with me."

"That will be for the doctor to say," said Atwood, a little stiffly.

"I am afraid," said Alfreda, "that will be for *me* to

216

say. She is, in effect, my patient."

"This hospital cannot—"

"She won't be able to accept this hospital. Or, indeed, any."

Betty could not stay hushed. "The girl we saw on Opal Street!" she cried. "She acted scared to death of doctors and nurses and hospitals. She looked as if she'd fly into a fit, and we had to give up. But that was *Alison?*"

"Of course. Of course." Alfreda sighed. "I told you. Alison steals Lilianne's whole psyche whenever she needs it. A wickedness. A great evil." The big woman's eyes flickered.

"But evil rebounds," she went on sternly. "Alison herself has little or no identity, now. A sick soul."

"You've seen Alison? Recently?" Dr. Prentiss pounced.

"Oh yes, quite recently. To speak your language, Alison is at this time on the verge of a nervous collapse with suicidal tendencies."

"Well, then," Dr. Prentiss said, "if you have spoken to Alison, we do seem to be sorting these girls out, at last."

"Providing," said Atwood, "that Dr. Dienst is right about the girl upstairs."

Alfreda smiled. "Still a doubter," she chided gently.

"I will believe it," said Atwood, "when she tells me, herself, who she is."

"Ah then, the simplest way," sighed Alfreda, "is for me to go now and wake her. But then I must take her. And you must agree to that."

She rose. Atwood got up. He made a pronouncement of his own. "The police must be informed."

"Why?" said Alfreda.

"Because, obviously, if you know that both the twins are alive, the dead girl must be Dorothy Daw."

Alfreda said, "I believe I have already said so. Al-

217

though the dead girl is not, and never has been, within my ken."

Dr. Prentiss seemed more amused than appalled. "You're going to have to talk to the police, Doctor," he said, with an air of kindly warning.

The big woman raised her brows. "I will speak to the police if I must — but only when I find myself able to take the time. I will not abandon a soul, to suit the law. A wooden structure, yes. A human soul, no. Never. Not even" — she slew Matt with a glance — "a *poor* soul." She looked at the door and said, "Which of you will take me to Lilianne?"

Dr. Prentiss put his hand on the doorknob. "I'll take you, Doctor."

"Thank you, Doctor."

Matt was at the woman's side. "I'd like to go with you, Dr. Dienst," he said intensely, "if you will please allow it."

That's the way, thought Betty. That's the way to speak to *her*. She saw Alfreda's look, now bent upon Matt. It was full of lofty pity. "Ah yes," said Alfreda, as if she waved a wand, "you have need. You may come with me."

She walked away with the doctor, and Matt followed.

Betty stayed where she was.

Hadn't he taken in the truth — that Peg had guessed, that Alfreda knew and had stated, that Betty herself had just stated? Matt didn't seem to realize that he had already met and spoken with a *well-practiced copy* of the girl upstairs. And she had turned his stomach. She had made him sick. Well . . . poor Matt.

Meanwhile, Atwood was after Lieutenant Tate on

the phone and he got him.

"This is Fred Atwood at Cooper Memorial Hospital. A Dr. Ruth A. Dienst is here who says that our sleeping girl is Lilianne Kraus or Hopkins, twin sister of Alison. Dr. Dienst also tells us that *Alison is alive* and she has spoken to her. Now, sir, you must see . . ."

Atwood began to listen. Betty was on her feet, making motions. "The address," she urged. "Tell him 438½ Opal Street. He can find Alison there."

But Atwood only rolled his eyes at her and did not repeat into the phone what she had said. He went on listening to Tate and after a series of "Yes," "Yes" and "No," he hung up and mopped his chin.

"They think," he told Betty, "that Mrs. Hopkins was choked before she was gassed and by the same hands that broke the neck of the girl in the truck. Tate has this Wimberholtz fellow now and is interrogating him. Wimberholtz *also* says that Alison is alive. Tate is having her picked up."

Betty relaxed.

"But Tate says," Atwood's voice began to sound a little frantically weary, "that they have received some information that leads him to suspect that Dorothy Daw may have been, or wanted to be, acquainted with the Hopkins clan. *He* isn't sure that our girl upstairs is not Dorothy Daw." Atwood mopped vigorously. "He does say that he now knows where all three girls *are* and that he will get them sorted out, once and for all, before this day is done."

Atwood began to shift some papers on his desk. "I only hope," he added, "that this hospital can be said to have done its full duty."

"You have duties now," said Betty. "I'd better leave you to them."

"Will you wait in the lobby?"

"I may. Or I may run over to tell Mrs. Cuneen."

"It will take time, I'm afraid."

219

"Will it?" said Betty. "She didn't seem to think so."

"Eh? Oh, no, not Dr. Dienst. I meant that it will take time to pick up the third girl in Yuma. Or on the way there. Whoever she is."

"But surely she is Alison!"

"I suppose I tend to think so," said Atwood pathetically.

Betty went into the corridor and walked along slowly. What would Dorothy Daw want with the Hopkins family? How would she know about them? Wait—Megan Royce had known that Alison was a double for Dorothy.

Betty came into the lobby and looked for Megan, to question her if she dared. But Leon Daw and Megan Royce were not there.

Betty sat down, feeling numb.

Tate said to Larry Wimberholtz, "We'll go over it again. Alison is alive, right?"

"That's right. I told you five times."

"And how come you've got her suitcase in your car, with her passport in it?"

"Because we forgot," raved Larry, pounding his thighs with his fists. "We *forgot!* I told you. She's alive. I took her to catch a bus. She got out and never said a word about the suitcase, and I *forgot* it."

"Uh huh. Why did you go to Opal Street so early this morning?"

"You don't believe me. What's the use? You don't believe a word I—"

"Tell me again."

"I wanted to see Lilianne. I thought I'd find Lilianne there."

"Why did you want to see Lilianne?"

"I told you. I just wanted to see her. All right. All right." Larry began to sob. "I went to tell her that her

220

mom was dead."

"You knew her mom was dead, eh? How did you know that?"

"Because I saw her, through the kitchen window."

"Now maybe we're getting somewhere. When was this?"

"I don't know. Five-thirty this morning."

"You saw her through the window in the dark?"

"*Yes,* in the dark! The oven door was open. You got to believe me."

"And why were you looking through Bobbie Hopkins' kitchen window at five-thirty in the morning?"

"Because . . . You're trying to mix me up."

"Because you had it in for Bobbie, too? Did Bobbie have a hunch you'd killed Alison?"

"No. No. No. I didn't kill anybody. Alison isn't even dead. I told you. She's pretending to be her sister. She's gone to Yuma."

"Maybe she *is* her sister," Tate said. "Or maybe she's Dorothy Daw."

"What's the use of telling you anything?" Larry screeched. "Don't *ask* questions, if you don't believe me."

"You knew I wanted to ask questions. Mind telling me why you ran away?"

"Because of just what's happening, right now. I can't *take* this. I knew I couldn't take this. I can't take this *any more*. I got nerves. I get sick. Go ahead, lock me up. I got a record. I got no rights. Do anything, only let me alone. Or I'm going to pass out on you. Right in this chair. Feel my pulse. Go ahead. See what you're doing."

"I might lock you up for a little bit," Tate said soothingly. "But, first, let's just go over it once more."

* * *

Megan said, "What a miserable *hut*. Come away, Leon. She isn't here. The neighbors might not like us breaking in."

Leon turned around. He was standing in the tiny alcove kitchenette with a knife in his hands. It was a sturdy kitchen knife with a seven-inch blade.

"Come. Put that thing down," she said sharply. "Don't touch things."

He said, "Your latest bright idea didn't work out either, did it?"

"Oh, come on." Megan walked out into the air. Her right hand twisted at her beads. She began to walk fast towards the car.

When Leon slammed the door of the little house behind her, she looked around. He was coming. She got into the car. He had the keys. She sat stiffly in the front seat. He went around to get in. He tucked the kitchen knife under the driver's seat. He didn't mention it.

Neither did she.

When they were on a through street, Megan said, "Could you drop me at the shop, darling? I really ought . . ."

Leon said, "No."

She didn't argue.

He said, in a moment, "You're going down, too."

"Nobody is going down. There is no connection between us and the truck. None at all. Not even Alison can say anything about *that*. They can't prove it. They can't prove anything."

"They won't wonder why we worked up an alibi?" he snarled. "Oh, you *are* intelligent!"

"They can't prove why."

"Oh, come on. Oh, come on. Oh, come on." Leon sounded at the end of his rope. "If I have to be dragged through a trial I'd rather . . . Where is Alison?"

"I don't know, darling," Megan said meekly.

"That cheap, brainless little movie queen — darling?" He mocked her.

"We're going home? Maybe that boy from the news-paper will find out something."

"Too late. For both of us." He banged the wheel. "For both of us, remember."

"Why I know that, darling," Megan said softly. "But don't worry. I don't intend for us to go down."

Time crept. Betty fidgeted. There was a man clean-ing up the lobby. He began to clean out ashtrays. After a while, Betty got up and drifted thoughtfully towards the phone booth.

Chapter Nineteen

Tony Severson was sitting in Peg's living-room, bemoaning his state. "Why are they always keeping *me* out? It ain't right, Mrs. Cuneen. Wasn't it my story in the first place? Well, I'm sticking to you, Mrs. Cuneen-darleen, because you're going to be told, the minute they do, or don't, identify the chick in the hospital. And you're a good friend of mine, which is more than I can say for some."

Peg was looking very tired. "Oh, our girl is Lilianne," she said.

"But how do you know that already, Mrs. Cuneen-sweetheart?"

"Because *she's* had such fits before," snapped Peg, "and that means a very high degree of probability."

"Oh, oh." Tony wasn't shocked. He pondered a moment. "So then, who do you think was staying in the shack on Opal Street and set the joint on fire, Sunday night?"

Peg shook her head. She was untangling embroidery cottons. Her hands were nimble.

Tony twitched. He looked at the time. He said, "Can you keep a secret?"

"I don't want a secret," Peg said, rather shortly.

He was quiet for forty seconds. Then he said slyly, "You ever wonder how come three girls all look alike?"

"It doesn't do much good to wonder."

"They were sisters," he said.

"Who?"

"All three. They were sisters. Same Ma. Same Pa."

Peg's hands stopped moving. "What are you talking about?"

"Oh, we can't print it," Tony said. "My boss got this from an inside source. We got to find this bird first and interview him. Since his only known address is Chicago, Illinois, that ain't easy."

"What bird?"

"If I tell you it won't go any further?" Tony was bursting and he didn't wait for a promise. "O.K. This morning some bird calls up, long distance, the police. Fella says his name is Kraus, Charles. He used to be married to Bobbie Hopkins and he is the legal and acknowledged papa of the twins. So he sees stuff in the paper or on TV or some place and he figures to be helpful. And when he hears Bobbie has had it, too, he breaks down and tells all. And he says he and Bobbie, they seemed to have kinda jumped the matrimonial gun, long ago, and there was another baby girl — about a year and a half older than the twins but without benefit of clergy, so they farmed *her* out to be adopted. In the East, mind you. So he says, what with this Dorothy Daw being such a dead ringer for her own two sisters, he is willing to bet that's who she is."

"Dorothy Daw was *adopted?*"

"Yup. Yup. Yup." Tony rolled his head in his hands. "The cops can dig that up. They got their resources. But Megan *knew* it. And why didn't *I* think of that?"

Peg was looking startled. "I knew she knew it was her child," she murmured.

"So now they got this Larry Wimberholtz," Tony went on blithely, "and no point in me hanging around, because everybody and his brother is waiting, now, on the results of the interrogation. But guess what came out already! Larry-boy has got a record. He was put away once, not long, for child-beating. And so, by the way, was his teenage wife, under the name of Alice Kraus Wimberholtz, which is — you wanna bet? — what our Alison was at the time."

Peg was looking horrified.

"Oh, the kid wasn't too bad off. They took it away and *it* got adopted."

Peg drew in a shuddering breath.

"But now do you see what it is all about? Alison must have been blackmailing the poor slob. She'll tell his new and pregnant wife, maybe? So he gets upset and does her in. Then it comes over him that Bobbie-girl, his ex-mother-in-law, she knows the whole story and probably is going to mention not only the story on him, but his motive for the murder of Alison. So he has got to do Bobbie in, too. And that wraps it up, hey? Don't worry They'll get it out of him."

Peg stared. "But wait," she said. "Then *who* was the girl on Opal Street?"

"Ah hah," crowed Tony. "See, there's a big fat cliché in this country. Let a kid be rich, she's bound to get done in for her money. But it ain't necessarily so. And there was no hanky-panky with the money. The girl on Opal Street is Dorothy Daw."

"Surely that can't *be*."

"Sure it can." Tony began to expound, his boxy eyes delighted. "Listen, Dorothy Daw fixed it to vanish, didn't she? All that jazz at the railroad station? Say Dorothy finds out she's got a real blood Mama and a couple of real blood sisters in this vale. O.K. She'd just as soon get to know them. But she wants no publicity about this. Which is reasonable. Well, now, she pulls her act at the Union Station —"

"There must be something you don't know," said Peg vehemently. "Or you've forgotten."

226

"Oh, wow," said Tony, "is there ever going to be a twist to this story. And I'm the only one that's on it. Me and Megan, that's all. Oh wow—the rich guys are going to turn out to be the good guys. Twist of the century! Nobody murdered the tenth-richest girl in the world . . . for her money or anything else. Dorothy Daw is still alive! And I know where to find her. That is—providing the chick in the hospital is honest-to-God Lilianne."

"I don't see . . ."

"All right. You can't figure it any other way." Tony was ready for argument but the phone rang.

Peg jumped. She excused herself and went out into the front hall to answer.

"Peg?" said Betty Prentiss. "Dr. Jon and Alfreda are trying to wake the girl up now. Matt's with them."

"Then you don't *know* . . ."

"I'm sure it was Alison we saw on Opal Street. You've guessed that, I'll bet."

"Yes, I . . . But Tony says that was Dorothy Daw. He says the rich guys are the good guys. He's here now."

"Then say something, quick. Say you'll bake a cake."

"I'll bake a cake," said Peg, slowly. "But why?"

"Because Tony's got ears like a fox." (Tony, whose ear was to the kitchen extension, grinned foxily.) "And we just can't put up with Tony's embellishments. Listen, Peg," Betty went on, "even in the smell of the fire on Opal Street I thought I could smell tobacco on her, somehow. Lilianne doesn't smoke. Alfreda is dead against it. She says *Alison* has to give it up."

"Yes?"

"And Peg—when we were up there this morning—didn't you smell tobacco smoke?"

"In the temple?"

"Uh huh."

"I . . . might have."

227

"Me, too. The police are trying to pick her up in, or on the way to, Yuma."

"But she's *not?*"

"Well, the point is — at least she *might* not be. So do you want to call Lieutenant Tate?"

"I'll do that," said Peg decisively. "You go up there."

"Go?"

"Because if she's there, she must be there all alone."

"Oh?"

"The quicker the police — You go and you *take* her to the police. Or I can go."

"No, no," said Betty with resignation. "I'll go, Peg. My car's here. I'll go right away."

"Or I could take Tony with me."

"She wouldn't know Tony," said Betty wearily. "Or you either, Peg. But she's met me. I'm the one who should go."

"Good girl," said Peg. *"Do it."*

She hung up and dialled the police number. She couldn't have said why she was doing what she was doing. She knew it must be done.

She wasted no time asking for Tate. She gave her message crisply. "Will you tell Lieutenant Clarence Tate, at once, that Mrs. Cuneen called to say this. He is looking for an Alison Hopkins. Tell him I have reason to believe that she is, right now, alone in a place called the Temple of Health Through Art, run by a woman named Dr. Dienst who calls herself Alfreda."

Peg took breath. Something made her hesitate.

"Do you know where that is?" she demanded.

"Yes, ma'am," the voice said calmly. It began to repeat her message.

When she was satisfied, Peg went into her living-room to deal with Tony's ears. But he wasn't there. She found him hovering over the extension telephone on the kitchen counter.

"Is it O.K., Mrs. Cuneen-mavourneen," he said, with cream on his whiskers, "if I make a little bitty phone call?"

"Of course," Peg said, dismissing suspicion.

So Tony turned his back and began to dial.

In the Spanish house, Megan was sitting, still and tense, in the big back room. Leon Daw would not let her upstairs or out of his sight. He had been roaming the downstairs rooms. He had been sharpening the knife he had brought with him, on the electric sharpener in the kitchen. Now he was standing at the glass door to the patio, slapping the flat of the knife monotonously upon his palm. The sound was getting on Megan's nerves.

She gathered her legs ready to spring and said boldly, "What in the world are you doing with that thing?"

"I have a hobby," he said bitterly.

"Oh, Leon, don't be so gloomy. You can't tell what will happen. Nothing may happen."

"I'm not particularly gloomy," he said. "I don't seem to have an awful lot to live for."

He heard her gasp and turned around.

"Except, of course, the publicity," he said.

"Leon, put that thing away and don't — "

"I am changing my *modus operandi*," he said and laughed. "Don't think I'm going down alone."

"You have in mind taking someone else along?" she snapped. The man was cracking up. She wasn't afraid of him physically. She was ready to fight for her life.

"Why not?" he muttered. "What's the difference? I'm not a murderer." He lifted his countenance and began to howl, as if to the moon. "It all started with that stupid, love-bitten little ignoramus — who had a silver spoon stuck in her mouth by luck, and never knew one

229

thing about earning a living. A *living*."

"Leon, darling," Megan tried again, "you mustn't go on like this. You're not *thinking*. Suppose the police come here? You can't talk to them if you don't pull yourself together a little bit. Why don't you go upstairs and lie down? Let me . . ."

The phone rang.

"I'll answer," she said quickly.

"No," he said. "No, you won't."

Peg had begun to clear a portion of the kitchen counter when Tony got his connection.

"Tony Severson, here. May I speak with your wife, please, sir? . . . No, I'd better talk to her.

"Hi, Mrs. Royce, I mean, Mrs. Daw. Listen, Dorothy is, right now, all alone in a place called the Temple of Health Through Art run by a Dr. Dienst who calls herself Alfreda. Now, I'll find out where it is and I'll go there my—"

Peg's hand cut the connection with a bang.

"Hey," said Tony, shocked.

She said, "You listened in!"

"But, Baby-doll, that's my business. Look, tell me where this—"

"I won't tell you a single thing," Peg cried. "You did *wrong*. I remember what you forgot. Megan Royce tried to poison that girl in the hospital."

"What! What!"

"*Yes*. Matt says so."

"Naw. He must have had some brainstorm."

"You shouldn't have *told* her."

"But listen—but wait—" Peg walked away and he trailed her, begging. "O.K., then let me go up there. Tell me where it is, and I'll go get her myself. I'll take care of her."

"No, you won't," said Peg. "The police will take care of her."

"You're blowing my story!" screeched Tony Severson.

"I hope so. I hope so."

"Now look, Mrs. Cuneen-*belovéd,* I can find out where it is. I can look in the phone book. So — save me five minutes? Angel? Precious?"

"No, I won't."

"I'll ask Information."

"Not on *my* telephone," Peg said craftily. Then severely, "This is serious police business and you can read about it in the newspapers."

Chapter Twenty

Dr. Prentiss waved the idea of regalia aside. The man on guard looked startled. Then grateful. He did not follow the three of them into the room where she was sleeping.

"Will you please disengage that thing?" Alfreda said.

Dr. Jon took away the feeding needle from where it was strapped to her arm.

Matt slipped around to the window side of the bed and stood well away, watching and listening. Alfreda gazed down. "Of course. I knew it would be she."

"You are sure? When her own mother was not?" said Dr. Jon. "Better wake her, if you can."

"You have been warned. I must, then, take her." Alfreda rolled her big eyes.

"We'll see. How will you do this, Doctor?"

"Her mother is dead." Alfreda pursued her argument. "Her sister is incompetent. I am the only one who can be responsible for Lilianne."

"Let *her* say so."

A faint contemptuous smile crossed Alfreda's lips. She stood close over the bed and began to speak. Her voice took on cadences that were somehow familiar. Matt glanced sharply at Dr. Prentiss and saw his craggy face turn sour with knowledge.

232

Alfreda was using the hypnotist's cadences, the hypnotist's language, the monotony, the insistence, and a great dominating attention.

"Lilianne, you are sleeping a good deep sleep. You have been sleeping a good long time. You have slept for a week. You are well rested, now. So, in a little while, I shall count to three and snap my fingers. When I have counted to three and snapped my fingers you will wake up, feeling well rested. You will not be afraid, because I am here. Alfreda is here with you, now."

The voice went on and on, repeating and repeating. The big woman was exerting a tremendous effort. She was stalking her prey, the girl's awareness. Matt was tense and becoming a little angry. He met Dr. Prentiss' eye and the doctor shook his head slightly, as if in warning. Sad warning. The scene seemed to drift away. It became unreal. Alfreda went on and on. The girl sighed. Her head moved slightly. It turned towards Alfreda's side of the bed.

But she did not wake.

Alfreda lifted her hands and flexed her fingers. She took in breath and began again. With an addition. "Lilianne, when you wake, I shall take you with me to the temple. When you wake, we shall go there. Lilianne, I shall take you with me to the temple and you may stay there with me. You may stay there all the time. Night and day. I shall count to three and snap my fingers. You will wake up and we shall go to the temple where you always feel so safe and happy and in tune. If you are ready, we shall go."

Alfreda stopped, watched, listened, seemed to divine the right moment.

"One . . . two . . . three . . ." Her fingers snapped.

Matt was not breathing. The room was so still the fingercrack seemed to echo on deep emptiness. Nothing happened for a moment. Alfreda did not move or speak. But she was projecting a force that Matt could almost see.

Then the girl in the bed opened her eyes. They were grey.

Alfreda said softly and cheerfully, "Come, my dear. Sit up now." She bent and as the girl began to lift her head, Alfreda slipped a strong left arm down behind her back and lifted. Matt jumped to activate the mechanism that would raise the head of the bed. The girl could see him. At least she was looking at him. But there was no reaction in her glistening eyes.

"Alfreda?" she said in the childish piping Matt had heard before.

"I am here," said Alfreda.

"May I question her?" said Dr. Prentiss. "What is your name, young lady?"

"Alfreda?" The girl's hands were tight on Alfreda's big right arm.

"It's all right. Tell him your name."

"Alison . . ." the girl said.

"Doctor?" said Dr. Prentiss.

"Just a minute, Doctor," snapped Alfreda.

The girl began to look terrified. "No," she moaned. "No, no, no doctors, no." She swayed from side to side as if to struggle out of bonds.

Alfreda said, "You had better let me deal with this. Now, Lilianne."

"Leading the witness, Doctor?" said Prentiss.

The girl began to heave dry sobs. "Hush. No doctors," said Alfreda. "I am here. Tell Alfreda. What did Alison do?"

"Alison stole my name. Alison wanted it."

"You must tell the gentleman your name," said Alfreda, "the one your daddy gave you."

"Lilianne," the girl said. Her eyes were on Matt and he had to believe that they were not intelligent eyes.

234

"Very well," soothed Alfreda. "Very well, my dear. Now, we shall go to the temple."

The girl began to smile. Her eyes glistened.

"But you must feel strong enough to put on clothing," said Alfreda. Strength surged obediently into the girl's body. She sat up using her own muscles and threw off the covers with one sweep of her arm.

"Just a minute," said Dr. Prentiss.

"I must take her, as you see." Alfreda seemed to be able to use a voice that the girl did not hear at all. Alfreda slid the white robe from her arm and put it on the bed. The girl did not touch it. She seemed to have been forbidden. She was held, like a child in a game of Statues.

"That girl will have to be institutionalized," said Dr. Jon softly, "and you know it."

"I must either put her back to sleep," said Alfreda calmly, "or take her with me. Otherwise, she will suffer. I warned you. There was a very strong conditioning."

"She must be under competent and accredited psychiatric treatment," said Prentiss. "If you won't put her there, I will."

"You can't talk to me about my patient." Alfreda was both shocked and offended.

"Your patient, to whom you did not come?" said Dr. Jon. "If you think that protocol, or anything else, will keep me from an obvious duty, you are much mistaken. I'll see to this temple, by the way."

"Threats, Doctor?"

"Responsibility, Doctor."

The girl began to sway and moan as if she were in pain. Matt dared not move.

Dr. Prentiss said to Alfreda sharply. "Steady her."

Alfreda's lip curled. "Your patient? Why don't you?" It was brutal. The girl was in pain. She seemed to be groping, like a wounded insect, with blind feelers.

235

Dr. Jon said coldly, "It may take a day or two to make proper arrangements. If you do not agree that arrangements will be made, then she must suffer. And I'll pull your temple down."

The big woman licked her lips. "And if I agree?"

"Take her. Forty-eight hours. No more."

"She does not suffer," said Alfreda defiantly, "when her spirit is in tune."

"She has no spirit," said Dr. Prentiss sternly. "It has been stolen. I seem to have heard that this is an evil."

Force was meeting force, a clash of Titans. But Matt cried out, "Why doesn't somebody *help* her?"

"I'll order sedation," Prentiss said.

But Alfreda turned. "Lilianne. Put on your robe, now."

Matt couldn't bear to see any more. He blundered past them and went out the door, while the girl groped eagerly for the white garment.

Alfreda said, to Dr. Prentiss, "I could, perhaps, prepare her for leaving me?" Her voice coaxed, now.

"Do that," snapped Dr. Jon, "if you have any mercy."

He came out into the corridor, beckoned to a nurse and sent her flying into the room. The girl shrieked. Alfreda began a controlling chant.

Matt said fiercely, "What *is* that?"

"I wonder," said the doctor. "Too many shock treatments? Addiction to the hypnotic state? I suppose there *is* a word for it. In the vernacular, brainwashing. I don't like knocking her out with drugs."

"You are going to let her go?"

"Dr. Dienst will do what's proper, or see her temple fall. I may pull it down anyway. Depends upon what else goes on in that place. We'll see." The doctor was full of anger. "I'll make a report."

"What can be done for . . . for Lilianne?"

"Not much, I suspect," said the doctor, full of hard truth. "I think she's a goner."

Matt said, "Do you need me?"

"No, no, I'll see the office. . . ."

Matt went away down the corridor. He went into a storeroom. There was no one there. He leaned his forehead on the wall. The girl was empty. No soul, no self. Stolen? Whether by her sister, or her mother, or by her experiences, her woundings, by some too zealous efforts to cure her, or finally by the power of Alfreda's greedy spirit — this body harbored no one. She was better off sleeping, he thought without tears. Better off as somebody's foolish dream.

He waited where he was. He didn't want to watch them go.

Betty parked her car. The land below was covered with a bluish haze but she got out into pale sunshine. She went up under the pillars and used the brass knocker. Nothing answered.

She moved to one of the big multipaned undraped windows and leaned tight to the glass. She could see all the way through the big empty room, where the floor cushions made their spots of color. There was nobody in the room. She put her palms beside her eyes and moved her head to see all she could, to right and left.

"I'm probably wrong," she said to herself aloud.

But she shifted along the façade of the building. She could not see very far into the small dark offices, with no glass wall at their opposite sides. She wondered if there was a bluish drift of smoke, there above the sill. She couldn't be sure.

After a while, she went back to sit in the car. She supposed she ought to wait and speak to the police. It was quiet up here and peaceful. There was nobody around.

237

The few other houses on this ridge seemed silent and empty on their perches. Betty simply sat there.

She'd only come here because Peg had told her to come. She was here. Why should she bother about anything more? Perhaps the police would be along. Perhaps not. She'd rather be here than waiting in the hospital. Why should she wait in the hospital? Nothing that was happening there could make any difference to her.

Leon said, "He didn't give the address."

"He doesn't *know* it. So much the better." Megan was full of energy. "That woman in the *thing,* the *robe.* It's *her* place. You heard what she said about some new market?"

"On Parsons Street," Leon's mouth worked.

"And there was a ground-slip? Parsons Street isn't far. It isn't long, either. You can find it."

"We can find it."

"No, no," Megan said. "He was cut off. He'll call back. I'll make sure he comes *here.* I'll keep him away from the place where she is. She's there alone, he said. Go talk to Alison, darling. Maybe it's not too late. Bribe her. Go, talk to Alison, quickly. I can—if you like—imply that you are lying down upstairs."

Leon had taken a step. At this last, he turned back and picked up the knife from where he had dropped it near the phone.

He said nothing. Nor did Megan.

When he had gone, she sighed. She began to rehearse, mouthing phrases. "Simply appalled. . . ."

When the taxi pulled up, Betty watched them get out of it. First Alfreda, who turned to pay the fare, fishing

238

money out of some mysterious fold of her robe. Then the girl. Barefoot. Wearing a long white robe with a white cord at her waist.

Betty tumbled out and ran towards them. She recognized this girl. Remembered her way of standing, the hair falling around her face, the forlorn air about her, the unappealing passivity.

Alfreda saw her and said sternly, "Not now, Miss Prentiss."

"Oh, hallo," said Betty.

The girl looked at her. "Oh, hallo," she said feebly.

Alfreda stiffened. It was as if she were offended because Betty had been recognized. "What is it?" she said to Betty impatiently. "Lilianne must be taken care of, as you can see."

"It's about the other one, the sis—"

"Be still," Alfreda commanded. The taxi moved off. Alfreda said irritably, "Come in, I suppose. Come in."

She used a key. As soon as the door swung open, the girl went past her on a straight line to a blue floor cushion. She sat down and bent her head and clasped her hands.

"She's quite all right, in this atmosphere," said Alfreda crossly. "Quite serene. Quite happy. As you see." Alfreda's fingers were automatically fixing the little lock button on the edge of the door.

"Dr. Dienst," said Betty, "if the . . . if someone else is here . . ."

"Don't speak."

"But please," Betty whispered. "Where can we talk?"

"Wait."

Alfreda took strides to a high panel in the wall, beside one of the arches. She opened it and pulled switches. The plain putty-colored curtains at the far end of the big room began to move on their tracks, to close. A light went on in the ceiling and a color wheel

239

began to move slowly over it. A pinkness deepened slowly to crimson, then crimson began to become purple.

Alfreda moved, in her white robe that became each of these colors as the wheel turned. She bent over and the girl smiled upward — happily, idiotically, pathetically.

Alfreda turned again and came, walking in indigo, to Betty. "In my office," she said grumpily.

As they went towards the small waiting room Betty looked back and saw the girl sitting quietly on the cushion — eerily blue.

"She is happy here," said Alfreda, "but perhaps *only* here. It *is* a burden. I suppose I must give it over. Others need me." The big woman seemed to have become uncertain, needing argument.

"Dr. Dienst, I came because of Alison. You know there may be danger."

"There is no danger whatsoever," boomed Alfreda, "in my sanctuary."

She opened the door to the inner office. The small room was full of tobacco smoke. The girl who was sitting there jumped up and cried out.

"Be still," said Alfreda. "I've brought your sister and it won't do . . ."

Betty said, "Alison?"

The girl said, "What's she doing here? That's not my sister." Her voice had an angry twang. "You brought her. You won't help me. I didn't think you would. You're just a fat rat-fink, like everybody else."

The girl was edging around to the far side of the desk in what seemed to be senseless panic.

Alfreda closed the door. "You forget," she said pompously, "I have promised." Then, to Betty, "Now, just what is it you want?"

"I only wanted her, Alison, to know," said Betty,

240

"that the police are looking for her."

"*Augh.*" The girl made an ugly sound.

"To protect her," Betty insisted. She looked at the girl. "We think they tried to kill your sister, while they thought she was you."

"This is absurd," said Alfreda.

"You *bet* it is," said Alison. "You damn phony!"

Alfreda said, "Miss Prentiss, go wait in the next room. Or preferably — just go away."

"I'm sorry," said Betty with some spirit, "but I know you have no car and no telephone. I can drive her to a police station. It's safer, Alison, believe me. *Don't* you believe me?"

"I haven't done one thing," whined Alison. "I haven't done one thing!" Both her hands went shoulder high. "And somebody better help me."

Alfreda's hand was heavy on Betty's shoulder. "Go and wait," she said. "Let me be alone with her. It is more important than you realize."

Betty was being pushed.

"This one can be saved," said Alfreda. "I can save her."

Betty couldn't help feeling frightened. There was something about the girl that was desperate. It wasn't that. There was something about Alfreda that was too full of glee, too well pleased, too swelling — Alfreda's hand was urging her through the now open door into the waiting room.

"Mrs. Cuneen is calling the police," warned Betty.

The woman's face hardened. "Don't interfere with what you do not understand. Now, sit down. Sit *there*. And do not, I warn you, so much as speak to Lilianne. Don't even let her see you. I shall deal with the police, when and if the time comes. And Mrs. Cuneen too. You leave my patients to me."

Betty was in the other small room now, and Alfreda

241

shut the door in her face.

Leon Daw's car nosed into the parking lot behind the new supermarket on Parsons Street. He got out and, shielding his eyes, looked at the raw steep bank where the earth had been cut away. His neck arched, his collar tightened, as he kept looking higher, tracing the ridge above, noting how to reach it.

Tony Severson was on the telephone in a drugstore. "I finally got the address, Mrs. Royce-I-mean-Daw, but I think it's too late—"

"Oh?" cut in Mrs. Daw. "Oh, mercy, I *don't* understand what has been happening. There's a Lieutenant Tate, here, from the police . . ."

"I'll be right over," said Tony, anguished. *"It's my story!"*

A single policeman in a car was proceeding as instructed, driving steadily, but not fast, considering placidly the best way up that hill.

Betty Prentiss didn't know what to do. She tiptoed to peek through the open door of the waiting room and could see, on a long slant, the girl in the robe, sitting on the cushion and watching the colors change with the enchanted expression of a small child who still believes in magic.

This is crazy, Betty thought. But she was afraid to disobey; she didn't know what might happen if the girl on the cushion were to turn around and catch sight of her. So Betty stepped backward and sat down on the edge of a chair where, by leaning forward slightly, she could still see.

Head down, feet dragging, Matt trudged the park path. When he opened the door of his mother's house, it hit soft obstacles. All the fat phone books of the Los Angeles area were scattered on the floor of the front hall.

"What in the . . ."

"She's Lilianne!" his mother said, appearing in the archway. She knew. Dr. Jon had called her.

"Yes, she is, Ma."

"Are you all right?"

"Sure. Fine." He didn't fool her. "What goes on here?"

"Oh, that idiot, Tony Severson!" Peg began to gesture dramatically. "Alison was up in the temple. Betty figured that out. We both smelled cigarette smoke up there this morning. But *that* must be how the house on Opal Street caught fire. So we knew. And Betty went to warn her and I called the police. But Tony had some *mad* idea and he called Megan Royce and told *her*."

Matt took in this spate of jumbled information as one lightning stroke. (He had forgotten! He had forgotten! There was a third one. One dead. One a goner. But a third girl!) "How long ago?" he demanded.

"A while," his mother said. "But Megan Royce and Leon Daw . . . There is no phone at the temple. It isn't listed. They don't know where it is."

Matt said, "Yes they do." He turned and fled out the door. He raced around the house and got into his mother's car.

Leon Daw walked softly and read the nameplate on

243

the pillar. This was the place. He went up to the door, but he did not touch the brass knocker. He slipped to his left; he looked in through the window.

There she was. The light was green.

Chapter Twenty-one

Betty, still on the edge of the chair, was falling into a strangely dreamy state. The slow changing of the colored light out there was hypnotic. The temple was very still. She could hear no voices from the inner office. The girl on the cushion in the big room was silent.

When Betty saw the front door opening slowly, in silence, her brain at first took no message. When she saw the figure of a man, colored emerald at the moment, she wondered, idly, locked in a passive state, what *man* was an intimate of Alfreda's, that he entered here without knocking. She saw him peering ahead of himself. When she saw his left hand stretch backwards along the door's edge to feel for the little button that would make it lock, she tensed. But it was not until the door was closed, and the figure was washed in paling green, that she began to guess who he was. The cut of his clothing? Those portly curves?

Betty stood up.

Matt pulled on the brakes of his mother's car. He saw Betty's Chevy. He saw the black car. He raced upon the temple's porch. He wrestled with the doorknob. The door was locked.

Betty saw Leon Daw begin to cross the shallow

foyer, walking as if he curled his toes to keep upright on ice.

The girl was sitting gracefully on her cushion. She did not hear him. She did not turn her head. The light was deep gold and slowly orange. When it began to be red, Betty saw the knife, ruby bright, in the man's hand.

She shouted.

Matt heard a shout. He jumped to the left, to the first window. Light was seeping over the interior, in changing colors. It was confusing. A body flung itself on his back, jolting his breath out. Matt twisted his head around. It was a policeman. "Wait," Matt gasped. *"Look—"*

Inside, the light was bluing and suddenly Matt, with his forehead on the cold glass and the cop's hand hard on his shoulder, could see plainly. Saw the bend of a pale figure near the floor, the bend of a darker figure over it.

And then a racing body hurled itself across his cone of vision upon the standing man.

He knew it was Leon Daw who straightened in violent shock, who turned and cast Betty's body off his back. He saw Betty flying helplessly. He saw, and felt, her crash into the wall.

Saw the man's face and teeth. Saw him turn to look for what had been knocked out of his hand. Saw the girl in the robe, standing. Blue was greening. He saw Alfreda's bulk, in the left corner of his vision, her robe catching the coming of the green. Lifted his leg and kicked out glass.

Felt rushing out of the place, like an explosion, a terrible force.

Saw, through shatters, the girl in the yellow-green robe stand high. Saw her hand and arm swing upward, as neatly as if she had been a trained assassin.

246

When through the window, shoulder first, glass shards cracking.

Swept his gaze once over the girl Alison's terror, where she huddled to his left.

Saw how Alfreda was wrenching the blackened knife from Lilianne's golden hand. Looked once at that girl's face and its childish smile, that sought and expected praise. Looked at the blood down the front of her robe as the light, going orange, turned it black.

Saw the fallen man and his black blood on the floor.

Went slithering to where Betty was crumpled.

Heard Alfreda's voice crooning, "Sleep, Lilianne. Go to sleep now. It is all over. Go to sleep." And by the tremor in the voice was confirmed in a knowledge that was not scientifically demonstrable.

Alison began to scream. *"She* did it! *She* did it! You saw it! Don't get *me* mixed up in it! *I* didn't do it! *I* didn't do anything!"

Heard the cop's, "Now, wait. Now just a minute, miss. Now take it easy."

Bent, in indigo, to Betty—and thought he would never bring his senses single—to hear her heart.

Then, mercifully, the colored lights stopped changing. There was a rasp of fabric and the curtains opened. In daylight, Matt straightened and looked behind him.

Lilianne was on a cushion in a corner, her head against the wall, her eyes closed, her hands passive in her bloodied lap. She slept?

Alfreda was standing beside one of the arches, her hands twisting and moving in agitation.

Alison was momentarily silent, standing free, with her feet apart, her face shrewd, yet torn into mask and underlay. Two-faced and tormented, she looked like her mother.

247

Matt caught at his brains and brought them to his clear duty in all this madness. He called to the cop harshly. "Get an ambulance."

"D.O.A. on this one," said the cop, who was looking down at Leon Daw.

"Get an ambulance, *please*."

Alison's feet stuttered on the floor and she began to run. The cop moved almost lazily and caught and held her. "I don't think so, miss," he said.

"I want *out!* I want *out!*" she shrieked. "It was my sister. I'm the *other* one."

Matt yelled. "Will you call an ambulance? This girl is badly *hurt!*"

Saw Alfreda take hold of the wiggling, struggling blonde whose underlying face was so ugly in its torment to escape.

Turned his head back and bent to Betty. Heard the door slam. Heard a heavy sigh.

Outside, the cop was talking in his car. The blonde girl began to run along the road. She stumbled and fell headlong, and lay still.

When the floor vibrated, Matt muttered, "Don't touch her."

Alfreda said over his head, "I am a doctor."

Matt looked up at her and said, "You are a killer."

He didn't wait to see her react. He bent to Betty, who was lying on the bare floor, looking as if she were asleep.

Peg Cuneen looked down at Megan's face in the Wednesday morning paper. "She still looks old and ugly and mean, to me." Peg's coffee cup shook in her hand. She'd been up all night long.

"She didn't fool *you*, Ma." Matt wanted to comfort her. "You saved a lot of trouble. The lieutenant was pleased, wasn't he?"

"In old clothes and that thing on her head! She was so snoopy and critical. She did open all the dresser drawers. I thought she was looking for something wrong with my house." Indignation perked Peg up. "As if I'd have had her in it!"

"She was planting the key. Now we know. With Alison telling how she *gave* the key to jolly old Megan, and you seeing through to the bone. Oh, Megan's had it. Accessory, twice over. She was a little too smart, telling Tate about Bobbie's phone message."

"She isn't smart. She's just intricate-minded." His mother was so tired that she began to sound like Sybil. (Potions and cryptic advices.) "It's not smart to think everybody else is stupid."

He said, "It's all over but Megan's trial, and that could be months from now."

"I don't suppose," said his mother darkly, "that it is ever going to be all over."

"No Daw money for Megan. Did you read Dorothy's will?" Money was a safe subject.

"I did not," Peg said. (His father used to say that.)

"Lots of Daw money to this Doctor Harkness and his noble project. Good. Fine. Until you get to the fine print, that is."

"What, dear?"

"There's a little joker." Matt was trying to sound cheerfully cynical. "He gets it if, and only if, at the time of her death, he was married to Dorothy."

"But he wasn't, was he?"

"There may be a fight. St. John Cotter will deal with the Daw money. Good luck to it." (His father used to say that.)

His mother looked at him with her fatigue-

249

smudged eyes and said deliberately, "Poor Dorothy."

(But Dorothy was dead. The Cuneens had never known her and never would. She was dead, now. Alison, alive, bore the mark that would not tan. And what marks Dorothy's body bore, that Tate had kept to himself, were, some of them, known to a Dr. George Harkness.)

"Mr. and Mrs. Larry Wimberholtz are in seclusion," Matt read loudly.

"What's to become of Alison?" Peg was looking at him in the same way.

"Nothing much," he said as lightly as he could. "Did you read *her* interview? Seems Alison only hopes that all this tragedy will deepen her art." Matt threw the paper to the floor.

"Tony," said his mother, "is just a little boy playing games. He's sick and astonished about Betty . . ."

Matt didn't want to talk about Betty Prentiss. "Alison says it was Larry who beat the baby. Larry says it was Alison."

"It was Alison." His mother spoke as if she knew for sure. She twitched her shoulders. "She didn't *do* anything."

Matt struggled to follow this. "To Dorothy, you mean? I know. That's why the law will let her off."

"She won't get off. She didn't *do* anything—when her sister was in trouble. Nobody gets off cheating."

"If you ask me," Matt said flatly, "Alison is only one jump behind her sister, on the way to the booby hatch." If Peg needed to be told that he was wide awake now, then he had better tell her. "And so much for the three of them. Because Lilianne is a goner."

"What will they do with Lilianne?"

"The law? Nothing. They can't convict her. It would be self-defense, if anything. But it wasn't anything. Alfreda pulled the strings."

"That can't be proven, can it?"

"No. I suppose it wouldn't hold up. Alfreda is doing penance. She won't 'save' any more young girls."

"You see?" his mother said. "It isn't going to be over. Things have changed."

"It's over, as far as we're concerned." This wasn't true.

"Are you going, now?" his mother asked pointedly.

He got up. "Are you coming?" he countered. (He'd have to go.)

"No. I saw her. I'll wait, now, for Elizabeth to get here. She'll want to see Betty." Peg turned away. "Give her my love."

"I will, Ma." But he hesitated.

He had been thinking, *trying* to think, most of the night, waiting in the hospital while they operated, while the surgeon undid the damages and succeeded, so they said, in restoring to working order the brain in Betty's head.

Thinking that if Betty had only stood still and screamed, Matt would have burst through that window and the cop behind him. But Betty hadn't known that they were there.

So it was done. And not to be undone.

So Leon had not killed poor soulless Lilianne, thinking she was Alison and there alone. He hadn't killed her, before three eye-witnesses. He had *been* killed. Alfreda had put her own furious reaction . . . to violence with violence . . . into a second-hand murder of a murderer.

Still, why had Betty done that? She hadn't thought, had she, hadn't gone over pros and cons, when she had simply hurled herself? People don't always think. Oh come, he had known *that*. He had

251

known that the brain was comparatively new in the universe.

But if she hadn't thought, then had she felt? And what could Betty Prentiss have felt for Lilianne Kraus? Was it, then, just an unwillingness to see harm done, pain given, death dealt? Was there such a thing as so powerful an unwillingness? An instinct? A civilization?

Or—and now he cringed to think what he was about to think again—had Betty felt for *him?* For Matt? For *his* dream? And in some old-fashioned, wicked sacrifice—No, no, incredible! It would also be unbearable. He writhed, even to imagine it. He didn't want to see her, lest it be so. His mother had seen her for a moment. He had not. He couldn't live with that. If it were so, he could never look at Betty Prentiss again. But she couldn't have. She was modern. The trouble was he had lost his faith.

Could he ask his mother? She wasn't very old; she might be wise; she'd had a life. (Matt remembered his father with a pang. Bobbie, Megan, and Alfreda. The names rang in his head, unbidden. So much for the three of them. Poor women. Only Peg had had a man like his father.) All right. His mother must be woman-wise. Maybe she could tell him.

He said, "Ma?"

Peg looked up, quickly.

"Why did Betty do that?"

His mother looked at him, examining the question.

"Did she do it for Lilianne?"

His mother pulled her brows together, questioning the question.

"She didn't do it for *me,* did she?" He was red in the face.

Peg's mouth opened to an O of outrage. "Don't be ridiculous!"

"But why—"

"She did it for *herself*. She *had* to. She couldn't *help* it. Oh, go *on*." Peg got up and began to collect the dishes with great indignant energy, as if to say, Have I such a fool, then, for a son?

Matt slunk away. He wasn't sure he understood, but he was feeling better as he walked through the park.

Tony Severson was sitting in the hospital lobby, looking dejected, with his hands between his legs. He leaped up. "How is she?"

"They say she came through fine."

"Can I see her?"

"I don't think so. Not now."

"When, then?"

"I don't know."

"Where are *you* going?"

"To see her."

"How come *you* rate?" Tony's face flushed.

Matt stood still a moment. "Come to think of it, I don't know," he said and turned away.

"Well, it ain't fair." Tony huffed behind him. "Listen, I'd have rather cut off my head! I want her to know . . . Hey, does she know?"

"They've told her the usual 'everything's all right.' No details, I guess."

"Well, don't *you* tell her, buddy-boy. I want to tell her myself—when I'm let—what a damn fool *I* turned out to be. Listen. I wouldn't have had old Betts get hurt for sixty million dollars!"

"All right," said Matt vaguely and walked away.

The nurse in the room turned out to be Selma

253

Marsh. He and she were ancient friends, on some level that couldn't be explained. She smiled at him tremulously and shook her head to indicate sad wonder over the events of the day before. Then she smiled a different smile, to indicate that Betty was going to be all right.

Betty was sleeping.

He went to look at her, where she was lying on her back with her head wound in white. A few freckles were sharp on her skin. Her eyes were closed. He couldn't see the color of her eyes. He knew them to be brown.

The room was very quiet. Peaceful. He stood waiting, brooding. Dr. Jon came in. He looked closely at Betty, nodded to Matt without smiling, and left them. The nurse twitched Matt's sleeve, smiled to say "Excuse me?" and went out after the doctor.

Old Betts.

It was a good body, a very pleasing female body. It was a good face. He seemed never to have seen it before; he knew it very well. In the round little skull under the white there was a good brain that would be as good as ever, so they said.

All of a sudden, he couldn't stand this. He panicked. His heart began to race. He had to see the spirit back into this body. He bent and put his hand around her wrist, her small dainty wrist. "Betty?"

At once, she stirred. She sighed. She opened her eyes. They were, for a moment, blank with sleep and Matt felt like dying. Then he saw the person seeping back. Saw the consciousness. *"I am me."* Saw the slow wondering, *"But why here? Why so?"* Saw himself recognized. Saw, as if in a mirror, the fact of his own existence.

"Hi," she murmured, peacefully.

A wave of what felt like homesickness hit him. He

254

said, "How are you, old Betts?" Wished he hadn't said that. Blurted, "What did you do that for?"

Saw she didn't even remember what she had done.

(Thought, But you do what you are. You have to. It isn't often you can help it.)

Said with joy and relief, "Never mind. Peg sends love. Your ma is flying down." Picked up her hand and squeezed it. "You're back, huh? That's good."

Ducked meeting brown eyes—that could meet and could see.

Couldn't say "I'm in love with you." He loved her dearly—but how could he be "in love" with someone he knew so well?

He was a dreamer. He hadn't known that, but he knew it now.

Felt the hand wiggle out of his. Saw her turn away, the eyes wide open. The spirit brooding upon itself, what it was? Dreaming after what it needed? Fierce bridegroom? Part-time father? The other half of wisdom?

Saw the body, turned in the lovely curve of woman.

Had never known her.

Held his breath.